SUSPENSE

ALSO BY PARNELL HALL

PARNELL HALL

- - - - - - - - - -

SUSPENSE

THE MYSTERIOUS PRESS

Published by Warner Books

A Time Warner Company

Mysterious Press books are published by Warner Books, Inc.,
1271 Avenue of the Americas, New York, NY 10020.

Visit our Web site at http://warnerbooks.com

 A Time Warner Company

The Mysterious Press name and logo are registered trademarks of Warner Books, Inc.
Printed in the United States of America
First printing: January 1998

10 9 8 7 6 5 4 3 2 I

Library of Congress Cataloging-in-Publication Data
Hall, Parnell.
   Suspense / Parnell Hall.
      p.   cm.
   ISBN 0-89296-624-6
   I. Title.
PS3558.A37327S8   1998
813'.54—dc2I   97-18188
                                                                  CIP

For Jim and Franny

1.

"I'm in danger."

Oh, dear.

If you're a private detective, that's an occupational hazard. People bring you their troubles. They expect you to fix them. They think that you can.

They watch a lot of TV.

Unfortunately, it isn't like that. I've been a private eye for years, and any resemblance between me and a TV detective is entirely coincidental and not to be inferred. I don't have fist fights or car chases, and don't even carry a gun. I carry a camera and take pictures of cracks in the sidewalk. Probably not that big a help to someone in danger.

I smiled at the young woman who had graced my office first thing on a Monday morning. Gave her my best apologetic I-am-not-a-TV-detective shrug. "I'm sorry," I said. "I'm not a bodyguard."

"I don't want a bodyguard."

"That doesn't matter. If your problem is you're in danger, you've come to the wrong place. I don't deal in danger. I deal in accidents. If you have an accident, I will come to your home, interview you, and photograph your broken arm or leg, so you can sue the City of New York. If you're in danger, I doubt if these skills will help you."

"Yes, yes," she said, impatiently. "I know all that. You do negligence work. Most private detectives do. But isn't that still investigating, solving problems, figuring things out?"

I hesitated. Not to disparage the work I do, but most of it requires no intelligence whatsoever. My duties for the law firm of Rosenberg and Stone consisted of driving around in my car waiting for people to call in response to their TV ads. When they did, the office would beep me and send me out to sign them up. But there was no discretion exercised, no thought process required. I was not called upon to judge the merits of the case. Whatever the client told me, I dutifully took down and passed on to Richard Rosenberg, who would eventually decide whether or not to keep it. Rarely was my opinion asked. Rarer still was it ever acted upon.

But I didn't really feel like getting into all that.

"Uh-huh," I said. "Thanks for your support. Still, I doubt if I'm equipped to deal with danger."

"How do you know until you've heard?"

I sighed, leaned back in my desk chair, sized her up. She had curly red hair, a sprinkling of freckles, green eyes, and a turned-up nose. She was wearing a scoop-neck pale blue pullover, and had very large breasts.

I have trouble dealing with women in general, and attractive women in particular. A redhead only complicates the problem. Throw in a pair of large breasts and I'm really in trouble.

I also realized I had forgotten her name. I'm terrible with names. "All right, look, Ms. . . . ."

"Winnington. Maxine Winnington."

"All right, look, Ms. Winnington," I said. "Frankly, I don't think there's anything I can do for you. But if you wanna tell me your story, tell it fast, because I have an appointment in Harlem in half an hour and I've gotta get out of here."

"You have an appointment?"

"Yes."

"Could you cancel it?"

"Not very well. But this is beside the point. Why don't you tell me. How are you in danger?"

"I've had threats."

"Threats?"

"Yes."

"What kind of threats?"

"Anonymous threats."

"Uh-huh," I said. "You wanna speed this along? What kind of anonymous threats? Who's making them? How are they being made? Don't make me ask all the questions, just tell me the score."

She looked irritated. "Because you have an appointment."

"That's part of it."

"Just part of it?"

"Well, it's a lot of it. It does happen to be a fact."

"You're saying you can't concentrate on my problem because you have other work?"

"I suppose that's one way of putting it."

"Work for which you are being paid?"

"Yes, of course."

"Uh-huh," she said.

She set her purse down on my desk, snapped the top open, reached in, and pulled out a huge wad of cash.

2.

You have to understand.

I run a business. The Stanley Hastings Detective Agency. Of which I am the sole proprietor and sole employee.

It is a profit-making organization. At least it was intended to be. It is supposedly the means by which I support my wife and child—not an easy thing to do in New York City—and fill in the gaps between my writing and acting gigs, which are what I think of as my real professions, as what I actually do. The private detective work, you see, is merely a temporary job. A full-time temporary job. Which I've been doing for years.

But that's beside the point. The point is, I'm in it for profit.

Why am I explaining all this? Well, because I'm not particularly proud of my reaction when Maxine what's-her-name pulled out the wad of money.

I should have told her to go to hell. I should have told her it made no difference. I should have told her I couldn't be bought.

On the other hand, the older I get, the less idealistic and more materialistic I seem to be. I don't know if this is a common trait or if it is just me, but it certainly seems to be true. Anyway, when Maxine whipped out the money, instead of throwing her out of my office, I decided to hear what she had to say.

Still, I put up a good front. "Never mind that," I said, waving the money away, as if it were the last thing on my mind. "I'm perfectly willing to listen. Just tell me what your problem is, so I can see if there's anything that I can do."

"I told you," she said. "I've had threats."

"What kind of threats?"

"I told you. Anonymous threats."

"What kind of anonymous threats," I said.

As I did, I realized my ignominy was complete. Having flashed the money, she had walked me through the identical series of questions I had balked on before. Clearly as an object lesson, to let me know who was in charge.

She didn't glory in her victory, however. Instead, I swear to god, she looked around, lowered her voice, leaned in confidentially, and said, "Phone calls."

I blinked. "Phone calls?"

"That's right."

"You've been getting threats over the phone?"

"Uh-huh."

"From whom? A man or a woman?"

"I don't know."

"You don't know?"

"No. It's a low hoarse voice. A whisper. It could be anyone."

"What does the voice say?"

"They're horrible messages. Horrible."

"I understand. Such as."

"You're going to die."

"What?"

"That's it. The whole message. I pick up the phone, say hello. This hoarse voice says, *You're going to die,* and hangs up."

"How many times has this happened?"

"That one, I think twice."

"That one? You mean there've been others?"

5

"Yes, of course."

"How many others?"

"I don't know. Maybe ten. Maybe a dozen. After a while I lost track."

"The same voice?"

"As far as I can tell."

"What are the messages?"

"All variations on the same theme. The underlying message is, *You're going to die. Die, bitch, die* was one. *Death to the bitch* was another. *Are you ready to die?* was another." She cocked her head at me. "You get the gist?"

"I think so. Tell me more. As many as you can remember."

"Why?"

"I want to see if there's a pattern to this."

"There's a pattern all right. Someone wants me dead."

"Beside that, I mean."

"Beside that I don't much care."

"You'd like to find out who's been making these threats, wouldn't you?"

"Yes, of course."

"So humor me."

"Okay," she said. "I think I've given you the general tenor. But as for specific messages, we have *Your death will be ugly.* We have *The end is near.* We have *You've been warned.* We have *Prepare to die.*" She turned to me expectantly. "So, what does that tell you?"

Not much. I had the general impression someone wanted her dead, but I doubt if she'd have been too thrilled with that assessment.

And there was that big wad of money.

"Well," I said. "One of the threats was rather revealing."

She raised her eyebrows. "Oh?" she said. "Which one is that?"

"*You've been warned.*"

"*You've been warned?* Of course I've been warned. What's so revealing about that? It seems to me every one of these calls is a warning."

"Yes and no," I said.

She frowned. Looked irritated. "Just what do you mean by that?"

"All of the other phone calls just tell you you're gonna die. They don't express it in terms of a warning, just as a statement of fact. The intention is not to warn you but to scare you."

"So what? *You've been warned* is the same thing. It's not supposed to warn me, it's supposed to scare me."

"Maybe so, but it introduces the concept. It's the only phone call that does, and it's a whole different idea. Because of the implication."

"What implication?"

"That there's something you could do about it. That's the whole intent of a warning. The implied *if. If you don't stop that, I'll kill you.* See what I mean?"

Her eyes were wide in disbelief. "Semantics?" she said. "You're giving me semantics?"

I certainly was.

"Absolutely not," I told her. "I'm just trying to make a point. *You have been warned* implies that there's a way out. At least in the mind of the person making these phone calls. That all these threats are conditional. That if you were to do something, or stop doing something, or in some way alter your behavior, these threats would no longer apply. See what I mean?"

She was looking at me with distaste. "Jesus Christ," she said. "Don't tell me you're a writer."

"You have something against writers?"

"You mean to say you are?"

"I've done some writing in my day. No big deal. Why?"

"Have you ever heard of Kenneth P. Winnington?"

I blinked. Who hadn't heard of Kenneth P. Winnington? His books were on the *New York Times* best-seller list every week, right up there with John Grisham and Mary Higgins Clark.

"The writer?" I said.

"Author."

"Huh?"

"The author. If you're unpublished, you're a writer. Or if you write for movies or TV. If you write books, you're an author."

Well, excuse me. I recalled that she had referred to me as a writer. I resented it. Particularly since by her criteria I was.

"Sorry," I said. "The author. And what has Kenneth B. Winnington got to do with you?"

"He's my husband."

3.

Alice was impressed. "Kenneth P. Winnington?"

"That's right."

"The writer?"

"Author."

"Huh?"

"He likes to be called an author."

"Then *call* him an author. Stanley, this is great."

"What's so great about it?"

"Are you kidding me? In the first place, it's money. In the second place, it's Kenneth P. Winnington."

"It's his wife."

"Same thing. You're sure to meet him, aren't you?"

"Yeah. So?"

"So maybe you could pick up something useful."

"Useful?"

"Yeah. Maybe you could learn something from him. About how to write."

"I don't *need* someone to tell me how to write."

Alice put up her hands. "No, no. I didn't mean that. Of course not. It's just that he's on the best-seller list."

"You ever read one of his books?"

"No."

"Neither have I."

"What's your point?"

"My point is if he doesn't write the type of book we would read, he probably doesn't write the type of book I would write."

"How do you know?"

"I have some standards."

"Oh? This from the man who wrote a karate movie with four hot babes?"

I grimaced. "That was different."

"How is it different?"

"That was the movies. Movies make you crazy. People do things they wouldn't normally do."

"Uh-huh," Alice said. "Anyway, you're gonna be working for this guy."

"For his wife."

"Uh-huh. Too bad you're not familiar with his books."

"Why?"

"Maybe you should read one."

"Alice, I don't need to read the guy's books to find out who's harassing his wife."

"How do you know? Maybe someone's pissed off about something he wrote."

"So they kill his wife?"

"Stranger things have happened."

"Yeah, sure. In a book."

"Exactly."

I opened my mouth. Closed it again.

"When do you start?"

"Tomorrow. If."

"If what?"

"If I take the job."

"You didn't take it?"

"I told her I had to talk to Richard."

"You didn't talk to him yet?"

"No."

"Why not?"

"I thought I should talk to you."

"Why?"

"To see how you felt about it. I mean, basically, the woman wants a bodyguard."

"No, she doesn't."

"Sure, she does. She's being threatened."

Alice shook her head. "If she wanted a bodyguard, she'd hire some beefy ex-cop who carried a gun. She doesn't want a bodyguard, she wants someone to figure out what's happening."

"That wasn't the job description."

"What *was* the job description?"

I wasn't sure. All I knew was the woman wanted help with her problem and was willing to pay five hundred bucks a day. If I was willing to help her, I was to show up at her apartment tomorrow morning at nine o'clock. If I wasn't willing to help her, I was to call her and let her know so she could get someone else.

I had hedged on taking the assignment by saying I would have to consult my employer. Instead, I had wound up consulting my wife. This was for two reasons. One, the case in Harlem was not far from home. And, two, I knew what Richard's opinion would be before I even asked him. Richard would want me to tell the woman to go to hell so I could continue to work for him.

I'm Richard's top investigator. Don't take that as bragging. What it means, basically, is I'm the only person with an I.Q. over a hundred willing to work for the wages Richard's willing to pay. After long years of service, I had raised that figure to a whopping twenty bucks an hour. And then, only on the provision I didn't tell any of his other detectives, who were still only making ten. I commanded the higher salary by virtue of occasionally getting the information right, and lasting more than a month. I'd hate to tell you how long it had taken me to figure this out.

"The job description is actually somewhat vague. Basically, I'm supposed to show up at her apartment tomorrow morning at nine o'clock prepared to work full-time until the matter is resolved."

"Are those your words or hers?"

"That's the gist of it."

"Is that your gist or hers?"

"Hers. She wanted me to clear all cases so I'd be prepared to work full-time on this."

"And from that you conclude she wants a bodyguard?"

"Well, it stands to reason."

"Was the word bodyguard ever mentioned?"

"Oh. Well . . ."

"Well what?"

"Actually, I told her I wasn't a bodyguard, and she said she didn't need one."

"From which you concluded she did," Alice said. "But of course. Women are such confused, fickle creatures, if they say they don't want something it must mean they do."

"Alice."

"So, the bodyguard thing was entirely your idea." She smiled. "That's so cute."

"Cute?"

"You saw yourself putting on fancy clothes. Taking her out to dinner. Escorting her out on the town. To all the fanciest places. Is that how you saw it? Kevin Costner and Whitney Houston?"

"Alice."

"That's adorable. What was it now? Oh, yes. Rule one: Never let her out of your sight."

"Alice."

Her eyes were bright. She looked at me impishly. "I-ah-I-ah-I will always love you-oo-ou-oo-ou."

4.

At least Richard didn't sing.

"A leave of absence?" he said. "You're requesting a leave of absence?"

"Just for a while."

"A leave of absence for an indefinite period of time. How nice."

Richard got up from his desk and began to pace around the room. That was a bad sign. Richard Rosenberg was a little man who wore his opponents down through a seemingly inexhaustible source of nervous energy. He was hard enough to deal with sitting down. Standing, he was practically invincible. Allowed to hit his summing-up-for-the-jury stride, he could quickly reduce me to jelly.

"We have an agreement, Richard," I quickly pointed out.

He wheeled on me, leveled his finger. "Exactly," he said. "That's exactly true. We have an agreement. Our agreement is you work for me. If you don't want to work for me, then you need to tell me why."

"I have another job."

"That's less than helpful."

"I have a *higher-paying* job."

Richard's eyebrows raised. "Now you're on my wavelength. What is this other job?"

I gave Richard a rundown of the situation, being careful not to use the word bodyguard.

"Interesting," Richard said.

"So what do you think?"

"I think you have a plum of an assignment. How much did you say you were getting?"

"Five hundred bucks a day."

"Just to find out who's calling this woman?"

"That's right."

"How hard could it be?"

"I don't know."

Richard nodded judiciously. "At that rate, it would behoove you not to find him."

"I beg your pardon?"

"This is the type of job that rewards failure. If she's going to pay you five hundred bucks a day to find out who's calling her, why find out who's calling her? As long as you don't you're still employed."

"That's cynical, even for you."

"Thank you," Richard said. "And she's married to Kenneth P. Winnington?"

"You've heard of him?"

"Who hasn't."

"Ever read one of his books?"

Richard made a face. "What, are you nuts. Why would I do that?"

"Well, he's on the best-seller list."

"Exactly," Richard said. "I have some standards."

"Oh? Such as?"

"I make a point of never reading any book I can buy in the airport."

"Ever read John Grisham?"

"Of course not."

"But he's a lawyer."

"So?"

"You're a lawyer. Didn't you ever get the urge to write a book?"

"Not at all. Why?"

"It just occurred to me you might read a John Grisham book and say, Hey, I can write better than that, and this guy's on the best-seller list."

"Never happen," Richard said.

"Why? Because you can't write?"

"Don't be silly. I could write if I wanted to. But what's the point?"

"The point? The point is the guy's on the best-seller list."

"So?"

"So he's making a fortune."

"By his standards, sure."

"By his standards?"

"Exactly." Richard looked at me. Smiled. "Stanley, if John Grisham had my law practice, he wouldn't have to write."

I grimaced. "Hey, good line, Richard. So, can you do without me for a few days? Or would you care to top the young lady's offer?"

"Of five hundred bucks a day? I'd go broke signing up trip-and-falls at five hundred bucks a day."

"That should make Mr. Grisham less envious."

Richard ignored the barb, said, "So, let me know what happens. Though there will probably be no need."

"What do you mean by that?"

He shrugged. "Well, it's Kenneth P. Winnington, isn't it? If anything comes of this, it will probably make the front page of the *National Enquirer*."

5.

I met the great man the following morning at nine o'clock when his manned elevator delivered me directly into the living room of his floor-through Park Avenue apartment. If I had to describe that living room in two words, they would be *spacious* and *ornate*. That's about as good as it gets from my point of view. What I know about interior decorating wouldn't fill a one-page brochure. I can barely tell gothic from modern, and am not sure if those terms even apply. At any rate, here you were talking high ceilings, wood paneling, marble fireplaces, French windows (I think), and oil paintings that gave the impression of being originals, though whether they were or not, I could not have begun to guess.

In the middle of the room stood a powerful man, impeccably dressed in a three-piece pinstripe blue suit, a gold watch chain draped across the vest. His wavy brown hair, medium long, swept back from a high forehead. Sideburns, impeccably trimmed, showed just a touch of gray. Though obviously a few years older than my client, he was not nearly as old as I'd expected. At least not for a best-selling author. I had a quick, fleeting pang of envy—younger than me and so successful. I repressed the thought, smiled.

"Mr. Hastings?"

"Yes, sir," I said. And immediately kicked myself for saying *sir*. There's deferential and then there's deferential. I extended my hand. "How do you do?"

"Fine, thank you," he said, with just a trace of a smile. Then, "Mr. Winnington is in the study. This way, please."

Feeling only slightly foolish, I followed whoever the hell it was who'd greeted me to a study twice the size of my living room that boasted a TV, a bar, and a pool table, just to name a few of its more obvious accoutrements.

It also boasted a massive oak desk, so large I couldn't help wondering how it had gotten through the door. While it was slightly smaller than the pool table, pool tables come apart. I can't recall the same being said of oak desks. At any rate, it was big and huge, looked like it weighed a couple of tons.

Seated at it was my second guess for best-selling author Kenneth P. Winnington. This man was closer to my age than that of my client. He was bald, with a fringe of gray hair, straight, medium long, hanging down over his ears. His gray beard was short and trimmed into what I guess is called a Vandyke—my knowledge of personal grooming only slightly exceeds that of interior design. A pair of half glasses hung from a cord around his neck.

He wore a faded, brown, plaid flannel shirt. When he stood up, I could see that it was not tucked in, and that he wore a pair of faded jeans. And when he came around the desk to shake my hand, I could see that he wore a pair of running shoes with the laces untied.

"How do you do?" he said. "I'm Kenneth Winnington."

"Stanley Hastings," I said, shaking hands.

"Yes. So Max said. She'll be right down."

"Down?"

"Yes. This is a duplex. The bedrooms are upstairs."

"Oh, I see," I said. And I did. A floor-through duplex. On

Park Avenue. Five hundred a day was beginning to seem a little cheap.

"Now then," he said. "About these phone calls."

"Yes?"

"The main thing is put her mind at rest. It's a terribly annoying thing, and it simply has to stop."

"Who do you think's behind it?"

"If I knew that, we wouldn't need you." He smiled. "But, obviously, some kind of kook."

"You don't think the threats are serious?"

"I hope to god they're not. But much more likely this is just some kind of crank."

I frowned.

"You disagree with that assessment?" he asked.

"Not at all. It's just if this is some crank, he'll be harder to stop."

"Why do you say that?"

"If the threats are genuine, the creep is gonna act on them. When he does, he's apt to expose himself and get caught. If it's a crank making anonymous phone calls, he's gonna be hard to find."

"That's why you're here."

"Uh-huh," I said. "Can I assume the reason your wife hasn't changed her phone number is because it's your phone number too, and you need it for your work?"

"Don't be silly," he said. "I've changed the number. The calls still come."

I frowned. "She didn't tell me that."

"You mean you didn't ask?"

I bit my lip. The job had barely started, and I was making a hell of an impression.

"Actually, there were several matters we didn't discuss. You see, there was some question of my taking the job."

"Uh-huh," he said. "Well, the fact is I have an unlisted number, I've changed it, and it does no good."

"And you think the caller is some kind of kook?"

"Of course."

"How would a kook get your new phone number?"

He frowned. "That's the troubling part, and that's where you come in."

"Who has access to your phone number?"

"I can't see how that's relevant."

"You can't?"

"No. These threats are particularly odious. No one I know would make them."

"And yet someone is."

"Which is why I hired you."

"Actually, I believe your wife hired me."

He opened his mouth to say something, closed it again. Nodded. "Yes, yes, of course."

"At any rate," I said, "I'm going to have to track down how this creep got your phone number. I trust I can count on your cooperation."

"Certainly. David will give you all the help you need."

"David?"

"My secretary. David Pryne. The man who saw you in. He would have all that information."

"Un-huh," I said. "Should I speak to him now?"

"No, no. Max should be right down."

We both looked toward the door, but Max was not forthcoming. That left me alone in the room with a famous author, who was not particularly forthcoming either.

I have to admit, celebrities make me nervous. I'm always afraid I'll act like a total boob. That, coupled with the fact that I'd been hired to do a job I wasn't sure I was capable of, made me somewhat less than comfortable. I fidgeted, glanced around the room.

On the opposite wall were a row of what at first glance appeared to be pictures. It was a moment before I realized what they were.

"Are those your book covers?" I said.

"Those are the dust jackets, yes."

I walked over, took a closer look. The covers, or dust jackets, as the author preferred to call them, had been framed so that both the front cover and the spine of the cover showed. As a result, the titles of each book appeared twice, once vertically and once horizontally. The titles formed Ls, due to the fact that the front cover titles were across the bottom rather than the top of the covers. On the top of each cover was the name Kenneth P. Winnington. As in the movies, the star had his name above the title.

I glanced at some of the titles. *Die, Lady, Die. Till Death Do Us Part. Fatal Indiscretion. Woman on the Edge.*

The predominant theme seemed to be women in danger. This was borne out by the cover art, which further defined the genre as Busty Women in Danger.

I turned back from the pictures to find my host looking at me, and realized a comment was in order. I almost said, "So these are your books?" but that seemed awfully dumb with the block letters Kenneth P. Winnington on each one. Instead, I said, "So you write mysteries?"

He winced slightly, managed a somewhat put-upon look. "No, actually I write suspense."

"Oh?" I said. "What's the difference?"

"Suspense sells."

"Oh."

"I'm sorry," he said, with what I'm sure was intended as a disarming smile. "That was a bit smug. Actually, when you talk about a mystery, generally you're speaking of a whodunit. You have a killer, the identity of whom is not known. And your police officer, private eye, amateur detective, or whatever, is attempting to unravel the mystery and solve the crime. Basically, find out who.

"Suspense is quite different. In suspense, the identity of the killer is often known, at least to the reader, if not to the protagonist. Because who the killer is isn't particularly important. What's important is who's in danger. Will the killer get them, or will they get away? The greater the danger, the more the suspense. See what I mean?"

"Uh-huh," I said. I groped for something to say, but not having read the man's books, I was somewhat at a loss.

Fortunately, at that moment my client showed up. She came gliding into the room in a purple pantsuit of some clinging material or other that emphasized her figure and suggested that she had neglected to put on a bra. She was obviously just out of the shower—her hair was wet, which made it seem more brown than red.

She hurried in, saying, "Kenny, Kenny, please." She kissed him on the cheek, turned to me. "You must forgive my husband. He's done so many signings and seminars, when he gets into his lecture mode, you can't get him out. Dear, Mr. Hastings isn't a fan, he's here about the phone calls."

"Yes, of course. We were just killing time waiting for you."

"Well, I'm here. Now, about the phone calls. I want you to listen carefully, see what you can tell from the voice."

"Listen? You mean you have them recorded?"

"No, but that's an idea." She turned to her husband. "Honey, is there a way to make the answering machine record the calls? I mean, when you answer it yourself—can it record the call without the beep and the message and all that?"

"I don't know."

"What about it, Mr. Hastings? Could it do that?"

I really wanted to one-up the guy and have the answer, but frankly I didn't know either. "That would depend on the machine," I said. "We can make some experiments."

"Well, maybe later," she said. "Meanwhile, just see what you can get from the voice."

I put up my hand. "I'm sorry. I'm not following this. What do you want me to listen to?"

"The phone call, of course." She frowned. "Oh, he didn't tell you? That's why I wanted you here at nine o'clock. The phone calls come in at nine fifteen. At least some of them do. We've had some in the afternoon. But nine fifteen, that's like a regular thing."

I glanced at my watch. It was nine nineteen. Of course, my watch is always five minutes fast, which made it nine fourteen, and—

The phone rang.

My client and her husband exchanged glances, then she looked at me. "Listen carefully," she said. "I'll put it on the speaker phone."

She crossed to the desk, pressed the button on the phone, said, "Hello."

There came the general electronic background noise from the speaker.

Then a hoarse voice saying, "Eat shit and die."

Then the click of the phone being hung up.

Then the dial tone.

My client pressed the button on the phone, shutting off the sound.

Then, as if on cue, she and her husband turned to me, expecting me to do something about it.

6.

"Is Caller ID legal?"

"Huh?"

"Caller ID—you happen to know if it's legal?"

MacAullif leaned back in his desk chair, cocked his head and scowled. "What the hell are you talking about?"

Sergeant MacAullif was a homicide cop with whom I'd worked on numerous occasions, no doubt more numerous than he would have wished. I'd done him a favor once, and had been taking advantage of him ever since. Perhaps that's putting it too harshly, but I'm sure that's the way MacAullif would have put it. In fact, I seem to recollect him saying something of the kind at one time or another.

At any rate, he was the cop I always applied to in any matters involving the police. And despite his grousing, MacAullif and I actually worked quite well together. In the past, with his help, I had even sent people to jail.

"I'm talking about Caller ID. You know, the system that tells you who your incoming calls are coming from. You familiar with that?"

"Is there a point to this?"

"There was a question on *Jeopardy!*, and my wife and I had this argument—"

"Fuck you. I got a full plate today, I got no time for this shit. You got a point to make, make it. Otherwise, take a walk."

"I got a point to make. It's just hard with you evading the question."

MacAullif nearly gagged. He opened his mouth, closed it again. Then he took out a cigar, unwrapped it, and drummed it on the desk. His doctor had made him give up cigars, but he always played with them in moments of stress. Or when trying to think something out. Or when restraining himself from slugging someone.

"I'm going to try to be calm," MacAullif said. "I'm not going to get exasperated, or upset, or anything of the kind. I'm just going to ask you nicely to tell me what you're getting at with the Caller ID shit."

"So you don't know if it's legal, is that right? I'm talking about Manhattan, the borough where you work."

"Hey, schmuck. I'm a homicide cop. I'm not a lawyer or an ADA."

"So you don't know," I said. "Well, in that case, I happen to have good news for you. Caller ID *is* legal, and you can get it. Provided your area is wired to handle it. And I was just on the phone with NYNEX, and they tell me Park Avenue is. Isn't that great?"

"It's made my day," MacAullif said. "You got ten seconds to connect this up with the real world, or you're goin' out of here on your ear."

"You ever hear of Kenneth P. Winnington?"

"No. Who the hell is that?"

"He's an author. His books are on the best-seller list."

"Oh. Well, I wouldn't know. I'm just an illiterate cop."

"Yeah, well, I haven't read him either, but apparently other people have. The guy's got a floor-through duplex on Park Avenue."

"Would this have anything to do with Caller ID?"

"Yeah. Guy's wife's been getting anonymous threatening phone calls. Hired me to handle it."

"That's your solution? Caller ID?"

"Why not? Creep's been calling regularly. I hook up Caller ID, next time he calls, I nab him, end of case."

"That's pretty smart," MacAullif said. "And they pay you a big bonus?"

My face fell.

"What's the matter," MacAullif said. "You didn't negotiate that? You don't get a lump sum for wrappin' it up?"

"I'm getting paid by the day."

MacAullif's grin was enormous. "You're getting paid by the day? Hold on, hold on. Let me be sure I understand this. You get no bonus for completin' the job, you're gettin' paid by the day—that's for starters. You come up with this bright idea on how to solve the case really fast. That's number two. Number three—and this is the part I love—you're here in my office—now correct me if I'm wrong—you're here to ask *me* to help *you* with some aspect of this in order to make it go faster still?"

"I was hoping you could trace the phone number."

"Of course," said MacAullif. "You wouldn't want to ruin your perfect record of never bein' able to solve anything by yourself without help."

"I don't happen to own a reverse phone number directory."

"No, I don't suppose you do," said MacAullif. "It's called a Cole's, by the way, just in case you want to impress your next client. Though how impressed they're gonna be when you don't happen to have one is hard to say."

"So, you won't help me with this?"

"Let me ask you something."

"What's that?"

"When'd you start this job?"

25

"This morning."

"You started today?"

"That's right."

"Any phone calls yet?"

"There was one."

"When?"

"This morning."

"What time?"

"Nine fifteen."

"Was that unusual?"

"No. They've been getting a lot of calls around then."

"That's what you meant by regularly?"

"Yeah. Nine fifteen, he usually calls."

"So you're expecting another call tomorrow morning?"

"That's right."

"This Caller ID shit—is that all installed?"

"Actually, I'm on my way to pick it up now."

"From the phone company?"

"No. They offered me an appointment next Thursday. I found an electronics store on Canal I can get it this afternoon."

"They have the equipment?"

"So they say."

"So, you're gonna go buy the stuff, hook it up to your client's phone, nine fifteen tomorrow morning when the creep calls in you'll get his phone number, know who he is—you'll call me with the number, I'll give you the name of the guy, and you'll have worked yourself out of the job?"

"I hadn't thought of it like that."

"I'm sure you hadn't. You've thought of it now."

"Yeah."

"How much they payin'?"

"Five hundred a day."

"At least you'll get two. Good goin'. You're such a schmuck,

I'm surprised you didn't suggest they just change their phone number, so they wouldn't have to pay you at all."

"Oh. Well . . ."

"Well what?"

"Actually, I did. Turns out they had. They changed the number, but the calls keep coming. That's why they hired me."

"I hope this is an unlisted phone," MacAullif said. "This whole thing's dumb enough without their phone bein' listed."

"No, it's unlisted."

"Well, that's wonderful," MacAullif said. "Couldn't be better." He was grinning from ear to ear. "So, if this pays off, not only will you have worked yourself out of a job in two days, but it turns out you had another way to go. If the guy's changin' his phone number and someone's gettin' a hold of the new one—well, I'm just a dumb cop, but it would seem to me, that would tend to indicate the desirability of questioning anyone who had access to the new number. That would certainly be a reasonable and logical way to go about it, and sure would be a nice way to justify a couple of weeks investigation at five hundred bucks a day."

"Don't rub it in."

"But you, oh master of the no cash bonus, will need only my cooperation to wrap this up before lunch tomorrow." MacAullif spread his arms. "What can I say? How can I refuse? Call me with the number, and I will be happy to supply you with the name of the perpetrator."

He held up his finger. "And, just because it's you, there will be no extra charge for this invaluable lesson on how to bill for your services."

MacAullif shook his head. Rolled his eyes. Chuckled.

"Wait'll the boys hear about this."

7.

I inspected the connections, set the box on the desk next to the phone, and stood up.

"Are you sure you hooked it up right?" Kenneth P. Winnington said.

"I followed the directions. If they're right, it's right."

"Yeah, but are you sure you got them right?"

I was in no mood for this. Not after my talk with MacAullif. Because, in point of fact, everything was coming off without a hitch. I'd picked up the Caller ID box from the electronics store, no problem, a bargain at sixty-nine ninety-five, and the guy told me hooking it up was a snap, any moron could do it, which I must admit had made me uneasy. But it turned out he was right, any moron could do it, and I was just the moron to prove it. There had been no problem whatsoever hooking up the apparatus that was destined to dork me out of a job.

"I'm sure I got it right," I said. As I did, it occurred to me, maybe I *hadn't* gotten it right. Which, the way things were, might actually be to my benefit. Though, I must admit, I wouldn't have enjoyed failing in front of Kenneth P. Winnington. Or in front of his wife, Maxine, or his secretary, David Pryne, who were also on hand to witness the installation of the miracle invention.

"We should test it," Maxine said. "Don't you think so, Mr. Hastings? Shouldn't we test it?"

"Sure," I said. "You have another line?"

"Huh?"

"Another phone line. Is there another phone in the apartment? I mean, with a different number."

"No. Just the one."

"Then we'll have to call from someplace else. That's the only way to test it."

"Of course," Kenneth P. Winnington said. "David, go call us."

"I beg your pardon?" David said.

"Go out in the street and call us on the phone. We need to test the Caller ID, see if it's gonna work."

"Yes, sir," David said. He turned and went out.

"You didn't have to do that," Maxine said.

Her husband frowned. "What?"

"You didn't have to send him out."

"I want to test the machine."

"You could call someone, ask them to call you back."

"Who?"

"I don't know. Your editor. How about your editor."

"Good idea," Winnington said. "I'll call her now."

He started for the phone.

His wife stepped in front of him. "Honey," she said. "Don't bother. David's on his way to call."

"Maybe this would be faster."

"Not really. And then David will get a busy signal."

"So?"

"That would be inconsiderate."

I thought so too, until Winnington said, "How can you talk inconsiderate when some creep is threatening your life? I just want to know if this works."

At that moment the phone rang. David Pryne had reached the pay phone, ending the argument.

The three of us crowded around the desk to watch the caller ID. It worked. By the second ring, the digital readout on the little box displayed the numbers 212-555-4968.

I don't know what it is about new electronic gadgets, but it must be something.

All three of us pointed.

All three of us said, "Look."

And all three of us grinned.

The phone rang a third time.

I said, "Okay, it works. Answer it and tell him to come back."

Kenneth P. Winnington nodded, pressed the button on the speaker phone.

A voice said, "Die, bitch, die."

There came a click of the phone being hung up.

Then the dial tone.

The three of us stood there, frozen in shock and horror.

I recovered first, pressed the button, hanging up the phone.

"Look at that," Winnington said. "That . . . that was him. Then that's his number. That's his number, right there."

The thought had occurred to me. I was already on the phone.

MacAullif answered on the second ring. "MacAullif."

"It's me. Stanley Hastings. I got the number."

"Are you kidding me?"

"No. It just came in."

"Are you telling me you got Caller ID, hooked it up, and the guy called already?"

"Yeah. I got the number. Can you trace it?"

"Of course I can. This gets better and better. You're now a candidate for Moron of the Month. You're not even gonna get paid for tomorrow. You're solvin' the case for five hundred flat."

It occurred to me I was damn glad I hadn't punched on the speaker phone. "Yeah," I said. "Let me give you the number. It's 212-555-4968."

"Great," MacAullif said. "What's the number there? I'll call you back in a few minutes, let you know you're off the case."

I gave him Kenneth P. Winnington's phone number and got off the line before MacAullif could make any more jokes at my expense.

"Okay," I said. "He's gonna call me back. When he gives me the information, we have to plan how to proceed."

"I know how to proceed," Winnington said. "We're gonna go over there and slap the motherfucker silly."

"That might not be advisable," I said.

"I don't care what's advisable," Winnington said. "This man is threatening my wife."

Maxine put her hand on his shoulder. "Yes, honey," she said. "And I know you're upset about it. But violence isn't going to help."

He looked at her. Relented. "Maybe not," he said, "but the man has to pay. We'll have him arrested, put in jail."

"If I could step in here," I said. "It's very important at this juncture not to go off half cocked. That's why I said we need a plan. Now you, Mr. Winnington, are a rich and powerful man. The creep who's making these calls is probably not. If you were to accuse him of something, harassment, threats of bodily harm, extortion, what have you, believe it or not, that would put him in the position to sue you. In the event you were not able to make your charges stick, since you are a wealthy man, he would be in the position to take you for a sizable chunk of change. You see what I'm saying here?"

Kenneth P. Winnington looked at me in disbelief. "You mean I have to just sit there and take it? You mean this man can threaten my wife, and I can't say boo?"

"Not at all. I'm just saying we need to proceed with caution. Before we make any accusations you might later regret. I would strongly advise you to consult an attorney. I would assume you have one."

"Huh?"

"An attorney. Do you have an attorney?"

"Of course I do. He handles my contracts."

"Uh-huh. An entertainment attorney might or might not be comfortable with this sort of situation. In the event yours isn't, I could put you in touch with a lawyer who would. At any rate, the only point I'm making is you should protect yourself. At the moment, we don't know why this person is making these calls. It might turn out the reason for the calls is exactly that—to goad you into making an accusation so the caller could sue."

The phone rang.

"That was fast," I said.

I snatched up the receiver before anyone could put it on speaker phone. MacAullif on speaker phone I didn't need.

"Hello," I said.

"Hello. Who is this? Do I have the right number?"

It wasn't MacAullif. And, I realized, the number now displayed on the digital readout wasn't MacAullif's number.

It took me a second to realize who it was. "David Pryne?" I said.

"Good, I got through," he said. "I've been trying to call, but the line's been busy. Anyway, does it work?"

"Yeah, it works," I said. "Come on back."

I hung up the phone. "David Pryne's been getting a busy signal. I take it you don't have Call Waiting?"

"No."

"Then let's keep the phone free for MacAullif. As I was saying, once we know who our man is, it's important we analyze the information before we go ahead. The name will tell us a lot.

It may be a name you know. In which case, you'd have something to consider. If you know who the person is, you may be able to figure out why they're doing what they're doing. If you know that, there may be a simple solution, maybe one that doesn't involve the law.

"On the other hand, if you *don't* know the name, then we need to put a face to it. Because, without knowing the name, you still might know the face. A crazed fan, perhaps, someone who goes through your signing line, who thinks they know you very well, though you don't know them from Adam."

He frowned. "Perhaps."

"At any rate, the important thing isn't to go rushing out and confront somebody before we know the situation. It would be better for you to get a look at them first. I mean both of you, of course. Now, if waiting in parked cars on stakeout isn't really your speed, I suggest you have me take some pictures for you to look at. So you can study the suspect's face without a chance of them ever seeing you."

I hoped that sounded reasonable and logical, and not like me desperately trying to talk my way back into a job.

The phone rang again. I figured it would be MacAullif, and this time I figured right.

"I got it," he said. "And let me be the first to congratulate you, because it happens to be a piece of good news."

"Oh, yeah? So, who's our guy?"

"I don't know."

"Huh? Why not? Don't tell me it's an unlisted number."

"Oh no, not at all. It's listed just fine."

"Well, what is it?" I said, well aware that my client and her husband were looking at me with ill-concealed impatience. "Come on, MacAullif, what's the scoop?"

"You get to keep your job. 212-555-4968 happens to be a pay phone on Thirty-fourth Street."

8.

Nine o'clock next morning found me on the northeast corner of 34th Street and Seventh Avenue, checking out the phone booth across the way. I say booth. I shouldn't. Phone booths in New York City have gone the way of the dinosaur. In fact, I believe in the first Superman movie there's a scene where Clark Kent's looking to change and, instead of a booth, he finds one of these pay phone stands they have now.

My god, was that a long time ago.

Anyway, that was the type of phone I was staking out now. A pay phone on a stick on the southeast corner, facing uptown. Anyone using it would also be facing uptown. And since this phone didn't have a wind screen or sound baffle, or whatever the hell they call those things around the pay phones now, I would have a good shot at the guy's face from my vantage point across the street.

That vantage point, by the way, consisted of a hot dog stand, manned by a swarthy gentleman of indeterminate origin but, in my humble opinion, excessive zeal. I mean, in New York City there are all types, and granted someone somewhere might want to buy a hot dog at nine o'clock in the morning, but I would doubt if there would be sufficient numbers to sustain a business. It occurred to me that perhaps the hot dog stand was a front for something else.

Anyway, I was camped out at the far corner of it, trying to look inconspicuous on the one hand, but not like I wanted to order a hot dog on the other.

I was alone, for which I was grateful, for it had not been easy. My client and her husband had both wanted to come, and it had taken a good deal to dissuade them. My first argument, that they needed to be there to receive the call, was countered first by the suggestion that they didn't *both* need to be there (ventured by Maxine), and then by the idea neither of them did since the speaker phone could be pushed on by David Pryne (put forth by Kenneth).

My next argument was if the caller knew them and spotted them, the jig would be up. He'd realize the calls had been traced, and he wouldn't make the call, and would vanish into the woodwork and we'd never find him again. I don't think they really bought it, because they both kept protesting that they would be careful and wouldn't be seen, but for once in my life I was firm. I would go alone, I would take pictures of the suspect for them to identify. Neither one of them liked it, but in the end they went along.

So there I was, hanging out on the corner with my Canon Snappy 50, ready to photograph the perpetrator when he made the nine fifteen call. The Canon is not a surveillance camera, of course; it is the one I use in my negligence work, to take pictures of people's broken arms and legs. It's a very simple, 35-millimeter, automatic-focus color camera. You just aim it and shoot. That's one of its features. Another is it's small and inconspicuous. I wear it on a cord around my neck, hanging down my left side under my jacket like a shoulder holster. That way I can reach under my jacket, whip it out, and fire off a few quick shots without anybody noticing, which is a good idea if you happen to be photographing, for instance, the front porch of some gentleman your client is planning to sue.

Anyway, I had had a lot of practice with the camera, and was confident I could use it to nail our man, my confidence only slightly eroded by the fact Alice had spent a good hour the night before trying to talk me into using her Nikon camera with the telephoto lens. While I had to agree with Alice that it was a better camera and could have taken better pictures and closeups to boot, I felt those advantages were outweighed by the fact that by the time I got the damn thing focused the suspect would have either spotted me or made his phone call and left. I don't think Alice was entirely convinced. Nonetheless, I was using the Snappy 50.

The only way the plan could go wrong, by the way, was if the guy didn't show. And by nine fifteen I was getting edgy. Apparently nine o'clock in the morning is not prime time for public pay phones. In the half hour I'd been there, only two people had used it, neither of them our man. The first one was a lady with shopping bags. Not a bag lady, just a lady who'd been shopping, though how she'd managed to do that much shopping that early in the morning was beyond me.

The second was a cab driver calling his wife. I know because I crossed the street just to make sure. After all, our guy could have been a cab driver. If so, he wasn't *this* cab driver. Because he had finished his shift, he was on his way home, and he wanted to make damn sure his wife waited for him before she went out on *her* shift, whatever that might have been.

Anyway, the point is, our man hadn't showed, and I was beginning to think we were going to have to hang it up and wash it out.

But then, nine twenty-two by my watch, nine seventeen real time, a man walked up to the pay phone and dropped in a quarter.

I was back across the street, too far to hear, but I could see him punch in the number as I came out from behind the hot dog stand, flipping my jacket open with my left hand, raising the camera with my right, and, in full stride, firing off shot after shot.

I knew I had him. I was used to shooting that way, firing from the hip. I often had to at accident sites where the camera couldn't be seen. So I could have sworn I had him in frame. But, taking no chances, I raised the camera to my eye, fired one off I *knew* was framed, all the while without breaking stride while crossing the street.

I hit the south side of 34th, stepped between two parked cars onto the sidewalk, and squeezed off two more shots of my man just as he hung up the phone.

He never saw me, of that I am sure. He just turned, headed across Seventh Avenue. I let him have a little head start, then gave chase.

Hot damn.

I must admit, I often have preconceived ideas about people that turn out to be wrong. But this time I hit it on the nose. The guy *looked* like a crank caller. He wore a gray suit, faded, of some sort of cheap, shiny material. His shirt was worn, and his tie didn't go. Even I, whose taste Alice ridicules, knew that. He was a middle-aged man with beady eyes, a pencil-thin moustache, and a little twitchy nose. I'm afraid my description of him doesn't do him justice. The man gave the impression that for him crank phone calls was a step up from his usual occupation of hanging out at the playground offering candy to schoolchildren.

I followed him across Seventh Avenue in the direction of Madison Square Garden and Penn Station. He wasn't going to either, however, just continued on 34th Street to the next corner, then headed up Eighth.

A couple of blocks uptown he went into a dirty book store. That figured. That was right in keeping with his image. I didn't follow him in, just took up my position on the sidewalk, and hoped the guy wouldn't be long.

The problem was I had to keep following him until I knew who he was. This could be accomplished in one of two ways.

Either he'd go home and I'd learn his address, or my client or her husband would see him and know who he was. In that event they'd have recognized him from the pictures I'd taken anyway and there'd be no need for this, but of course there was no way to know.

Not unless I managed to call them up and get them down here. Which wasn't a bad idea, what with the guy holed up in the porn shop.

I looked around, spotted a pay phone on the corner. I hurried to it, fished a quarter out of my pocket, dropped it in.

And the guy came out of the porn shop and headed up the street the other way.

I hung up the phone—which failed to give me my quarter back, what a surprise—and tagged along.

Three blocks up the street he turned into an OTB. Classy guy. Makes a crank phone call, looks at dirty pictures, and bets on a horse.

There was a pay phone on the corner. I went to it and called the Winningtons.

David Pryne answered the phone.

"It's Stanley Hastings," I said. "Let me talk to my client."

But it was Kenneth P. Winnington who grabbed the phone. "Hastings," he said. "Where are you? What are you doing?"

"Relax," I said. "I'm on the job. Did you get the call?"

"Sure we got it. Nine fifteen, same as always "

"On the nose?"

"Give or take a minute. What's the big deal? Where are you?"

"Don't worry," I said. "I got him spotted. I'm on his tail."

"What?"

"I picked him up when he made the phone call, and I'm following him now."

"Then you must be psychic," Kenneth P. Winnington said dryly. "He called from another phone."

9.

"It's a pay phone on East Fifty-seventh Street."

"Oh, is that right?" Kenneth P. Winnington said.

I indicated the phone I'd just hung up. "According to my friend on the police force. It's a phone booth on the corner of Fifty-seventh and Third."

"And do you plan to stake it out tomorrow morning?" Kenneth P. Winnington said. I can't do justice to his line reading. It wasn't exactly ironic, but it was in the form of a taunt, made me want to wipe the superior smirk off his face.

I exercised great control, said calmly, "I think we probably should. Also the one on Thirty-fourth Street. Even though it will probably do no good. It would be foolish to pass up a bet."

"What bet? The man's using different phones."

"True, but we don't know why. The supposition is he's doing it so he can't be traced. Which is entirely likely. But it's not certain. He could have called from different phones just because he happened to be in those areas at the time. See what I mean? In which case, if he happened to be in one of those areas, he might use the phone again."

"That's not logical," Winnington said.

"It's merely a supposition," I said.

"But it's not a logical one. The guy's calling us nine fifteen as a regular thing. Which means the calls are planned. And if he's planned *when* he's making the calls, he's probably also planned *where*."

"While that's logical, it's not necessarily true." When Winnington started to object I put up my hand. "Highly likely, I admit. Frankly, I agree with you. I'm just saying we should take precautions and provide for the possibility we might be wrong."

"That's logical," Maxine said, and I could have kissed her. I was having a hard time dealing with her husband, who was obviously used to getting his own way. "So, tell me, Mr. Hastings," she went on. "What is it you think we should do?"

"As I said, I think we should stake out these phones. Now, I can take one and either you or your husband can take the other, or I can hire another man."

"I'll do it," Maxine said.

"No, you won't," Winnington said. "I'll do it."

"But I *want* to do it."

"It isn't a case of what you want. I'm going to do it."

"But, Kenny—"

"No," he said. "Flat out, no. I'm not trying to spoil your fun. Just stop and think. If this man should show up—and I don't think he will—but even if there is the slightest possibility that he might, let's not forget you're the one he wants to kill."

"And I think that should settle the matter," I said. "I'll take one phone. Mr. Winnington will take the other. If it comes to that."

"What do you mean, if it comes to that?" Maxine said.

"We're talking about tomorrow morning. Let's see what we can accomplish now."

"What do you mean?"

"To begin with, I want a complete list of all the phone calls. Times, dates, and what was said."

"I can't do that," Maxine said.

"Why not?"

"Are you kidding? I can't remember them all."

"It doesn't matter. Do it to the best of your recollection." I turned to her husband. "And you do it to the best of yours. Then we'll compare notes."

"That's silly," he said. "Why don't we talk it out together? Refresh each other's memory."

"Because then we'd only get one list," I said. "I want to get two. Compare them to each other. *Then* let you talk it out and refresh each other's memory."

"What's the difference?" Winnington objected.

"Because that way you don't influence each other. Maybe you're thinking of one phone call, she's thinking of another, but you manage to make each other think you're both talking about the same one. Then that phone call's the only one that gets listed, and the other one gets lost."

"That makes sense," Maxine said, and I could have kissed her again. Not that I really thought it could make that much difference. I just liked winning an argument with her husband. Which shows what sort of frame of mind I was getting in.

"Okay, so we make the list. That's one thing. Next I want to pin down who had access to your new phone number."

"I don't like that," Winnington said.

"Why not?"

"Because it's all my publishing people. My editor, my agent, my publicist. I don't like you bothering them."

"Yes," I said. "But, as you pointed out, the man's threatened to kill your wife. So who has your new number? You mentioned your editor, your agent, and your publicist. Is that all?"

"Of course not. I just mentioned them as the people I don't want you to bother."

"And who are the people you'd *like* me to bother?"

Winnington looked at me sharply.

I kept my expression neutral, waited him out.

He took a breath. "I don't know everyone we gave the number out to. David Pryne would."

"Then let's ask him," I said.

Winnington stared at me a moment to put me in my place, then crossed to his desk and pressed some concealed button, invisible to the naked eye.

Seconds later, the secretary came in.

"Yes, sir," he said.

"He wants to know who we gave our new phone number out to. Do you know just who that was?"

"Yes, of course."

"So tell him."

"Sure." David Pryne turned to me. "Abe Feinstein. That's his agent. Elizabeth Abbott—his editor. And Sherry Pressman, his publicist."

"You're kidding," I blurted.

David Pryne looked surprised. "Why should I kid about a thing like that?"

"You have a publicist named Pressman?"

"Yes," Winnington said. "Is that all right with you?"

It was fine by me. I just couldn't believe they didn't find it funny. A publicist named Pressman? That was a natural.

"Who else?" I said.

"Well," David Pryne said. "There's some others, but they don't really matter."

"I'll be the judge of that."

"Now, just a minute," Winnington said. "Are you telling me the others *do* matter?"

"No, no, not at all," David Pryne said. "It's just . . . they're important. The others are unimportant. At least relatively, if you see what I mean."

"Uh-huh," I said. "And if you could just tell us what those other unimportant ones are."

"Yes, of course. Well, there's the maid. She has the number in case she has to call in sick."

"What's her name?"

"Rose."

"What's her last name?"

"I don't know."

"What's her last name?" I asked Winnington.

"I don't know. I would have to look it up."

"Uh-huh," I said. "I take it you don't pay by check? Perhaps a little lax about withholding tax?" When Winnington didn't say anything, I turned back to David Pryne. "Anyone else?"

"Well, there's the video store."

"I beg your pardon?"

"The place they rent videotapes."

"Why do *they* have our number?" Winnington demanded.

"Remember the tape you had me rent last week?" David Pryne said. "It wasn't in, so I reserved it. I had to leave our number so they'd call when it came in."

"Great," I said. "Anyone else?"

David Pryne looked embarrassed. "Actually, my girlfriend. I gave her the number in case she had to reach me."

"Damn it," Winnington said. "I'm not paying you to gab on the phone."

"It was just for emergencies," David Pryne said. "So far she hasn't used it."

"Uh-huh," I said. "Is that all?"

"I think so," David Pryne said. "Of course . . ."

"Of course what?"

"Well, I know my girlfriend hasn't given it out. But the others . . ." He shrugged. "They could have told anyone."

10.

Abe Feinstein looked like an agent. Or at least someone's stereotypical idea of an agent. A little man with a big cigar, he kept his hat on right through lunch, the gray and black tweed hat with the little red feather, which covered what I presumed to be a shiny bald head.

"Let's do lunch," Abe had suggested when I called, and now he was ensconced at a table at his favorite deli, the cigar in one hand, and a gigantic pastrami sandwich in the other. I thought smoking in restaurants had been banned in New York City. If so, no one seemed to care.

If they had, I doubt if Abe would have noticed. He took a huge bite of sandwich, chewed noisily, then took a slug of coffee.

"So what's the deal?" Abe said. "Kenny says talk to you, I'm gonna talk to you. But it isn't business, so what's the deal?"

"Someone's threatened his wife."

"So he said. This to me makes no sense."

"Me either. That's why I'm here."

His eyebrows raised. "Me? You look at me?"

"Not at all. But I need some background information, and who would know better."

"About his wife? What am I, some secret stud? I barely know his wife."

"What do you think of her?"

"Nice girl. Quite a looker. He could have done worse."

"I know she's pretty. I was wondering what she's like."

"Pretty is what she's like. Aside from that, I wouldn't know." He took a puff of his cigar, blew the smoke out from between clenched teeth. It occurred to me I was glad I wasn't negotiating a deal with him.

Turned out I was.

"Now see here," he says, jabbing a cigar at me. "What I'm getting at, the point I was trying to make, is this is not a business lunch. I'm here because you want to ask some questions. All well and good. And for this I should buy you lunch? Does that seem reasonable to you?"

"All right," I said. "If that's the way you feel about it, *I'll* buy *you* lunch."

With regard to that magnanimous gesture on my part, I must admit it had occurred to me I could put it on my expense account and charge it to Kenneth P. Winnington.

Abe Feinstein put up his hand. "Let's not go overboard. You buy your lunch, I'll buy mine. As it should be. Separate checks."

"We didn't ask for separate checks."

"No big deal. We figure it out. Hey, Sammy, more coffee."

The waiter came over, filled his cup.

"So what's this about someone wants to kill Kenny's wife?" Abe said.

The waiter smiled.

I blinked. Coughed. Held my cup out for a refill.

As the waiter moved off, I said, "Could we keep this somewhat quiet?"

Abe shrugged. "What's the big deal. I always talk like that.

45

It's a plot idea. It's a book. You think I sit at this table a lunch goes by I don't talk about who's trying to kill who?"

"I'm sure you do," I said. "This time it happens to be real."

"I find that hard to believe."

"So do I. But it happens to be true, and that's why I'm here."

"Uh-huh," he said. "So why don't you fill me in?"

I gave Abe Feinstein a rundown of the situation.

He frowned. "I don't get it."

"What do you mean?"

"It's a lousy idea. The woman keeps getting phone calls. Big deal. If nothing else happens, you got no plot."

"It's not a book."

"I know. And it wouldn't be, either. You'd have your readers falling asleep."

"A woman's life has been threatened."

"So what? Happens all the time in books, and a lot better than that. Where's your failed murder attempts? The hit-and-run accident doesn't come off. The popping sound, the whine like a bee beside her head, and next day you find a bullet lodged in her front door. Or she gets a package in the mail and a cobra jumps out." He put up his hand. "Even the warnings could be better. A bloody knife stuck in the wall. Or a letter cut out of newspaper headlines."

I shifted uneasily in my chair.

Without knowing it, Abe Feinstein was touching a nerve.

As a failed writer, I had sometimes considered the possibility of getting published by writing up my exploits. What stopped me was the realization that real life wasn't nearly as interesting as fiction, and frankly no one would care.

I had resigned myself to the fact that publishers would be unimpressed by the adventures of Stanley Hastings. I could have done without Abe Feinstein underlining the point.

"So," I said, "you find these phone calls very unlike fiction?"

He looked at me in surprise. "Yes, of course. Why?"

"Your client writes suspense novels. I was wondering if this scenario might resemble anything he's ever written."

"Certainly not."

"How can you be so sure?"

"Are you kidding me? For all the reasons I just said. This telephone business wouldn't make a decent plot."

"And your client is too skilled to come up with anything that clumsy?"

Abe Feinstein cocked his head, looked at me for a moment. He put up his hand. "I have to remember you are not a potential source of income. You are a hired employee, doing your job, who couldn't care less. I take it you are not a personal friend of Kenny's?"

"Never met him in my life."

Abe Feinstein smiled. "Then it gives me great pleasure to tell you the man is a total putz, can barely write his own name."

I blinked. "I beg your pardon?"

"The man owes his career largely to me. He wrote a first novel that was uncommonly bad. Fourteen other agents turned it down. Not me. Why? I knew one editor at one publishing house who I knew would have a soft spot for the woman who was the lead character in the book. I signed Kenny up, took that manuscript and presented it to that editor and that editor only, being careful to lay just the right spiel on him. Here was an amateurish first effort, with a terrific lead character, and all the potential to be a runaway hit. A rough gem that just needed polishing."

"He bought it?"

"He bought it, he rewrote it, and the rest is history."

"He rewrote it?"

"Well, he had to. It was dreadfully bad."

"I thought writers rewrote their own work."

"Those that can, do. Doug worked with Kenny until Kenny couldn't cut it. Then Doug simply wrote what he wanted."

"Doug?"

"Doug Mark. The editor with two first names."

"What happened with the book?"

"Like I said. It was a runaway hit. Reached number twelve on the *New York Times* best-seller list. Paperback reached number eight."

"Uh-huh," I said. "But this Doug Mark. He's not Mr. Winnington's editor anymore."

"No, he's not."

"How come?"

"Kenny dumped him after the first book."

"Why'd he do that?"

"Because he could." Abe Feinstein shrugged. "Lots of things, power things, you do because you could. Kenny's first book was a best seller. Everyone in the world wanted his second book. He didn't have to stay with the same publisher. He sold the book to the highest bidder."

"Didn't that piss Doug Mark off?"

He shrugged. "I would assume. But that sort of thing happens all the time in publishing."

"But if the guy was responsible for the success of his first book . . ."

"Hey, you're expecting loyalty from an author?"

"That's not what I mean. The first book was a best seller because this guy rewrote it. So how does he write without him? Does his present editor rewrite him?"

"No, of course not. She asks for rewrites, and edits him. Par for the course."

"So, you're telling me he learned how to write?"

Abe looked at me in surprise. "No, of course not. His stuff is dreadful as ever. What I've read of it." He shrugged. "You reach a point, I send the manuscript out, if I haven't read it, who's to know?"

My mind was totally blown. "But aren't his books best sellers?"

"Yes, of course."

"How can they be best sellers if they're no good?"

Abe Feinstein made a face. "Good? What's good got to do with it? You don't know anything, do you? His books are best sellers because his books have always *been* best sellers. And always *will be* best sellers. That's the way it is. He could copy the phone directory, and enough book stores would order enough books to put it on the best-seller list.

I blinked. "Why are you telling me all this?"

"Are you kidding me? How often do you think I get to talk like this? Everyone I talk to is in the industry. I gotta put on a happy face, hawk the next Kenneth P. Winnington book. It's nice every once in a while to be able to say the man's a doughnut, wouldn't be anywhere at all if it weren't for me."

"Does he know you feel this way?"

"What, are you nuts? I told him the facts of life from the word go. Kid, you can't write, but I can help you. What, you think I kiss his ass, tell him he's the great pooh-bah? From other people, that he'd believe. Not from me."

"How come he hasn't fired you?"

Abe Feinstein's eyes narrowed. "How come you ask me that?"

"If you're the only one who tells him like it is, why would he want you around?"

Abe nodded. "Good point. But it is for exactly that reason. I'm like a reality check. Plus I have him under long-term contract. I'm not as dumb as I look."

"How long have you known him?"

"Ever since his first book."

"How long is that?"

He shrugged. "Seven, eight years. You should talk to his publicist."

"I intend to."

"Good. She'll know for sure. She can give you a press kit, covers all that."

"Uh-huh," I said. "And his wife?"

"What about her?"

"How long have you known her?"

"I don't really know her. I've been acquainted with her since the marriage."

"When was that?"

"You don't know?"

"Actually, I don't."

"Two or three years ago."

"Were you at the wedding?"

"Yes, I was. So were all his publishing people."

"Are they the same ones he has now?"

"Huh?"

"You mentioned him changing houses and dumping his editor. Did he have the same one then he has now?"

"Oh, sure. He's been with her the last three books."

"Is that one a year?"

"I wish. Kenny's not that fast. With him it's every other year."

"Uh-huh," I said. "Now, about his phone number."

"I have the new number," Abe said. "Is that a crime? I'm his agent, I should have his new number."

"Of course," I said. "And when did you get it?"

"I got it when that putz called me. That male secretary. What's-his-name. And what's the deal with that? I mean, a famous author should have a guy secretary instead of a nice-looking piece of fluff?"

I looked at him. "Is that something that changed since the marriage?"

"What do you think?"

So. Abe Feinstein resented my client for preventing her husband from hiring an attractive young secretary. Somehow I doubted if that was sufficient motive to want to kill her.

"Uh-huh," I said. "What about the phone number?"

"What about it? The guy called and gave it to me."

"When was that?"

"How should I know? Some time last week."

"Could you be more precise?"

"No, but what's the big deal? Doesn't *he* know?"

"Who?"

"The secretary. He called me. Wouldn't he know?"

"He says it was Thursday afternoon."

"Well, there you are. Why ask if you already know?"

"I like to verify the information. Just 'cause someone tells me something, it isn't necessarily true."

"Uh-huh," Abe said. He shoved the last bite of sandwich into his mouth, signaled for the waiter. "Hey, Sammy, lemme have a piece of pie."

"So, to the best of your recollection you've had the new number since Thursday?"

"If you say so."

"Would you care to contradict that?"

"Not at all. Why would I do that?"

"And who did you give the new number to?"

"What?"

"The new number—who'd you give it out to?"

"I didn't give it out to anybody."

"Are you sure?"

The waiter took Abe's plate, slid a piece of lemon meringue pie in front of him. Abe picked up a fork and went to work.

"Am I sure?" he said between mouthfuls. "Sure, I'm sure. Who would I give it out to? Why would I do a thing like that?"

"How about a publisher or an editor? Couldn't there be a business reason?"

"Hell, no." Abe jerked his thumb at his chest. "I'm the agent. People work through me. You think I want them callin' the guy direct? Why the hell would I want that? First thing you know, someone's trying to make a deal behind my back, cut me out of my percentage."

"Uh-huh," I said. "So you wouldn't normally give out your client's number. I'm just wondering if for any reason at all you might have done so in this case."

"Yeah, well, I didn't. Of that I am sure."

"Then let me ask you this. Where were you at nine fifteen this morning?"

Abe Feinstein looked at me. Blinked. "I beg your pardon?"

"I thought that might give you a chuckle. The old staple from detective fiction. What were you doing on the night of etcetera, etcetera. In this case it's this morning at nine fifteen."

"Are you serious?"

"Absolutely. Someone made a threatening phone call at that time. Whoever made it was someone with access to the new number."

"Well, it wasn't me."

"Yes, but you didn't give it out to anyone. Which narrows the field of who it could be."

Abe made an irritated gesture. "Just because *I* didn't give it out doesn't mean it wasn't given. That numbnuts secretary probably told the whole world."

The waiter slid the check on the table. Abe snatched it up with a proprietary air. He held it at arm's length, squinted at it, scowled. "Well, now," he said. "We can add this up, or just split it down the middle. Of course, I may have had a little more."

Good guess. I'd had coffee and a toasted corn muffin. But I wasn't about to argue.

"Down the middle's fine," I said.

"Good," Abe said. "Why don't you give me the cash, I'll put it on my credit card."

"Sure."

I gave him the money, and he took out the card. It was his business credit card. As he handed it to the waiter, it occurred to me just how many ways the man was making out on the deal. He was pocketing my cash, which was an excessive amount, covering much of his lunch. Plus, he would doubtless be charging Kenneth P. Winnington for a business lunch on the one hand, while getting a receipt and writing it off his taxes on the other. Not bad for half an hour's work.

Perhaps it was that cynical assessment that caused me to say, after the waiter had left with the credit card, "Thought of an answer yet?"

"Huh?"

"Where were you at nine fifteen this morning?"

"You want me to answer that?"

"Yes, I do. Don't take it personally, but anyone who had access to the new number is gonna have to answer that."

"I was in my apartment. Which is also my office. Where else would I be?"

"Anyone can vouch for that?"

Abe frowned irritably. "I work alone. I am a one-man show."

"How about phone calls?"

"What?"

"Any business calls? Anyone call you at your office, can vouch for the fact you were there to answer the phone?"

"No, they didn't. Which is not unusual. Most people are considerate, don't call before ten."

"So you have no alibi for nine fifteen?"

Abe Feinstein squinted his eyes, crinkled up his nose. "What, are you nuts? You think I'm a suspect. I mean, do I look like a good suspect to you?"

"Frankly, you don't," I said. I smiled. "But it's not a book, it's real life. So I have to take what I can get."

11.

Elizabeth Abbott didn't look like a very good suspect either. A tall woman with angular features and piercing eyes, she certainly seemed intimidating enough, but I flunked her out on her voice. Elizabeth Abbott had a sharp, high-pitched, irritating voice, with which she didactically made her various points, and I just couldn't reconcile it with the hoarse whisper I'd heard on the phone.

I wondered if I should ask her to whisper. It occurred to me at some point during the investigation I might have to have all the suspects do that.

"A good editor has to know what the readers want," Elizabeth Abbott declaimed. "More to the point, a good editor has to know what *Kenneth P. Winnington's* readers want."

I might have asked her, "More to *what* point?" since I hadn't asked her anything of the kind. But since the woman seemed to need no prompting, I was happy to sit back and listen. At least for a while.

"Uh-huh," I said, figuring that was all that was necessary on my part.

It was.

"Absolutely," she said. "The readers have certain expectations. If you fulfill them, you're fine. If you don't, you're dead."

"And you know what those expectations are?"

"Of course. Take his latest book, *Woman on the Edge*." She looked at me. "Have you read it?"

"Actually, I haven't."

"That's not surprising. Most of his readers are women."

"Is that right?"

"Oh, yes, of course. Most of *all* readers are women. But his in particular."

"And why is that?"

"Because that's who his books appeal to. Always have. Ever since *Die, Lady, Die*. That's what set the standard. A likable female protagonist, sympathetic yet strong. Gets 'em every time."

"This is a continuing character?"

She looked at me as if I were an idiot. "Certainly not. You can't do suspense with a continuing character. If you know the character's going to continue, where's the suspense?"

"So when you talk about setting the standard, and the strong female protagonist?"

"*That's* the standard," she said. "The strong female protagonist. He always has one. It's just not the same one."

"Uh-huh," I said. "But . . ."

"But what?"

"Well, if he always has a strong female protagonist, and if you know she's gonna survive, because the strong female protagonist survives in all the books, where's the suspense?"

The look Elizabeth Abbott gave me was not kind. "You don't know publishing," she said. "One works, the other doesn't. It's as simple as that."

"You were telling me about his latest book."

"Yes. With regard to what the public wants. If you haven't read it it won't mean as much. But the fact is, Mr. Winnington made a mistake in that book. He wrote something his readers wouldn't have liked. I pointed it out to him and he fixed it. If you read the book, you wouldn't know it was ever there. But if it had gone out . . ."

"What would have happened?"

"Nothing immediate. In terms of sales. Some reviewers would have picked up on it. But that doesn't matter, no one reads the reviews anyway. Not for a best seller. They buy it because it's there. Anyway, sales of the book wouldn't have suffered."

She held up one finger. "But the *next* book. Next time out, you'd have seen a big drop-off. How big, how small, hard to gauge. But when you're talking best seller, even a ten percent drop is huge. It's also the difference of being near the top of the best-seller list and the bottom. And I don't have to tell you how a drop like that would affect the *next* book going out."

"Uh-huh," I said. "And does Mr. Winnington know this?"

"I beg your pardon?"

"I mean, yes, he knows you asked for the change. But does he know the effect of it, the way you're telling me?"

"Ah, yes, I see," she said. "That's a good point. I've *told* him the effect of it. Whether he took it to heart or not is another matter."

"Uh-huh," I said. I remembered what Abe Feinstein had said about Kenneth P. Winnington's callousness in dumping Doug Mark. I wondered just how secure Elizabeth Abbott's position was. Or how secure she *thought* it was. And whether she worried about it.

"Now, then," I said. "With regard to the present situation."

"That's a fine way of putting it," she said. "I would think I would have to edit that. Present situation? Didn't you tell me someone threatened his wife?"

"Yes, I did."

"Well, that's not the present situation. That's awful. That's horrible. That's shocking, and something should be done."

"That's why I'm here."

"That's fine, but has he notified the police?"

"Not yet."

"Why not?"

"He'd prefer to keep it quiet if he can."

"I suppose. But it's such a scary thing. Celebrities are so exposed."

"It's his wife who's been threatened."

"Yes, but it's because of him. Isn't that right? I mean, who'd want to threaten her?"

"Do you know her?"

"Not really."

"Were you at the wedding?"

"I had to be. I'm his editor."

"What do you think of her?"

"Why?"

"I don't know. In a way, I'm piecing together a puzzle. I need as many pieces as I can get."

She frowned. "Are you a writer too?"

"Actually, I am."

"Well, then, lay off the puzzle pieces. Doesn't sound true to life, makes it seem contrived."

"Thanks for the hint," I said. "Could you tell me about Mrs. Winnington?"

"Too young, too pretty."

"What do you mean?"

"That says it all. Sometimes you do best with an economy of words. Too young, too pretty may sound catty, may sound short, but is surprisingly apt."

"You've dealt with her, then? Aside from the wedding?"

"Yes, of course," she said. "Mostly on the phone. I'll call Kenneth and get her."

"How does she react?"

"What do you mean?"

"At having another woman call her husband on the phone?"

"Don't be silly. I'm his editor."

"Would that make a difference?"

She frowned, pushed her wire-rimmed glasses up on her nose. "I think you're off on the wrong track. The point is, my relationship with Mr. Winnington's wife is virtually nonexistent and will not help you. Now, is there anything else that might?"

"There's the phone number. That's the main thing I'm concerned with. The new number."

"Yes, I have it. No, I have not been making threatening phone calls. I don't know what else I can tell you."

"When did you get it?"

"The new number?"

"Yes."

"I got it Thursday afternoon."

"Are you sure?"

"Absolutely."

"How do you know?"

"Because I called Thursday morning and the number had been changed. Which was a fine how-do-you-do. He had a new unlisted number, and the phone company won't give it out, no matter who you are."

"So how'd you get it?"

"The secretary called. David Pryne. I gave him a piece of my mind."

"Why?"

"What do you mean, why? He called me Thursday afternoon to give me the number. Well, I needed it Thursday morning. *Not* Thursday afternoon."

"I take it you made that clear."

Her chin came up and she looked at me narrowly, as if to see if I were making fun of her.

I pretended not to notice, said, "So, who did you give it to?"

She blinked. "What?"

"The new number. Who have you given it to?"

"No one."

"Are you sure?"

"Sure, I'm sure. Who would I give his number to?"

"I don't know. An assistant. The copy editor. Someone in the art department."

She waved it away. "None of them deal with him. He only deals with me."

"What about the publicity department?"

"They deal with his publicist. Never with him."

"How do you know that?"

"Huh?"

"How do you know one of them didn't call him direct?"

"How do I know anything? Because it isn't done. That's on the one hand. On the other hand, they wouldn't have the number."

"No, but they could get it."

"How?"

"All right, you tell me. What's his new number?"

"What?"

"What's Kenneth P. Winnington's new number?"

"You want his number?"

"I want you to tell me what it is."

"I don't know offhand."

"I wouldn't think you did. I assume it's written down?"

She said nothing, glared at me.

"Where is it written down? Where do you keep his number?"

"On the Rolodex."

"So," I said, "any time you weren't in your office, anyone could walk in here, flip through the Rolodex, and get his new number."

"They'd be seen," she said irritably.

"Maybe so," I said. "But if they were someone who had a right to be there—perhaps your assistant—no one would think anything of it."

"My assistant is not making crank phone calls to Kenneth P. Winnington's wife."

"No, but she might have given the number to someone else."

"What makes you think my assistant is a she?"

"All right, *he* might have given the number to someone else."

She frowned. "My assistant *is* a woman. There's just no reason to assume so. Anyway, the idea is ridiculous. No one here would be involved in such a thing."

"I'm glad to hear it," I said. "Would you mind showing me the new number on the Rolodex?"

"Why?"

"I'd just like to see it."

Grudgingly, Elizabeth Abbott swiveled around and reached for the Rolodex. Her hand grasped the knob, but didn't turn it. And there was a strange look on her face. It took me a few seconds to realize it was embarrassment.

I stepped up next to her and looked.

The Rolodex was flipped open to the card with Kenneth P. Winnington's new number.

12.

It occurred to me if this were a mystery novel, Sherry Pressman was the one who would get killed. Kenneth P. Winnington's publicist had to be one of the most irritating people I'd ever met. A tiny person, she seemed determined to make up for her lack of size in any way whatsoever. Talking to her was an ordeal at best. Several times I came close to strangling her myself.

"You haven't read his books?" she said for the fourth time, peering over her wing-tipped glasses and jabbing a bony finger in my face. "How can you work for the man and not read his books?"

"I just started yesterday," I said defensively. And was instantly angry with myself. Why the hell should I be defensive?

"That's no excuse," she said. "What did you do when you got home last night? Got into bed, turned on the TV. And do you know why? Because you're lazy. You and ninety-five percent of the population. Do you know how many Americans actually read? And do you know why?"

"Would television be a good guess?"

She actually slapped at my jacket, as if from an elderly woman of her stature there was something charming about physical abuse. "Don't be a smart aleck," she said. "No one likes a smart aleck. The fact is, you went home last night and turned on the TV. The same day you got hired by one of our greatest living American authors."

Good god. It seems I'd insulted the next Ernest Hemingway.

"I was working all day," I said. "Not hanging out in the bookstores." And kicked myself in the head again. Yet another defensive statement.

"And what about your wife?" she said. "I bet your wife reads."

Not Kenneth P. Winnington was the immediate response that came to mind. The fact is, Alice does read. So do I, for that matter. But I didn't want to talk about it.

"We have a serious matter here," I said.

"Yes, we do," she said. "And you're to blame. If you won't read Kenny's books, who will?"

It occurred to me what charming publicity this woman must generate. Still, she was damn effective.

"I promise I'll buy one today," I said. "As soon as I get off work. But I won't get off work until you cooperate, so whaddya say?"

"You'll buy Kenny's book?"

"That's what I said."

"His *new* book."

"I beg your pardon?"

"His new book. *Woman on the Edge.* That's the one you should buy. The book came out, just made the list. Debuted at number fourteen. We can do better than that. So buy that book. Help us move up the list."

It occurred to me that would be his new *hardcover* book. What it might cost, I hated to imagine.

"Fine," I said. "Now, if you could help me out."

"Anything," she said. "Anything for Kenny. Such a sweet man. Don't you agree? Isn't he the sweetest man?"

Sweet is not how I would have described Kenneth P. Winnington. But Sherry Pressman was the type of woman who wouldn't let anything go.

"He's quite nice," I said.

"*Nice?*" she said. "What a lukewarm word that is. That's damning with faint praise. Nice. You think that's the type of word I'd quote from a review? You know what type of word *nice* is? *Nice* is the type of word, the *New York Times* calls the book *nice*, you use the *Publishers Weekly* quote instead."

"That's very interesting," I said. "Now, with regard to the phone call—"

"I don't understand this at all," she said. "Someone's playing a practical joke, and you're all making a big fuss."

"It's not a practical joke."

"Sounds like a practical joke to me. Calling on the phone. The type of thing that schoolboys do."

"Death threats are not a prank."

"Real ones, no. But if the caller is only kidding."

"That's the point. At the present time, there's no way to tell."

"Yes, well, if you don't mind my saying so, you're handling it all wrong."

I *did* mind her saying so.

"I beg your pardon?"

She looked at me as if I were a moron. "Hushing it up. This is the type of thing, you play it right, you make the front page of the *Daily News*. You can't *buy* publicity like that."

"Mr. Winnington wants to keep it quiet."

"I know he does, and I can't talk him out of it. A sweet man, but no business sense."

I looked at her in surprise. "You discussed this with him?"

"Yes, of course."

"When did you do that?"

64

"Just now. Right after you called me. Before you came up."

Up was Sherry Pressman's West 57th Street apartment, in the living room of which I was currently being abused. I'd called her from Elizabeth Abbott's office on Madison Avenue and 62nd Street and come right over, so the fact she'd discussed this with Kenneth P. Winnington was somewhat remarkable. She'd had at best a fifteen-minute window of opportunity.

"You called him and advised him to go public?"

"Of course I did. Why do you think I get the big bucks? I'm the best there is. And don't you forget it."

"And Mr. Winnington is having none of it?"

"Very short-sighted of him, but what do you expect? He's an artist. A creative type. Impractical, the whole lot of 'em."

"That must be very distressing," I said. "But the fact is, it's Winnington's call. If he wants it kept quiet, that's what we have to do."

"Yes," she said. "But you could reason with him. If he's concerned with his wife's safety, you might point out that the right type of publicity might scare this person off."

"I assume you advanced that theory?"

"He's not gonna take it coming from me. But you're a detective, right? If you think that's the way to go, it would lend more weight."

"I doubt if I'd have any influence."

"The other thing is, you could do it yourself. Leak the information. Or simply go to the police. Once the police are involved, everyone will know."

Not quite. I'd already been to the police, if you wanted to count MacAullif, and so far nobody'd said a word.

But I wasn't about to tell her that. "Why don't you leak the information yourself?" I said.

Her eyes shifted. "Oh, I couldn't do that. It wouldn't be ethical."

Ethical? Somehow I couldn't imagine this woman stopped by ethics. I thought a moment. Smiled.

"Oh, I see," I said. "You don't *dare* leak the information, because if Winnington found out, he'd fire you. Even if you leaked it anonymously, he'd figure it was you. So your only safe play is to have someone else leak it, that it can be traced back to. If I put out the story, you're off the hook."

I swear she ground her teeth together before speaking. "Some detective," she said. "Shouldn't you be thinking of your client's best interests, what's best for her? I mean, who hired you, him or her? And then you say, well, we have to do what Mr. Winnington wants."

I cocked my head. "What makes you think there's any difference of opinion?"

"I didn't say there was."

"You implied it."

She waved it away. "Please. I just asked a question. You tell me. What does your client want?"

"She wants this cleaned up as quickly and quietly as possible."

"There's another one, no head for business. How's about you talking some sense into her?"

"I'll make your opinion known to her," I said.

"You'll tell her it's a good idea?"

"I'll advance the opinion. That's the best I can do."

Sherry Pressman's attitude implied it wasn't good enough, but she begrudgingly let the matter drop.

"Now," I said. "Getting back to the matter at hand. I'm interested in when you got the new number."

"Why?"

"Because someone is making those calls. Whether they're a

prank, or whether they're on the level, the fact is someone is making them. That person has the new number, and I have to find out how they got it."

"Well, it wasn't from me."

"I'm glad to hear it. Now let's pin that down with some facts. When did *you* get the new number?"

"I believe it was Wednesday afternoon."

"Wednesday?"

"Wednesday or Thursday, I'm not sure. I mean, it's not as if it was particularly important."

"Well, can you fix the event by anything else that happened? Perhaps your business calendar."

"I fail to see how that would help," she said. Still, she picked up an appointment book and flipped it open. "Let me see, Wednesday of last week. Actually, it couldn't have been Wednesday. I was out all afternoon. It was either Tuesday or Thursday. I don't think it was as early as Tuesday."

"If it was Thursday, what time would it have been?"

"Sometime in the afternoon. The secretary called me, said Kenny changed his phone."

"Did he tell you why?"

"He said there'd been crank phone calls. I didn't think anything of it. Crank phone calls happen all the time. Now, if he'd told me there'd been death threats. But no, I have to find that out from you."

"So you got the number Thursday afternoon. And where did you write it down?"

"In the book. Where else?" She flipped the appointment book open to the address section in the back. "I wrote it right in the book."

"Actually, that's what I was going to ask you. Did you write it *right* in the book? I mean, right when he gave it to you? Or did you write it on a piece of paper first, and then copy it into the book?"

"What's the difference?"

"Are you saying that you did?"

"I'm not saying anything. I'm asking you what the difference is."

"The difference is, if you wrote it on a piece of paper, then there would be a piece of paper with that phone number on it. And I would be interested in knowing where that piece of paper went."

She cocked her head. "You have got to be kidding."

"But I'm not. Someone is making those phone calls. That person has access to the new number. They had to get it somewhere. The sources are limited. Fantastic though it might seem to you, it is possible that you were that source.

"For instance, I assume you have other clients. And they visit you here in your office. Suppose another of your authors, who didn't happen to like Kenneth P. Winnington, or perhaps was jealous of him, came up here and sat in the chair where I'm sitting now, and on the coffee table in front of them was a piece of paper with the notation *Kenneth P. Winnington* and a phone number. Well, if that author happened to be the person who was making the crank phone calls, he would realize at once that this was Kenneth P. Winnington's new number. In fact," I said, "if they already knew the number had been changed, they might have come to your office just for the purpose of trying to find out his new number. You see what I mean?"

Her eyes were wide. "You really suspect another author?"

"I don't specifically suspect anyone. We have an impossible situation. The phone number is changed, and yet the calls still come. There must be an explanation, so we have to explore all possibilities."

"I see," Sherry Pressman said.

"So let me ask you. Were there any authors up here since Thursday afternoon who might have seen that number written on a piece of paper?"

"I didn't say I wrote the number on a piece of paper."

"No, you didn't. But whether you did or not, you wrote it in your book. So, if an author was up here and you went into the kitchen to get a cup of coffee, he could have flipped your address book open to *Winnington*, and copied the new number. Isn't that right?"

Sherry Pressman said nothing, just glared at me.

"So, have there been any authors up here since you got that number?"

"Authors, no."

"*Authors*, no? How about anyone else? Who *was* up here since Thursday?"

"What's the difference? That doesn't fit with your theory."

"Yes, but it's just a theory. The caller doesn't have to be an author. It could be anyone. So who was here?"

"I had two prospective clients."

"Prospective clients? I thought you said no authors. You mean these were unpublished authors?"

She waved it away. "There's no such thing. *Unpublished author* is an oxymoron. These were wannabes."

"Wannabes?"

"Yes. They wannabe authors, but they're not. They're aspiring writers, at best."

"What would an unpublished writer want with a publicist?"

She looked at me. "Are you kidding? Where have you been? I can hype a book to an agent, an editor, a publisher. Even the press. A new writer, just starting out, trying to get published, you have no idea what good word of mouth means before that first manuscript makes the rounds."

"Did either of these two people sign with you?"

She shook her head. "No. Couldn't cut the mustard. I charge seventy-five hundred for the first six months."

My mouth dropped open. Good lord, was I in the wrong line of work.

"Well," I said, "if they knew that, why did they come to you?"

Her eyes shifted slightly before she said. "For evaluation."

"Evaluation?"

"Yes."

"You mean of their manuscripts?"

"That's right."

"Wait a minute, wait a minute," I said. "Are you telling me you read people's manuscripts, and then offer career advice?"

"Yes, of course."

"And you charge a reading fee?"

"Well, I can't work for nothing."

"How much do you charge?"

"Why? Do you have a manuscript?"

"Not at the present time. But I've certainly considered it. How much do you charge?"

"Five hundred dollars."

"Five *hundred* dollars?"

"That's right."

"And two people just paid you that?"

"Yes."

"For you to read their manuscript and tell them what you thought?"

"That's very reasonable. Some people charge a thousand."

"Good lord. Tell me, were either of the manuscripts any good?"

"Why do you ask?"

"Actually, I'm just curious. But I suppose it might make a difference. So were they any good?"

"No, they weren't. In point of fact, neither one was publishable."

"And did you tell them that?"

"Not in those terms."

I studied her a moment. "Of course not," I said. "You told them the manuscript needed work, and it would probably be advisable to generate some publicity before handing it over to an agent or editor."

"That's unkind," she said. "In each case, I actually gave quite helpful and practical advice on rewrites."

"And how did they take the criticism? Did either of them seem unbalanced enough to hold a grudge?"

"Not at all," she said irritably, "and I've resented the implication from the start. One of them is a very sweet woman with a mystery novel about cats. Totally unpublishable, which gives you an idea of how bad the writing was—pretty hard to miss when it's a woman with a mystery about cats. The other was a man with a thriller. Equally bad. Depressing, sadistic, a holy mess."

That sounded promising. "What's he like?" I said. "Tough, macho type?"

"Hardly. Mr. Penrose is a sweet little man, quite harmless, I assure you."

"But if he's writing a gruesome thriller . . ."

She waved it away. "Don't go by that. That's just the flavor of the month. He's also done a P.I. novel, a courtroom drama, and a cozy. All equally bad. The man has no talent whatsoever. But that doesn't seem to stop him."

"I see," I said. "Of course, you keep encouraging him with your evaluations."

She set her jaw defiantly. "I am not leading him on, I am merely trying to be kind."

"I'm sure you are," I said. "The fact is, this is a repeat customer, which is why you feel you can vouch for him."

"You really suspect Mr. Penrose?"

I shrugged. "As I say, it could be anyone. A man who's failed that many times could resent someone who's succeeded."

"So he threatens his wife," Sherry Pressman said sarcastically. "That's worse than one of Mr. Penrose's plots."

"That might be," I said, "but I'm going to need his address and phone number. Him and the other one. The woman with cats."

Sherry Pressman gave me the names and addresses and I copied them down. She did so very reluctantly. It was clear the woman was hugely frustrated by the fact that no one was going to let her publicize the death threats.

It occurred to me it would be particularly frustrating in the event that she was the one who had arranged for the death threats in the first place.

13.

Early next morning I was in my favorite position behind the hot dog stand on West 34th Street waiting for the creep to make the call. But this time I was somewhat more prepared. I was wearing my beeper, the one I usually wear for my job with Rosenberg and Stone. Today I was wearing it just for me. I had given the number out to Maxine Winnington, with instructions to beep me the minute the call came through. I could call her, get the number, and know immediately if the guy had called from the phone I was watching, the East Side phone Kenneth P. Winnington was watching, or another phone altogether.

It wasn't the best of all possible worlds. In fact, if Richard Rosenberg, whose beeper it actually was, had sprung for the newer, better beeper I'd requested, which allows the person beeping you to punch in a number that will be digitally displayed on your beeper, then I could have gotten the number instantaneously without even having to make the call. But Richard, in his infinite wisdom, felt it was his beeper, his office was the only one he cared to have beeping me, and why should he pay extra just so I could be beeped by somebody else?

As usual, I had found Richard impossible to argue with, so I still had the old beeper, which couldn't do anything but beep. If it beeped this time, I would know it wasn't the office, because the office knew I was on a leave of absence. It would be Maxine, wanting me to call her. As I say, it was the best I could do.

Long about nine fifteen a rather shady-looking individual used the phone, but with my track record from the day before, I didn't jump to any conclusions, just waited to see if my beeper went off. It didn't, and I let the gentleman go about his merry way.

My beeper went off about five minutes later. The good news was the call had come through. The bad news was, it wasn't from my corner. At the time I got beeped, there was no one on the phone at all.

I crossed the street, dodging cars, and called my client.

The phone was answered on the second ring. But no one said hello. There was just suddenly a loud, empty, echoing sound that meant the connection was open.

"Hello," I said. "Maxine, are you there?"

Then I heard her, over the speaker phone. "Oh, thank god it's you. We thought it was him."

"Him? What, calling back?"

"Back?" she said. "What do you mean, back?"

"Didn't he just call you?"

"No," she said. "He hasn't called. That's why we thought it was him."

"Then why did you beep me?"

"Beep you?"

"Yeah. Why did you beep me?"

"I didn't beep you."

"Yes, you did."

"Don't be silly. I would know if I had beeped you. I didn't beep you. I've gotta hang up now, so we can keep the line open."

And she hung up the phone.

Damn. What a revolting development that was. The beeper malfunctions, making me look like an asshole in front of my client.

If it *had* malfunctioned. But that had to be it. The only other person who might have beeped me was Alice. But it couldn't be her, because the beeper has two tones, intermittent and steady. Alice always beeps me on steady—that's how I know it's her.

The office uses intermittent. Which is the main number. The one I'd given Maxine. If she hadn't beeped me, the only one who could have, presumably, was the office. And, as I say, they wouldn't have, because they knew I wasn't working.

But it occurred to me, Richard Rosenberg's switchboard girls weren't that swift, and I suppose it was conceivable one of them might have forgotten I wasn't on call.

I dropped in another quarter, called the office.

"Rosenberg and Stone," said either Wendy or Janet. The two switchboard girls, in addition to being incompetent, happened to have identical voices, so it was impossible to ever know who you were dealing with.

"Hi," I said. "It's Stanley."

"Stanley," Wendy/Janet said. "You're on the beeper. I thought you weren't working."

"I'm *not* working."

"Then why are you on the beeper?"

"I was using it for something else. Did you beep me?"

"Of course I did. Who else would beep you? But I didn't expect you to answer."

"Then why did you beep me?"

"Oh. Richard told me to."

Richard told her to? That didn't compute at all. Richard knew I wasn't working. And Richard was competent.

"Then you don't know why?" I said.

"No."

"Then I'd better speak to Richard."

"Just a minute."

Wendy/Janet put me on hold. Seconds later, Richard Rosenberg came on the line.

"Stanley," Richard said. "Why are you on beeper?"

"It's a long story, Richard. Why did you have me beeped?"

"I thought it couldn't hurt. It didn't occur to me you'd have the thing on."

I felt as if my head were expanding. "Richard," I said. "Pardon me, but that doesn't make sense."

"Maybe not," Richard said, "but that's the situation. You answered the beeper, now I'm on the hook. Where are you?"

"I'm at a pay phone on the southeast corner of Thirty-fourth Street and Seventh Avenue."

"Yeah, well, stay there," Richard said. "They'll pick you right up."

"They? Who's they? Richard, what the hell is going on? Why'd you beep me?"

"Just one of those unfortunate things," Richard said. "Seems you're wanted by the police."

14.

I must have been wanted very much by the police, because I hadn't been standing there more than five minutes when a cruiser with the lights on pulled up and two uniformed cops got out.

"Stanley Hastings?" the older of the two said.

I tried to ignore the little knot that always seems to form in my stomach when I hear a cop call me by name. "Yes?" I said.

He opened the back door of the cruiser. "Get in."

I did, and the cops did, and away we went.

No one said a word.

I assumed this was the silent treatment, trying to get the suspect to crack. Since I wasn't sure what I was suspected of, it wasn't working.

"Where are we going?" I said.

No one said anything.

"Aw, come on," I said. "I'm a citizen. I have my rights."

The older cop who was driving said, "He has his rights."

The younger, shorter, stockier cop said, "Yeah, right." He half turned in the seat, said, "You have the right to remain silent. If you give up the right to remain silent . . ."

I blinked. Miranda? The guy was reading me my Miranda rights? What the hell was going on?

I waited till he was finished, said, "What am I charged with?"

"Now, now," the older cop said. "No one said you were charged with anything."

"Then why read me my rights?"

"I thought you asked for them."

"No, I just asked where we were going."

"I don't think that's in the Miranda rights, is it?" the older cop said. "The right to know where you're going?"

"Not that I recall," the short, stocky one said. "Should I read it again to make sure?"

Great. As if I didn't have enough troubles, I'd drawn a pair of cynical, wiseass cops who were under the mistaken impression that they were funny. I shut up and sat quietly in the back seat, while the car tooled downtown. The silence was oppressive, and it was a huge relief when the police car finally pulled to a stop.

Initially.

I tried to open the back, but of course it was locked. For a second I had a flash of panic that they were just going to go off and leave me there. Then the older cop came around and opened the back door. I stepped out gratefully onto the sidewalk.

And found myself face to face with Sergeant Thurman.

My heart sank.

I must explain. And apologize. I've had many dealings with the police in my less than illustrious career. And contrary to popular detective fiction, in almost all instances I found them to be clever, capable, intelligent men, far better equipped for solving crime than I could ever hope to be.

Then there was Sergeant Thurman, the exception that proved the rule. A walking cliché, straight out of a private eye novel. A cop so dense he couldn't solve the crime if you xeroxed the solution and handed it to him. I'd had the misfortune to work with him before. I'd prayed devoutly that I would never work with him again. And yet, here he was, my nemesis, standing before me, large as life, and whatever the hell he wanted, it couldn't be good.

"Well, well, well," Sergeant Thurman said. He was a bull-necked man who looked and talked like a prizefighter who'd taken one too many blows to the head. "So, Rosenberg gave you up."

I blinked. Richard Rosenberg had indeed given me up, if only through the bad luck of my wearing my beeper. Still, it was interesting Thurman looked at it like that.

"Come on, Thurman," I said. "What's up? Why did you pull me in?"

"As if you didn't know," Thurman said. It was one of his favorite expressions. And one of my least favorite.

"If I knew I wouldn't be asking. Come on, what's up?"

"You know where we are?" Thurman said.

Actually, I had no idea. I'd hopped out of the police car, seen Sergeant Thurman, and been unable to focus on anything else. I was vaguely aware we were in front of a white stone building of some sort, but what it was I couldn't have ventured a guess.

"No," I said. "Where are we?"

Sergeant Thurman put his hand on my shoulder. "Come on."

We went upstairs, inside, down a hallway, around a corner, downstairs, through a swinging door. We were in a wide corridor with florescent lighting and a marble floor.

The smell of formaldehyde hit my nostrils.

I blinked.

"What is this, the morgue?"

Thurman said nothing, kept his hand on my shoulder,

pushed me along. We went down the corridor, took a left through another swinging door.

And confirmed the fact we were in the morgue. In it were two marble slabs. One was draped with a sheet. At the other, a doctor was slicing up a corpse. He was using an electrical circular saw, and had just cracked the chest. Blood was everywhere.

I'd never been present at an autopsy before, and I sincerely hope I never am again. At first glance, my knees grew weak, my legs got rubbery, and my stomach did a back flip. I think the only thing that kept me from keeling over was not wanting to give Sergeant Thurman the satisfaction of seeing me do it. That and the desperate need to know what the hell was going on.

I made myself look at the face of the body, trying to place it. He was a young man with dark hair, a swarthy complexion, moustache and sideburns. I was pretty sure I'd never seen him before, but poor as I am with faces, that wasn't necessarily true.

"Hi, doc," Sergeant Thurman said. "Sorry to bother you again, but I got someone here I'd like to have take a look."

The doctor was a white-haired gentleman, appeared to be around sixty-five. I found that encouraging. Now that I'm older, so many doctors I meet seem too young to be doctors, if you know what I mean. Anyway, I found the white hair reassuring, the elderly features strangely comforting. Were it not for the blood-splattered gown and gloves, I could imagine this man about to examine my eyes, ears, nose, and throat.

"Oh, sure, go ahead," the doctor said, barely glancing up from the body.

Thurman grunted his acknowledgment, pushed me over to the other slab.

So, no wonder I hadn't recognized the body. That wasn't it.

Thurman took hold of the sheet covering the slab and pulled it down.

I took a look and blinked.

Lying there, staring up at me, was the body of Sherry Pressman.

15.

"My god, it's true," I murmured.

"What's that?" Thurman said.

"Nothing," I said, mentally kicking myself.

"Nothing? What do you mean, nothing? You said, My god, it's true."

"I was in shock. Seeing the body."

"You ever seen it before?"

"Not as a body."

"You mean you've seen her alive?"

"Should I be answering these questions? I mean, am I a suspect here?"

"No one said you were a suspect."

"No one said I wasn't. Should I have an attorney present?"

"You have the right to an attorney. I can't see why you'd need one."

"You can't."

"No. *I* don't think you killed this woman. In spite of how much evidence there is."

"Evidence?"

"I don't think you did it."

"There's evidence against me?"

"I think you're innocent, and I can't see why cooperating's gonna hurt you at all."

"What's the evidence against me?"

"Well, now, that's not really my place to say. That's something you'll have to take up with the ADA."

"The ADA? What's going on? Am I being charged here?"

"Not at all. Like I say, I think you're innocent. But I don't want to get in trouble giving out stuff I wasn't supposed to give."

"Jesus Christ. Thurman—"

He shook his head. "Sorry. My instructions are to show you the body and bring you in. Which I intend to do. And I wasn't even gonna discuss it. Except for the rather extraordinary statement you made about it being true." He looked at me. "Isn't that what you said?"

I took a breath. "If you can't talk, I can't either. Let's go see the ADA."

"Suits me," Thurman said.

He yanked me out of there, stuck me in a police car, drove me down to the criminal court house. We went inside, went up in the elevator to the sixth floor.

The corridor he was taking me down seemed familiar. So did the door we stopped in front of.

"Who's the ADA?" I said.

Thurman said nothing, pushed the door open, escorted me inside. I walked inside, stopped and blinked.

Déjà vu all over again.

The man sitting at a desk was ADA Baby Face Frost.

16.

ADA Henry Frost was a plump young man who always looked like some kid who was trying on his father's three-piece suit. The cops called him Baby Face, never *to* his baby face, but behind his chubby back.

I'd had occasion to work with Baby Face Frost in solving a string of murders. The reason for that occasion was the fact I'd been arrested for several of them. But since I hadn't been guilty of any of them, and since those arrests had largely been due to the ineptitude of Sergeant Thurman, and since the matter had eventually come to a satisfactory conclusion with the killer behind bars, there was really no reason for Frost to think unkindly of me.

Was there?

"Well, here he is," Sergeant Thurman said. "And wait'll you hear what he has to say."

"I can't wait," Frost said. "Do come in, Mr. Hastings. Please sit down. Forgive me if we skip the amenities, but we have this murder here. Just what is Sergeant Thurman alluding to?"

I sat in a chair, put up my hands. "Whoa. Time out," I said. "You may have a murder here, but I have my rights. I'd like to know if I'm a suspect, a witness, or what. Sergeant Thurman says there's some evidence against me."

ADA Frost frowned. "You weren't supposed to say that, Sergeant," he said. As always, when displeased he looked sulky.

"So there *is* evidence against me."

Frost waved it away. "Let's not quibble. I know you, you know me. I don't for a minute think you committed this crime. So why should we argue over words?"

"Great," I said. "Why is it, I hear that, my first reaction is I better call my lawyer?"

"That's what's known as a guilty reaction," Frost said. "You should try to control it. The more guilty reactions you have, the harder it is to appear innocent."

"Thanks for the hint," I said. "Should I get Rosenberg down here, or you wanna level with me and let me in on what's goin' on?"

"I really don't think you need a lawyer at this time, but it's your call. Would you like an attorney present?"

"Not so far. Of course, that might change. For the time being, I'm willing to listen to what you have to say."

"Actually, I was more interested in what *you* have to say."

"Then perhaps I *will* need an attorney. You wanna keep sparring, or you wanna get into it?"

"Well, let's kick things off," Frost said. "Did you recognize the woman you saw in the morgue?"

"Before I answer that question, I would like to know exactly what is meant by the suggestion that the police have evidence against me."

Frost frowned, again appeared to sulk. "Nothing, really. Your name on a piece of paper, that's all."

"A piece of paper?"

"That's right. The name Stanley Hastings. In what would appear to be the victim's own handwriting."

"And just where was this piece of paper found?"

"Well, actually, that's the bad part."

"Oh?"

"It was in her hand."

"What?"

Frost nodded. "I'm afraid that's right."

I stared at Frost. "The victim was found clutching a piece of paper with my name on it?"

"You got it."

"My god, it's like something straight out of a mystery novel."

"Yes, isn't it. I understand the woman dealt in them."

"You think there's a connection?"

"To you, or to mystery novels?"

"This may surprise you, but I don't find any of this particularly amusing. Would you mind telling me where the body was found?"

"In her apartment."

"That figures."

Frost looked at me. "Oh? Why do you say that?"

"She struck me as the type that didn't go out much."

"Then you *had* seen her before?"

"I'd seen her *alive*, yes."

"And just when was that?"

"Yesterday afternoon."

"Around what time?"

"I dunno. Somewhere around three."

Frost whistled.

"Why?" I said. "When was she killed?"

Frost just smiled.

"All right," I said. "That does it. My cooperation is withdrawn." Even as I said it, I realized I was locking the barn door after the horse was out.

"No reason for that," Frost said. "The woman was probably killed some time yesterday afternoon. We'll be able to pin it down a little better when we get a full autopsy report. But, while you *could* have done it, once again let me assure you I don't for a minute believe you did."

"I find that less reassuring all the time," I said. "Just for a point of reference, *how* was she killed?"

"You couldn't tell from the body?"

I hesitated.

"Aw, come on, take a whack at it," Frost said. "No one's gonna make fun of you if you're wrong."

"That wasn't really my concern," I said. "But if I had to hazard a guess, I'd say she'd been strangled."

"You'd say right," Frost said. "And I assure you your knowing that doesn't make you any more a suspect in my book."

"Glad to hear it," I said. "Any more a suspect and I'd begin to wonder why I'm not wearing handcuffs. Tell me, how'd you track me down?"

"I called Richard Rosenberg, told him I wanted to talk to you. He said you weren't working today. I asked him to beep you. He said that would do no good because you wouldn't be on the beeper. I figured that was a hollow ruse, and told him to do it anyway. He did, and here you are."

"It wasn't a hollow ruse. He didn't know I was on the beeper."

"Just a bit of bad luck, I guess. Well, now, we've talked about everything you want to talk about. How about talking about what I want to talk about?"

"And just what is that?"

"Why did you happen to call on Sherry Pressman yesterday afternoon at three o'clock?"

"Oh, dear."

"You got a problem with that? I hope not. Just when we were getting on so well."

"Speak for yourself."

Frost frowned. "Let's not be like that. Haven't I been totally frank and forthcoming, and told you what you wanted to know?"

"Yes," I said. "And you probably didn't hurt anyone, violate any professional ethics, or put yourself in a position to be sued."

"Is that what we're looking at here?"

"I have no idea. I'm not a lawyer."

"Again with the lawyer. Must I remind you you are not accused of any crime?"

"Can you give me your blanket assurance that anyone I mention won't be?"

"Don't be silly."

"There you are."

Frost frowned again. "I'm afraid I'm going to have to insist on an answer to that question."

"Then I'm going to call my lawyer."

17.

Richard Rosenberg listened to my story, grimaced, cocked his head. "Can't you do anything right?"

"Richard. It's hardly my fault the woman was killed."

"I don't mean that. I mean spilling your guts to the cops."

"I couldn't help it. When I saw her face it was a shock."

"Right. That's when you made your first damaging admission. That should be your first clue. That's when a bright person says, uh-oh, I made a damaging admission. Now I'm in trouble, I better call my lawyer. But you, you don't do that. Do you know why?"

I said nothing, waited for him to finish. But Richard wasn't going to let it go.

"Well, do you know why?"

"No," I said. "I think I'm too damn smart?"

"Not at all," Richard said. "You *know* you're too damn *dumb*. You make a damaging admission to the cops, which is why you ought to call your lawyer, but you don't, because you're too embarrassed to admit to me you made a damaging admission. So, like a moron, you try to carry on and patch it up yourself. So what happens, before you know it you've dug your grave a little deeper, and now, instead of one damaging admission, we have three. You knew the murdered woman, you've been to her apartment, and you were there just about the time she was killed."

"I also knew she'd been strangled."

"Right," Richard said. "A fourth damaging admission. You're having a hell of a day."

"Still, I called you."

"Right. After your fourth damaging admission, you made the call. Nice going."

"Don't I get some credit for calling? According to you, the more damaging admissions I make, the more reluctant I am to tell you about it."

Richard looked at me. "You're taking this awfully well. If you don't mind my saying so, you don't seem at all concerned."

Richard was right. Maybe it was the fact I knew both Thurman and Frost. Or maybe it was the fact neither one of them was inclined to think I was involved in the crime. But for once I did not feel personally threatened, despite the rather unfortunate position I found myself in.

"Right," I said. "I didn't kill this one, and knowing that makes me drunk with power. Listen, Richard, you wanna stop beating me up and tell me what I ought to do?"

"Well, now, there's the problem," Richard said.

"What do you mean?"

"I'm your attorney. But I'm not your client's attorney. And I'm not your client's best-selling husband's attorney. So I'm representing your interests and not theirs."

"So?"

"It is in your best interests to see that you are not convicted of this crime. Even if it meant convicting your client or her husband. On the other hand, it is in your best interests to see that your client or her husband don't sue the shit out of you for violating professional ethics by implicating them in a crime."

"How can they sue me? I have no money."

"More to the point," Richard said. "It's important here that your client and her husband are not put in the position to sue *me* for advising you to tell the police things that might implicate them."

"So you're advising me not to talk?"

"Don't be silly. You've already talked. If you stop now, it's a red flag. The cops will find out who you were working for, and that person will become prime suspect number one. No, what you want to do is tell your story, making a frank and full disclosure in the spirit of helpful cooperation, and do it in such a way that your client becomes such an unlikely suspect it's ridiculous to assume she ever could have had anything to do with it."

"So you *want* me to talk."

Richard grimaced. "Well, that's the other problem. I understand that your clients don't want any publicity."

"Mr. Winnington would prefer it."

"That's fine. Whether he gets it or not is another matter. The important thing is, if there is any publicity it doesn't come from us. So, while I would like you to talk, I don't want you to say anything."

"Richard."

Richard put up his hand. "Please don't worry about that. I'll tell you how to do it. It's a little messy, but it can be done. There's just one thing."

"What's that?"

"It's gonna take lawyers."

18.

It took three of them. Four if you counted Baby Face Frost. Aside from him you had Richard Rosenberg, representing me; Barney K. Rancroft, representing Kenneth P. Winnington; and Morton Steinway, representing Maxine.

When I say representing, don't get the wrong idea. My client and her husband were not present. Only the attorneys, ADA Frost, and me.

ADA Baby Face Frost viewed the array of attorneys with distaste, and said, "For the record, could the parties present please state their name and their connection to the current case, that is the murder of one Sherry Pressman."

"Certainly," Richard said. "I am Richard Rosenberg, attorney at law. I represent Stanley Hastings, who has been questioned as a witness in this matter."

Barney K. Rancroft cleared his throat. Being a man with several chins, that took some time. When he felt he had harrumphed enough, he said, "I am Barney K. Rancroft, attorney at law. And I am not willing to concede my interest in this matter at the present time. Therefore, let me state for the record that it has been made known to me that the police are conducting an investigation into the death of the decedent; that in the course of this investigation, they will naturally be interested in any persons connected in any way to the decedent; that the decedent made her living working in the field of publishing, in the capacity of what is commonly known as a publicist."

Rancroft looked around the table, as if to make sure everyone understood and agreed with this assessment of the facts, then raised his hand. "I put forth the hypothetical situation, that it is possible that one of the authors represented by the decedent Sherry Pressman is also a client of mine. In that event, I would certainly wish to protect my client's rights, particularly in terms of any invasion of privacy, especially one which might result in adverse publicity. I am here to guard against that happenstance."

ADA Frost blinked. "You are here," he said, ironically, "on the off chance we might wish to know something about an author who might happen to be a client of yours?"

"Thank you," Barney K. Rancroft said suavely, "for such a clear understanding of the situation."

Frost nodded grimly, turned to the other attorney. "What about you?"

Morton Steinway was tall and rather good-looking, with wavy chestnut hair.

I wondered how well he knew my client.

I chided myself for the thought, and realized I needn't have had it. The minute Morton Steinway opened his mouth, he transformed himself from the macho stud lover into the boring, stuffy, nitpicking lawyer.

"I'm Morton Steinway, attorney at law. And I'm not even willing to concede that I'm actually here."

"I beg your pardon?" Frost said.

"Well, hypothetically, now," Morton Steinway said, "suppose the only reason I were here at all was as a result of phone calls made by Richard Rosenberg, largely—and here, please understand I am making no accusation, this is merely speculation and hypothetical—but suppose I was brought here by Mr. Rosenberg largely to divert suspicion from his own client and thrust it onto others. Well, now, my very presence here could do that. Therefore, I am not willing to admit to my presence, in so much as it might in any way involve any client I might have, real or imaginary, living or dead, in any aspect of this case."

ADA Frost opened his mouth, closed it again. "I was going to say run that by me again," he said, "then I realized I don't want to hear it. I get the gist of what you are saying, and quite candidly, I don't appreciate it. We have a murder here. I would expect some cooperation. I would prefer to proceed without the double talk."

Frost might have preferred that, but it was simply not to be. Not with three separate attorneys with three separate clients all maneuvering for position. In point of fact, it was a good forty-five minutes of hypothetical bullshit before we ever got down to brass tacks.

Even then, it was a battle for every inch.

"Now then," Frost said, his exasperation showing. "Mr. Rancroft, we have conceded for the sake of argument that hypothetically you might be the attorney for Kenneth P. Winnington, who is a best-selling author."

Barney K. Rancroft raised his finger. "The best-selling author part is not hypothetical. Mr. Winnington is indeed on the *New York Times* best-seller list."

"Good for him," Frost said. "And you, Mr. Steinway," he said to the other attorney, "might hypothetically be representing his wife—and, yes, I understand this is not a hypothetical wife, it is an actual wife—and in the event the investigation should have anything to do with her, you would wish to represent her interests, though you have absolutely no reason to imagine why it should."

Frost cocked his head. "How'm I doin' so far?"

"Fine by me," Richard said. "Would you care to proceed?"

"Thank you so much," Frost said. "Now then, there was also the hypothetical possibility that all these parties might in some way be involved with the witness, Stanley Hastings. Would you care to take it from there?"

"Absolutely," Richard said. "To begin with, I think this might be an excellent time for Mr. Barney K. Rancroft and Mr. Morton Steinway to advise my client to make a full and frank disclosure to the police of any connection he may have had with either Mr. or Mrs. Winnington."

Rancroft and Steinway both lunged to their feet, ready to object.

Richard took no notice, went on as if there had been no interruption. "Because, in the event that they don't, the police will undoubtedly drag their clients down here and simply ask them instead. And being hauled into the police station's probably not the swiftest move for anyone attempting to control publicity."

The attorneys shifted uncomfortably, looked at each other.

"However," Richard said, "it's entirely up to you. If you don't want my client to say anything about your clients, just say so, and I will advise him not to answer any questions."

At which point Richard sat down, took a newspaper out of his briefcase, and began reading it, as if he had lost all interest in the proceedings.

The two attorneys looked at each other, looked at me, went off in the corner, huddled for a few minutes, then came back and did exactly what Richard wanted. They instructed me to tell anything I knew about my dealings with their clients.

So I did. I told them the whole schmear. The crank phone calls. The caller ID. The tracking down the new number.

"So, that's very interesting," Frost said. "Only a handful of

95

people had access to the new number. One of them is Sherry Pressman, and Sherry Pressman is dead."

"I'm not willing to concede that," Barney K. Rancroft said.

"It's not a concession," Frost said. "It happens to be a fact. You can argue whether or not it means anything. But it is certainly true. Now then, is there any connection whatsoever between the crank phone calls and the death of Sherry Pressman?"

"Only one I can think of," I said.

All heads turned to me. I must say, the looks the lawyers gave me were not kind.

"Well?" Frost demanded.

"Me," I said. "I'm the connection. I called on the woman, asked her about the phone number. Right after that she was killed. Holding a piece of paper with my name on it. There's your connection right there."

"Obviously," Frost said. "But is there any other connection?"

"How can there possibly be?" Rancroft said. "It simply makes no sense. The woman was a harmless publicist. So what if she had my client's unlisted phone number? Is it your theory now that she was killed before she could divulge who she gave that number to?"

"It's not that far-fetched if that person was contemplating murder," Frost said.

"Yeah, but you heard what he said." Rancroft jabbed a chubby finger in my direction. "She didn't give the number out to anybody, and the only people she saw were two aspiring writers who came to discuss their manuscripts."

"Right," Frost said. He turned to me. "I don't believe you mentioned their names."

I fished my notebook out of my pocket. "One's Wilber Penrose, the other's Linda Toole."

"There you are," Rancroft said. "These are the people you should be investigating."

"I assure you we will," Frost said. "For the moment I'd like to continue this discussion. Now then, Mr. Hastings, you called on Sherry Pressman yesterday afternoon at approximately three o'clock?"

"That's right."

"And before that, where had you been?"

"Haven't we been over this?" Rancroft said.

"Yes, but I'd like to work backward now, if you don't mind. Now, where was that, Mr. Hastings?"

"I'd been at the editor's. Elizabeth Abbott."

"Uh-huh. And prior to that?"

"With the agent. Abe Feinstein."

"Yes. And you met him in a deli?"

"That's right."

"And prior to that?"

"I was at my client's apartment. Getting the names and addresses of these people."

"Uh-huh," Frost said. "And the reason for that was your plan to track the anonymous phone caller through Caller ID had failed, due to the caller using pay phones, so now you were attempting another line of inquiry."

"Exactly."

"I find that rather interesting."

"Really," Rancroft said. "Frankly, I find it remarkably dull. In point of fact, I haven't heard a fresh idea in the last half hour. When are you going to let us leave?"

Obviously Barney K. Rancroft had never dealt with Baby Face Frost, or he would not have made such a deliberately inflammatory statement. I *had* dealt with Baby Face Frost, and figured the odds of Rancroft leaving anytime soon had just sunk to zero. But aside from a slight crinkling around the eyes, Frost gave no sign.

"Oh, don't go just yet," Frost said. "Let me tell you what I

find interesting. Mr. Hastings began calling on people yesterday due to the failure of Caller ID. That failure became clear
yesterday morning, when a phone call was identified as coming
from another phone. It was at that point that Mr. Hastings
went to Mr. Winnington's apartment, to discuss the fact that
Caller ID was not working, and that he should go at it from a
different angle. It was then—and correct me if I'm wrong, Mr.
Hastings—but it was then for the first time that you heard of
the existence of the decedent, Sherry Pressman. Is that right?"

"Yes, it is."

"You see why that's interesting?" Frost said. "Sherry Pressman doesn't even come into this until yesterday morning. Assuming there's a connection. Yesterday morning, when all else
failed, Mr. Hastings gets a lead to Sherry Pressman. He calls
on her by three o'clock yesterday afternoon. Immediately after
that, she is killed. If there is a connection—more to the point,
if there is a cause and effect, that Sherry Pressman has the
number and is being investigated for having the number, and
that is why she is silenced—well, in that event, the killer not
only knew that Sherry Pressman had the information, but also
knew that Mr. Hastings was after it."

"That's incredibly far-fetched," Rancroft said.

"Maybe so," Frost said. "But it's probably true. Because if it
isn't cause and effect, then it has to be the most monumental
coincidence. And I, for one, do not believe in coincidence."

I suppressed a smile, wished MacAullif had been there to
hear that. Not believing in coincidence was one of his pet say-
ings.

Rancroft's face retreated behind two of his chins, gave him
the look of a turtle pulling his head into his shell. "Say that's
true," he said. "So what?"

Frost beamed. "Well, then. We would have something to go
on, wouldn't we? Because whoever killed Sherry Pressman

would have to be aware of what Mr. Hastings was doing. And there would be a very limited field, since Mr. Hastings didn't know what he was doing himself."

"Thanks a lot," I said.

"What I mean is, you had no intention of doing so until the very day. Will you grant me that?"

"Yes, of course."

"So there you are. Hastings huddles with his client and her husband, decides to track down the number by calling on these people. He spends the day calling on three of them. The last one he calls on dies. Almost immediately after his visit. If we assume the killer was someone who knew what Mr. Hastings was doing, then we have a very narrow field. And one we must investigate." He turned to me. "Mr. Hastings, who was present when you had this discussion yesterday with your client?"

"My client, her husband, and his secretary, David Pryne."

"The secretary knew the new number?"

"Yes. In fact, he was the one who supplied it to the various parties, including the decedent."

"Okay," Frost said. "Let's have 'em in here."

Barney K. Rancroft and Morton Steinway were on their feet at once, spouting objections.

"Now see here," Rancroft said. "We've given you our full co-operation, precisely because this is the situation we wished to avoid. It's why we cooperated." Jabbing his finger at me. "It's why we had *him* cooperate." Jabbing his finger at Richard. "It's the stick he beat us with to make *sure* we'd cooperate. Controlling publicity, keeping our clients out of it, not having them dragged in here. And now you propose to do precisely that."

Frost smiled. It was a beatific smile, dimples forming on his chubby baby face. Only the eyes were hard.

"Sorry."

19.

It was a zoo.

First you had Kenneth P. Winnington and his lawyer. Then you had Maxine and her lawyer. Then you had me and my lawyer.

David Pryne didn't have a lawyer, but that didn't stop Barney K. Rancroft or Morton Steinway from interceding in his behalf at any given opportunity.

Had I been ADA Frost, I would have taken these people one by one. Apparently, that wasn't Frost's style. So, instead, we had a zoo.

"You have no right to drag me in here," Kenneth P. Winnington asserted, a typical, pompous, windbag declaration that showed how much *he* knew about it—ADA Frost not only had the right to drag him in there, it happened to be his job. The fact that he refrained from saying so showed great restraint on his part.

"I'm sorry to inconvenience you," Frost said, "but we do have this crime. Cooperate and I'll have you out of here as quickly as possible. And, I might add, as quietly as possible. I've been told you'd all like to control publicity. As far as I'm concerned, there's no reason for you to get your names in the papers. Unless of course you refuse to cooperate, and things become complicated."

"I will not have my client threatened," Barney K. Rancroft said hotly.

"I'm glad to hear it," Frost said. "And if anyone threatens him, I'll be the first to instruct them not to. Now then, if we could move on, I'd like to go back to yesterday morning when you had the discussion of the anonymous phone call. As I understand it, Mr. Hastings had been out in the field, staking out a suspected phone, but it proved not to be the one used that morning. You called him in and had a conference. Present at the conference were you, your wife, your secretary, and Mr. Hastings. Is that right?"

Mr. Winnington, not about to give Frost the time of day unless pressed, looked at his attorney.

"I think you can answer that," Rancroft said.

Grudgingly, Winnington said, "That is essentially correct."

"Essentially?" Frost said. "What's wrong with it?"

"If you want to be technically correct—which I'm sure you do—then I take exception to the suggestion that I called him in. And the implication that I was the one who precipitated the discussion. In point of fact, Mr. Hastings came in on his own accord, and tracking down these people was his idea."

"Now that's very interesting," Frost said. "Talking to these people was his idea?"

"That's right."

"Can you tell me how the subject came up?"

"Simple enough. He admitted his plan of using Caller ID wasn't working, and suggested we try something else. Figuring out who had access to the new number."

"Uh-huh," Frost said. "And what did you think of the idea?"

"I beg your pardon?"

"Did you think that was a good idea?"

101

"Certainly not. It was an absurd idea. No one I know would be involved in such a thing."

"And yet someone was making the calls. And your publicist is dead."

"I didn't know that then."

"You know that now. Does that change your opinion of the matter?"

"I still can't understand how this could have happened. I can't believe she had anything to do with it."

"Uh-huh." Frost turned to Maxine. "And you, Mrs. Winnington? Does your recollection coincide with your husband's?"

She smiled. "I don't see where there's any matter to dispute."

"How about your opinion? Do you also feel it's ridiculous this woman might have been involved?"

"It seems far-fetched. But the idea *anyone* might threaten me seems far-fetched."

"Good answer," Frost said. He turned to the secretary. "What about you, Mr. Pryne? I understand you were there for the discussion. What did you think of the idea?"

David Pryne cleared his throat. "Frankly, I found it ludicrous. Of course, in light of what has happened . . ."

"Exactly," Frost said. "We have to reassess. So now, I understand you were the one who supplied the phone number to the decedent?"

"Yes, I did."

"And did you do that in person?"

"No. Over the phone."

"You called her and gave her the number?"

"That's right."

"And when was that?"

"It was Thursday afternoon."

"How do you fix it in your mind?"

"Well, for one thing, I was the one who arranged for the new number. The number was changed Thursday morning. I gave it out Thursday afternoon."

"And who did you give it out to?"

"Sherry Pressman. His agent, Abe Feinstein. His editor, Elizabeth Abbott. The maid. The video store where we rent tapes. The cleaner that does his shirts. And my girlfriend." David Pryne took a piece of paper from his pocket. "I have a list of names and addresses here."

"Thank you," Frost said, taking the paper. "Now then, what time did this conversation take place? The one where you gave Mr. Hastings the names and addresses."

"Yesterday morning, sometime between ten and eleven."

"Uh-huh," Frost said. "And what time did Mr. Hastings leave?"

"As to that, I'm not exactly sure."

"Can you approximate?"

"Perhaps eleven. At least between eleven and twelve."

"Uh-huh," Frost said. "And what did you do then?"

"I beg your pardon?"

"You supplied the names, the conversation broke up, Mr. Hastings left. And what did you do then?"

"I went back to work. I had some typing to get done."

"Would that be before lunch?"

"Yes. Why?"

"Then where did you go to lunch?"

David Pryne frowned. "Now see here. Am I a suspect in this case?"

"I'd certainly like to eliminate you as one," Frost said. "Where'd you go to lunch?"

"I didn't. I had work to do, so I had lunch brought in."

"Brought in?"

"Yes."

"You mean you had lunch delivered?"

"Sure. I called the deli, had them send up a sandwich."

"Was that unusual?"

"I beg your pardon?"

"To work through lunch?"

"Not at all. When I'm busy, I like to keep working. I call for lunch maybe half the time."

"From the same deli?" I said.

All heads turned to me.

ADA Frost looked peeved. "If you don't mind, Mr. Hastings, I'm asking the questions here."

"Then you might ask him that one."

"Why?"

"Most places that deliver food ask for the address *and* the phone number."

One look at David Pryne's face showed that shot had hit home.

"Is that right?" Frost said. "Did they ask for the phone number?"

"As a matter of fact, I believe they did."

"And was that the first time you'd ordered from them since the number was changed?"

"I don't think so."

"Then why didn't you mention it before?"

"I didn't think of it."

"You thought of the cleaners and the video store."

"Yeah, but that was different."

"How is it different?"

"I was there. I went there to do business. During the course of which, I gave out the number. This calling for a sandwich— it wasn't business, it was personal, and it just slipped my mind."

"But the fact is, you gave out the number?"

"The fact is he ordered a sandwich," Kenneth P. Winnington

104

put in hotly. "There's no need to browbeat my secretary. You really think my publicist was killed by someone from a deli?"

"At this point I have no idea," Frost said calmly. "I'm asking questions to try to find out. I'm interested in anything that sheds light on the situation. The suggestion that I not ask certain questions does not really advance things." He turned back to David Pryne. "Is there anyone *else* you gave the number out to that you've neglected to mention?"

"No, there isn't."

"Are you sure?"

"Yes, I am."

"Good. On the other hand, should anything come to mind, do speak up. At any rate, you had lunch brought in?"

"Yes, I did."

"So you didn't go out to lunch. Did you go out for any other reason?"

"Yesterday afternoon?"

"Yes, of course."

"No, I didn't."

"You worked straight through?"

"That's right."

"From when to when?"

"From the time Mr. Hastings left till the time I went home."

"What time was that?"

"Five thirty. That's when I usually get off."

"Usually?"

"Sometimes if there's more work I'll stay later."

"Yesterday there wasn't?"

"No, I left at five thirty."

"So you were there all afternoon?"

"Yes, I was."

"I assume your employer can vouch for this?"

David Pryne blinked. "I beg your pardon?"

"Do you have any corroboration? Anyone can vouch for the fact that you were there?"

"I was typing. In my office."

"Your office?"

"Yes. I suppose technically it's a maid's room. It's set up as my office. It's a room in the back hallway where I can work undisturbed."

"The back hallway. Then no one would see you and know you were there?"

David Pryne gulped. His eyes were wide. He actually ran his finger inside of his collar. "I don't know what you're getting at," he said. "I swear I had nothing to do with this. I spent the whole day typing. I can even show you the work."

"Oh? And what were you typing?"

"Letters, mostly. Answering his fan mail."

"Fan mail?"

"Sure. Mr. Winnington has lots of fans. They write him care of his publisher. The publisher forwards the letters. Not one at a time, but as they accumulate. A batch came yesterday. Maybe twenty, twenty-five. Mr. Winnington likes to answer his mail personally. So I read all those letters, and typed responses for his signature."

"Wait a minute," Frost said. "You answered the letters?"

"That's right."

"As if you were him?"

"Yes, of course. People want a personal response. I go through the letters, find one item in each one to respond to. That way people know they're not getting a form letter."

"How nice for them," Frost said. "And did you have to consult with Mr. Winnington on any of the replies?"

"For fan mail? No, it's just routine."

"Uh-huh," Frost said. "Then he can't vouch for your presence yesterday afternoon."

David Pryne, who had relaxed somewhat while discussing the fan mail, looked betrayed.

"And you can't vouch for his," Frost said. "Mr. Winnington, what were you doing yesterday afternoon?"

"Don't answer that," Barney K. Rancroft put in.

ADA Frost made a face. "Haven't we been over this? Your client is cooperating to keep his name out of the press. I don't for a moment believe he's a suspect, but I have to ask these questions. Am I going to hear the answer, or read in the paper why I didn't get one?"

"That sounds like a threat."

"Then I hope it's effective," Frost said. "Are you going to allow your client to discuss what happened yesterday afternoon?"

"I have nothing to hide," Kenneth P. Winnington said. "The idea that I had anything to do with this at all is absurd. Aside from the business with Mr. Hastings, yesterday was a normal day. After he left, I went back to work."

"Work?"

"Yes. I'm a writer. I'm working on a book."

"You spent yesterday afternoon writing?"

"That's right."

"So you were home all day?"

"No, actually I went out to the park."

"Oh?"

"Yes. I like to walk in Central Park when I'm working out ideas. It helps me relax, think, clear my head."

"You spent yesterday afternoon in the park?"

"Part of it."

"What part?"

"I don't know. I went out for a couple of hours in the middle of the afternoon."

"Could you be more precise?"

"I don't know." Winnington turned to his wife. "What time did I go out, dear?"

"Around two."

"So you were out from two to four?" Frost said.

"Don't answer that," Rancroft said. He turned to Morton Steinway. "And you might want to advise your client also. You want to earn your fee?"

"Now see here," Steinway said.

Frost put up his hands. "Please. Gentlemen. Life is too short. Do I have to make another speech about how we're all cooperating, or could I move on? Now then, Mr. Winnington has already stated that he went out for a couple of hours around two o'clock. Mrs. Winnington, what were you doing at that time?"

"You make all the speeches you want," Morton Steinway said. "But I'm still going to advise my client. Mrs. Winnington, do you wish to confer with me before answering that question?"

"No, I do not," Maxine Winnington said. "This is getting ridiculous. Let's move things along. Yesterday afternoon I was home until about two. Then I went shopping. Grocery shopping. At the Food Emporium."

"For how long?"

"Quite a while. This was not just running out to the store. This was a major shop. Close to two hundred dollars worth of food. I had it delivered, so the store may have a record of it, if you really care. So I can prove I wasn't killing someone, I was buying frozen peas." She rolled her eyes. "Good god, I can't believe this is really happening."

ADA Frost nodded. "So you were out for most of the afternoon." He turned to Kenneth P. Winnington. "And *you* were out for most of the afternoon."

He spread his arms and shrugged. His baby face was beatific.

"So none of you can vouch for each other at all."

20.

MacAullif threw up his hands when I came in. "Oh, for Christ's sake. Look who's here. Look who comes walkin' in the door large as life, as if he didn't have a care in the world."

"What's the matter with you?"

"What's the matter with me? The man asks what's the matter with me. What do you think's the matter with me?" MacAullif leaned back in his chair, cocked his head, and said with elaborate irony, "I'm sittin' here at my desk, mindin' my own business, trying to solve a homicide or two, and what should happen but the phone rings. Which is not that unusual an event, seein' as how I happen to be in charge of a number of murder investigations, and people do call me now and then when they have information relating to one of them. So I am pleased when I answer the phone, because I think, hey, whaddya know, this just might be a clue." MacAullif raised one finger in the air, which despite his smile gave him the look of a dynamite stick about to explode. "And guess who was on the phone?"

"ADA Frost?"

"Bingo, right on the button." MacAullif jabbed his finger. "It was old Baby Face himself, and guess what the gentleman wanted to know?"

"About your involvement in the Sherry Pressman murder?"

"You really know how to turn a phrase, don't you?" MacAullif said. "Yes, that's *exactly* what he wanted to know. You know what that's like for a homicide investigator—to have an ADA question his involvement? Do you have any idea?"

"You're not involved."

"Tell it to him, why don't you? Hell, you told him everything else. What, you couldn't tell your story without mentioning me?"

"I was acting under advice of counsel."

"Who, Richard Rosenberg? I should have known. I swear to god that guy is out to get me."

"Oh, quit grousing, MacAullif," I said. "So you traced a couple of phone calls. You think anybody really gives a damn? It's not like it had anything to do with the murder."

"Then why the hell bring it up?" MacAullif said. "Look, I know you, you're a straight arrow, an ADA questions you you're gonna tell the truth. Tellin' the truth is one thing. You don't have to tell him your life story."

"Hey, why do you think I'm here?"

"You probably need a lead."

"I came here to warn you. I'm sorry he got to you first."

"You don't need a lead?"

"Well, now that you mention it."

MacAullif shook his head. "You're unbelievable."

"So how's about ten minutes of your time?"

"Ten minutes?"

"Sure. In return for which I'll tell Baby Face to go easy on your interrogation."

"Oh, you're really pushing your luck."

I shrugged. "Well, I'm in a good mood. No one really thinks I did this one. Anyway, how much do you know about it?"

"Just what I got from Frost. Somebody croaked a woman you called on tryin' to find out who had access to that guy's phone number."

"Let me bring you up to speed."

"Yeah, well, make it snappy. You got ten minutes, and the clock is running."

I gave MacAullif a rundown of the case. I can't say he looked particularly thrilled.

"So, what's your assessment?" I said.

"My assessment?"

"Yeah."

"It's a load of shit."

"I had hoped for more than that."

"Then you should have given me more than that. I just call 'em as I see 'em."

"Fine," I said. "You wanna assess this load of shit? From what I told you, what's your take on the crime?"

"Off the top of my head?"

"Sure."

"Off the top of my head nothing you told me means anything and the motive isn't there."

"You're saying she just happened to get killed?"

"Not at all. No one just happens to get killed. I'm sayin' she was killed for a reason, but the reason is not apparent from what you know."

"How do you know that?"

"I don't. You told me off the top of my head. That's only one solution, and it doesn't have to be right. Another solution would be the answer's right there in the load of shit. That, stupid as it seems to me, the murder was the act of some anonymous phone caller who had gotten the phone number from her, and who bumped her off to prevent you from discovering their identity. That solution shouldn't be discarded just because

111

it sounds like a bad novel. Also, it gives you something to work on, whereas without it you got nothin'. Now, if that was the case, you say there were two people called on the woman could have learned the number."

"That's right."

"And who would they be?"

"They're both writers. Or would-be writers. One's an old man, keeps writing books, paying this woman to read them. His name's Wilber Penrose. He'd just given her his fourth or fifth manuscript at five hundred bucks a whack."

"Five hundred?"

"That's right."

"This woman charged him five hundred dollars to read his book?"

"And tell him what to do with it."

"I'd tell *her* what to do with it. Five hundred bucks. Jesus Christ. Just to read his book? Four or five times? That would be justifiable homicide. Who's the other suspect?"

"These aren't really suspects."

"Don't quibble. Who's the other one?"

I consulted my notebook. "The other is Linda Toole."

"Sounds like a transvestite stripper."

"You're all heart, MacAullif. Linda Toole happens to be a perfectly nice woman with a mystery novel about cats."

MacAullif made a face. "Then I hope she did it."

"What?"

"They're the worst, these cat women. They're the ones give people the idea cops are stupid jerks couldn't solve a crime if it weren't for some fucking cat."

"I'm sure it's not as bad as all that."

"Well, it isn't good. You got a whole generation of people raised on a steady diet of *Murder She Wrote* who think crime isn't solved by cops, it's solved by mystery writers who are so much smarter than cops because they spend all their time thinking up solutions to things. I got news for you—the only crimes mystery writers can solve are the ones they write themselves. If this woman has any theories on the case, I'd watch out for her."

"Oh, come on, MacAullif."

"I'm not kidding. If I were you, I'd set my sights a little higher on Linda Toole."

"Any more bright ideas?"

"How does the secretary strike you?"

"What do you mean?"

"What's his story? You think he could be in on this?"

"Of course not."

"Why of course not?"

"He was there when the calls came in."

"He could have had an accomplice. Besides, the caller doesn't have to be the killer. The two things don't have to be related at all. Anyway, what's his story?"

"He says he was typing letters all afternoon."

MacAullif waved it away. "No, no. I don't mean his *alibi*. I mean his *story*. What's he doin' there? What makes the guy tick?"

"He's doing a job."

"Yeah, but why? Why that one? What's the guy want out of life?"

"I have no idea."

"Then how can you judge him as a suspect? These other two, at least you know what they want. They're trying to sell their books. But this guy—" MacAullif shrugged. "What the hell does *he* want?"

"Okay," I said. "Any other ideas?"

"What about those other two?"

"What other two?"

"The other two you told me about. The editor and the agent. What about them?"

"What do you mean, what about them? *They* didn't get killed."

"Exactly. And if I understand you correctly, you called on them before you called on her. Which means they not only knew what you were up to, they knew where you were going."

"But, but, but—"

"But what?"

"But they *had* the number. They had it themselves. They didn't *need* to get it from someone else."

"Yeah, but there you go again assuming the phone number had something to do with it. The phone number was the reason you called on these people. It doesn't have to be the reason one of them died. Suppose it's not the phone number, but just the idea you're poking into their business at all. And one of these other two says, Uh-oh, wait'll he gets to her, there's gonna be hell to pay, and tags along behind you and bumps the broad off."

"Why?"

"How the hell should I know? I haven't got a single fact. I only know what you told me, and you don't know shit. Now then, I hate to break it to you, but your ten minutes is almost up."

"Any more suggestions?"

"You're not gonna wanna hear this, but the most likely suspects are your client and her husband."

"Why wouldn't I wanna hear that?"

"Don't be a jerk. They're payin' the bills. Anyway, they top the list. They got no alibi, and they're the most involved."

"What's the motive?"

"How the hell should I know? We got no information yet. You get some more, you work it out."

My beeper went off. "Mind if I use your phone?"

"Oh, sure, why not. Just move right in. Take over the whole office."

I called the Winningtons. Maxine answered the phone.

"It's Stanley Hastings. Did you beep me?"

"Yes, I did. Can you get over here?"

"Why?"

"We got another call."

21.

"It was on the answering machine when we got home," Maxine said.

"The answering machine?"

"Yes."

"You didn't tell me that on the phone."

"You didn't ask."

"No, I don't suppose I did. This guy left a message on the answering machine?"

"That's right."

"What's the message?"

"Prepare to die."

"That's it?"

"That's it."

I had been following my client from the front door of her apartment to her husband's study. He was conferring with his secretary when we came in. He looked up, saw me, and declared, "This has got to stop." A typical Winnington statement, asserting his authority in matters over which he had absolutely no control.

"I understand the caller left a message," I said.

"He sure did," Winnington said. "Only we weren't here to get it because you got us dragged downtown."

"Where's the message?"

"On the answering machine."

"Is it still there?"

"Where else would it be?"

"I don't know, but you better take it out before it gets recorded over."

Winnington glared at me. You could tell he knew it was the right thing to do, but didn't want to do it because I was the one who had suggested it. After a moment he said, "David, take it out."

"You want to play it for me first?"

"You think we should risk that?" Winnington said ironically. "What if he were to accidentally erase it?"

"Oh, I don't think he will. Go on. Play it."

David Pryne stepped up to the machine, pressed the button. There came the whir of the tape resetting, then:

"Prepare to die."

It was a low hoarse whisper, the same voice we'd heard before. Only then it had just seemed strange and unsettling. In light of what had happened it was positively chilling.

"Okay," I said. "Take it out. You call the cops?"

"The police?" Winnington said. "No. Why?"

"They're gonna want that tape."

"Well, I'm not sure they should have it."

I stared at him. "What?"

"The more we give them, the more they're going to think we're involved. I've already been dragged in once. I don't want it to happen again."

I put up my hand. "I think you're missing the big picture here. That ADA is cooperating with you on this thing. The only reason you don't have every reporter in town at your door is because he agreed to control publicity. Now, you wanna turn around, kick him in the teeth by withholding evidence, you wouldn't believe how quickly that cooperation will be withdrawn. Now then, you gotta call. It's evidence. In all likelihood it's a voice print of the murderer. And you're gonna give it to the cops."

"I don't like being told what to do."

I smiled. "It's all right. I'm not telling you what to do. I'm telling you what *I'm* gonna do. I know it's evidence, and I'm turning it in to the cops."

"You have no right to do that."

"Oh, yes, I do. I not only have the right, I have the responsibility. Now, you wanna take the position that's your property and I have no right to touch it, well, that's fine, I won't. I will merely tell the cops you have it. After that, it's between you and them."

Winnington stood there blinking, as if he couldn't believe I'd said that. I could see him groping for the appropriate response. Clearly, he didn't want to lose face in front of his secretary and his wife. But, short of firing me, which seemed a distinct possibility, there wasn't much he could say.

That didn't stop Kenneth P. Winnington. After a moment's hesitation he made an abrupt about-face, and embraced my opinion as if it were his own. "He's absolutely right," he said. "This has to go to the cops. David, call and tell them we have it. And get it out of that damn machine."

David Pryne took the tape out of the answering machine and made the call. He hung up the phone, said, "They'll be right over."

"Who'd you talk to?" I asked.

"The assistant district attorney."

"He's coming over?"

"I don't think so. He said someone."

Someone turned out to be Sergeant Thurman. He stomped

in not ten minutes later and unceremoniously demanded, "Where's the tape?"

"Right here," David Pryne said. He held up a white business envelope. "I sealed it in this."

"Uh-huh," Thurman said. He turned to Winnington. "This was on the answering machine when you got home?"

"That's right."

"You all heard it?"

"Yes, we did."

"And?"

"And what?"

"Same guy?"

"As nearly as we can tell. You have to understand, it's just a hoarse whisper."

"Uh-huh. And when was the message left on the tape?"

"This afternoon. While we were all downtown."

"Are you sure of that? This couldn't be a message left yesterday you just never listened to?"

"No. It came in today."

"Uh-huh," Thurman said. "Which means it came in after the murder. Which is bad news. The killer strikes once, now the killer's targeting you."

"Not me," Winnington said. "These threats are being made to my wife."

"Right," Thurman said. "The killer's targeting you, Mrs. Winnington. Under the circumstances, you should be very careful. I would prefer it if you didn't go out. And the same with you, Mr. Winnington. We're dealing with a crank caller and a killer. That's a very sick combination. Until we know more about it, we gotta be careful."

Winnington blinked. "You're telling me not to go out?"

"That would be best."

"Excuse me," David Pryne said.

Thurman ignored him, but Winnington said, "What is it?"

"You know you have a signing tonight?"

"What?"

"With all that's happened you probably don't remember, but you have a signing scheduled."

"For today?" Winnington said. "You mean today?"

"I'm afraid so."

"What's a signing?" Thurman said.

"A book signing. I'm signing my books."

"At a bookstore?"

"Of course."

"Then you'd better cancel."

"Cancel?" Winnington said. "They've advertised it. They've ordered the books." He turned to David Pryne. "Christ, who is it?"

"Barnes and Noble."

Winnington made a face. "Shit. If it was just a little book store, what the hell. But I'm not gonna piss off Barnes and Noble."

"What time's the signing?" Maxine said.

Her husband turned on her. "*You're* not going."

"Yes, I am."

"No, ma'am," Thurman said, holding up his hand. "I don't think you understand. We're dealing with a killer here."

"Give me a break," Maxine said. "You expect me to stay in my apartment till you catch this guy?"

"No, ma'am. But I expect you to take reasonable precautions."

"Don't be silly," Maxine said. "I'm perfectly safe in a public place. I always go to signings. I like signings, and I'm going to go."

"I may not even do it," Winnington said.

"If you cancel, you cancel," Maxine said. "If you go, I go."

"I can't cancel Barnes and Noble."

"Then I'm going."

I stayed out of it. Not that I didn't have an opinion, just that I didn't want to get involved.

Then suddenly I was.

"If she goes, you go," Winnington said.

It took a moment to realize he was talking to me. "I beg your pardon?"

"If my wife refuses to listen to reason—which I wish she would—but if she insists on going, I want you to go with her."

"As a bodyguard?"

"Exactly."

I could see Sergeant Thurman rolling his eyes. I wished to god he hadn't been there. I figured I'd better point out my deficiencies before he did.

"A little bit out of my line," I said. "I don't even carry a gun."

"Gun?" Winnington said. "Don't be silly. I don't expect you to shoot anyone. Just be on the lookout for anyone hassling my wife."

"Oh, come on," Maxine said. "It will be fun."

I blinked. As a private detective, I try to have a good opinion of my clients. It was a little hard to reconcile someone in her situation talking about having fun.

"What time is the signing?" I said.

"I don't know. What time is it, David?"

"Eight o'clock."

When I hesitated, Maxine said, "Don't worry, we'll pay you. Put in for a double day."

A double day?

I must admit, in the midst of all the chaos, my mind zeroed right in: five hundred plus five hundred equals a grand. If you can't appreciate that, you must not be trying to support a wife and kid in New York City.

"All right," I said. "If that's what you want, I'll go to the signing."

Sergeant Thurman stuck his chin out. He didn't look pleased. I guess he wasn't having a thousand-dollar day.

"Me too."

22.

I got back to my apartment building to find Alice coming out the front door.

"Hi," I said, "where you going?"

"I'm at a meter."

"Huh?"

"I couldn't get a parking space. The car's at a meter."

"Listen, I got a lot to tell you."

"Not now. I'm gonna get a ticket."

I didn't argue. In New York City potential parking tickets take precedence over anything. At fifty bucks a whack, they command your attention. If your parking meter's running out, you do not stop to chat.

Alice hadn't. She was already hotfooting it toward Broadway. I took a hop skip and caught up.

"Where you going?" Alice said.

"I'll help you move the car."

"I'm a big girl. I think I can handle it."

"Humor me."

The car was parked on the corner of 104th in front of the Suba Drug Store. The meter was red, but the windshield was bare. I looked up the street, and Lovely Rita, Meter Maid, was half a block away. Some days you get lucky.

"You want me to drive?" I said, but Alice had already stepped out in the street.

"I'll drive," she said. "Get in."

We got in the car and started doing the parking space shuffle, the late afternoon fun game that sometimes can take upward of an hour.

We went down Broadway to 103rd. Right on 103rd across West End Avenue to Riverside Drive. Up Riverside to 104th. 104th across West End and back to Broadway. Broadway to 105th. 105th across West End to Riverside Drive. Riverside to 106th. 106th to West End. South on West End to 104th. 104th to Broadway. Broadway to 103rd, and the whole loop begins again.

We made it several times. While we did, I filled Alice in on the events of the day. Which took a lot of doing, as there were a lot of events. Throwing in a murder didn't help.

I must say I was impressed by Alice's concentration. She often kids me that I can't walk and chew gum at the same time. That isn't true—I just don't often chew gum. Anyway, she had no problem driving the car and paying attention to what I said.

"So, the bottom line is you're not a suspect."

"Not officially."

"Officially or unofficially. The cop and the ADA—no one thinks you did it. Which is pretty remarkable. You call on the woman at about the right time. And she was holding a piece of paper with your name on it—that really happened?"

"So they say."

"You see," Alice said, "that would tend to indicate to me that someone was trying to frame your client."

"My client?"

"Not her. Him. Winnington."

"The paper had my name on it."

"Sure, but like you say, no one thinks you did it. So if it was supposed to frame you, it simply didn't work. Kenneth P. Winnington is another story."

"How do you figure that?"

"A corpse clutching a piece of paper with a name on it is straight out of a book. It's what a writer would come up with. I bet the cops like him for this much more than they like you."

"They *don't* like me for it."

"So they say. Which doesn't have to be true. It's really what's-his-name—the dumb one?"

"Yeah. And Baby Face Frost too."

"He's not so dumb. If he doesn't think you did it, you're in the clear."

"True."

"So basically, you could butt out on this one."

"Yeah, except for one thing."

"What's that?"

I told Alice about the book signing. Her eyes widened, and she almost stopped the car. "Why didn't you tell me?"

"I just told you."

"Yeah, after everything else under the sun. You're making a thousand dollars today?"

"That I am."

"For being a bodyguard?"

"Are you going to sing again?"

"And you weren't going to mention it?"

"Hey, you make it sound like I was boring you with idle chitchat. There happened to be this murder."

"Which nobody thinks you did. Where's the signing?"

"Barnes and Noble."

"Which one?"

"This one. Upper West Side."

"What time?"

"Eight o'clock."

"Damn."

"What's the matter?"

"I can't go. I got a meeting at Tommie's school."

"So skip it."

"I can't skip it. I'm the class parent."

"Oh."

"You didn't know I was the class parent?"

"I *know* you're the class parent. I have a lot on my mind."

"So I can't go. Damn."

Alice spotted a parking spot half a block away. She floored it, nearly giving me whiplash. She screeched the car to a stop alongside the precious space, and proceeded to back in.

Alice got out of the car, slammed the door harder than necessary, and said, "Damn, it would have to be tonight."

"You really want to go to the signing?"

"Of course I do. It sounds like a lot of fun."

I sighed. Christ, it had been a long day.

"Don't bet on it."

23.

"Kimberly stumbled blindly down the dark street, her blond hair streaming out behind her, her blouse rustling in the breeze. The rough wind slammed into her face, caked the salty tears upon her cheeks, rubbed her skin raw.

"She barely noticed. Gasping for breath, she filled her lungs with air, then exhaled in sharp, choking sobs that shook her limber body as she forged on.

"Beneath it all her mind was churning, even as her heart was pounding, around and around the endless spiral of self-doubt, thrust upon her like a red-hot branding iron, the overwhelming revelation of seeing Brian, the one man she could count on, the one man she could depend on, the one man she could trust, in the arms of another woman.

"And not just any woman.

"But her.

"The vixen.

"The bitch.

"Her nemesis.

"Sabrina.

"The echo of her name went through her like a knife. Her whole body shuddered and she lost her balance, staggered, nearly fell, before bracing herself against the light post on the street corner. She clung to it for dear life, embraced the splattered, battered, paint-peeling pole, oblivious to the faint scent of dog urine wafting up from the street below. Steadied herself, tried to get a grip.

"A sound from the street made her spin around.

"A man with a knife?

"No.

"A bum with a deposit bottle.

"Only we don't call them bums now, we call them homeless, Kimberly told herself, then half-smiled at the irony that she should have this thought just now.

"She backed away from the pole, away from the man. Away from the street light that was creating patterns on the pavement, and into the dark shadows near the row of shops. The butcher and the laundry, familiar places in the light, now intimidating in the dark, or was everything just scary now, since her world had been turned upside down?"

In the back of the audience Sergeant Thurman jabbed me in the ribs. "This guy's good."

That figured. To me it was absolute drivel, so it was only natural Sergeant Thurman would think it was good. For my money, the only good thing about it was the delivery. Kenneth P. Winnington was a better actor than a writer, and seemed to get a kick out of reading his work. Though how anyone could possibly enjoy reading those lines was beyond me.

Kenneth P. Winnington was reading his book in the Barnes and Noble on Broadway and 82nd Street. About fifty chairs had been set up in a corner of the second floor, but it wasn't nearly enough. There must have been at least a hundred and fifty people there. They crowded around, squeezed between the shelves of books, to listen to the great man.

Fortunately, by getting there early, Maxine Winnington had

a seat. She was fourth row, center, and very visible in a red silk dress that didn't look bad from the back where Sergeant Thurman and I were standing, but must have looked terrific from the front, with a plunging neckline with a tendency to gape. Anyway, there she was, safe and sound in plain sight, and with Sergeant Thurman and me there to keep an eye on her, any danger she might be in seemed minimal at worst.

Which is why my mind wandered as I listened to her husband read his work. Not that surprising, considering what he was reading, and considering how many things were going through my head.

It occurred to me, this was the book. The one that not two days ago Sherry Pressman had coerced me into agreeing to buy. My only concern then had been how much it would cost. The estimation was I would be out about twenty bucks. Now, irony of ironies, the woman was dead, because of which I was standing here making five hundred.

Should I buy the book, fulfilling my promise? Be content with a four hundred and eighty dollar profit?

And if I did buy the book, should I have him sign it? If he did, I wondered what inscription he would write. The mind boggled.

I was aroused from my musings by the sound of applause, indicating Kenneth P. Winnington had finished his reading. That was good news. Now he could sign his books and get out of here.

Only not just yet. First he took questions from the audience. Which he also seemed to enjoy, judging from his gratified smile when, "Are there any questions?" was greeted by a dozen hands.

The first question was, "Where do you get your ideas?" Apparently, that wasn't a favorite question, because Winnington winced perceptively when he heard it, but recovered quickly and launched into what sounded like a fairly stock answer.

Beside me, Sergeant Thurman said, "This guy's sharp."

It was all I needed. To be forced to listen to Kenneth P. Winnington on the one hand, and Sergeant Thurman's approbation of him on the other.

Winnington finished with that question, then fielded a string of what purported to be questions, but consisted largely of nothing so much as people raising their hands and telling him how much they liked his books. This seemed rather boring to me, but from the smile on Winnington's face, and the graciousness of his replies, I gathered this sort of sycophantic response was exactly what he was looking for.

Anyway, it was a good ten minutes by my watch before anyone asked anything even slightly substantial.

"Do you ever write in the first person?"

The man asking the question had a round face with thick glasses and a bald head fringed with curly yellow hair. I had noticed him before, because he had had his hand up from the start, but hadn't been called upon till now.

"I'll tell you why I ask," he said. He had a whiny, sort of irritating voice, with a slight edge to it. "I ask because all the books of yours I've read are in the third person. So I'm wondering if you ever write in the first."

"Certainly not," Winnington said.

"Oh? Why not?"

Winnington's smile was condescending. "You can't write suspense in the first person."

As the man opened his mouth, Winnington pointed his finger, "And I'll *tell* you why not," which prompted a laugh from the audience. He smiled, said, "Why can't you write suspense in the first person? Well, it simply doesn't work, and I'll tell you why. To begin with, what are the basic elements of suspense?

130

Well, the basic element is danger. Putting the protagonist in danger. The basic premise of suspense is, will the hero be killed, or will the hero get away?"

Winnington smiled again. "Naturally, the hero gets away. Otherwise you have a depressing book that no one wants to read. However, there is still the possibility—and the reader buys into it—that the hero could indeed be killed.

"And that is what sustains the suspense. The underlying possibility. The fact that it could happen."

He held up his finger. "On the other hand, you take a first-person narrator, you *know* they're not going to die, otherwise who's telling the story?"

Winnington spread his arms, smiled, and looked around at the audience, who were all smiling back.

Except for the guy who asked the question, who didn't look at all convinced. "Is that the only reason? Come on, give me a break. You say yourself the hero's not gonna die, so what's the big deal? I mean, is that the only element to suspense?"

"It's a major one. But even setting that aside, there's another reason why first-person narrative simply wouldn't work."

"Why?" the man said, in a quarrelsome tone.

There was rumbling from the audience. Clearly the author's supporters didn't like this.

Winnington put up his hand. "No, no," he said. "It's a perfectly good question. I'd be happy to answer it. You see, there's another key element to suspense, probably more important than the one I just mentioned. Basically, it's this. Suspense doesn't just consist of putting the hero in danger. It consists of putting the hero in danger that is known to the *reader*, but is not yet known to *him*."

He looked around. "Do you see what I mean? I'll give you an example. The classic example is the bomb in the building. You start a bomb ticking in a building, send the hero in. The reader knows the bomb is there, the hero doesn't. You got him searching the place, opening doors, looking in one room after another, and all the time the reader's going, No, no, you fool, get out of there!"

He broke off, smiled and shrugged. "Now that's suspense, but it only works in the third person. The reader knows the bomb is there because you wrote a scene where the bad guy goes in and rigs the bomb. But the hero doesn't know that. He wasn't there, he didn't see it. Obviously, this doesn't work with a first-person narrative. You can describe only what the hero sees, what he knows. So you can't deliver the ticking bomb, so you can't have suspense."

The man looked totally unconvinced, and was probably prepared to argue the point, had not Winnington quickly called on someone else.

When that happened, the man got to his feet. Even with his back to me, his body language told me he was miffed.

I nudged Sergeant Thurman, said, "Watch him," very much as if the sergeant were an attack dog I was putting on guard.

I needn't have bothered. Thurman was already on the scent. With amazing agility for a man that large, he picked his way swiftly through the seats and within seconds had managed to put himself between his quarry and my client.

If the man noticed, he gave no indication, just pushed his way to the side of the row he was sitting in and disappeared among the shelves of books.

Sergeant Thurman gave chase.

In the back of the audience I shifted around to a position from which I could watch them go.

The man went straight to the escalator at the far end of the store.

Sergeant Thurman followed with all the subtlety of a steamroller, nearly pushing a woman into the remaindered rack, and elbowing his way onto the escalator in front of a young couple, who appeared miffed, but probably weren't going to do anything about it, considering the sergeant's size.

For me, Sergeant Thurman's exit was a bit of a surprise. I'd meant for him to watch the man, not learn his life story. My only concern was that he keep away from my client. Once he went the other direction I didn't really care.

But, as I suddenly realized, with Sergeant Thurman off on a wild goose chase, I was now solely responsible for Mrs. Winnington's safety.

Fortunately, it wasn't that tough a job. The rest of the signing proceeded without incident. Winnington fielded a few more questions, all of a congratulatory nature, accepted a round of applause, then retired to a table that had been set up in the corner of the store. A line formed, and soon about a hundred people were snaking their way toward the table, clutching copies of Winnington's books.

I moved in close to keep my eye on Maxine, so I had a good chance to observe the best-selling novelist in his interaction with his fans. I must admit, he was rather good, smiling, nodding, looking up at them in a modest, self-deprecating way. I wasn't close enough to hear the conversation, but I was sure it consisted largely of him acknowledging compliments. And when he signed a book, I noticed he usually did not just sign his name, but elicited the name of the fan, and then wrote a personal inscription.

I observed all this while keeping an eye on Maxine. She stood behind the table off to the left, watching her husband sign. She was smiling and keeping up a good front, but the tension was evident. Every once in a while she would let her guard slip, and I could see the irritation, the strain, the resentment.

Resentment.

It was about halfway through the signing when I noticed

that Maxine Winnington looking less than pleased seemed to correspond with Kenneth P. Winnington signing a book for a particularly attractive young woman. Winnington was going through his usual smiling, nodding, adorable, aw-shucks routine, just as he did with all the women he signed for, but while with some of the older ones it seemed merely charming, with this young one it came off as flirting.

At least my client seemed to perceive it as such.

I wondered if I was imagining it.

If not, I wondered if it was tremendously important, or not important at all.

I mean, as an extreme example, could it be that the woman I was witnessing now just happened to be Kenneth P. Winnington's mistress? Was a domestic triangle being played out right before my very eyes?

Not likely. Just like that, the woman was gone, clutching a signed book and heading for the escalator, and, lo and behold, the same situation seemed to develop with another attractive woman some twelve or thirteen people later.

Which seemed to tell the story. Maxine Winnington had no particular rival, but was well aware of the fact that her husband had roving eyes.

Sergeant Thurman returned about then, came sidling up to me, jabbed me in the ribs, and said, "Anything going on?"

Thurman was so crude and obvious it occurred to me Winnington might as well have put up a sign announcing he was being watched by the police. But no one seemed to notice.

I considered his question. Decided against alluding to any potential jealousy on Maxine's part.

"Not much," I said. "It would appear to be a waste of time."

"Maybe not," Thurman said. "That guy might be a live one."

"He got away?"

Thurman looked offended. "Are you kidding? I got him pegged. I'll check him out later. Right now I want to see if there's any action here."

There wasn't. Things went smoothly, and within a half hour the last book had been signed. All that remained was for me to take the Winningtons home.

We went out on Broadway and hailed a cab. We all got in the back, Maxine in the middle, Winnington and I on either side. The cab headed east, went into the park at 81st Street.

No one said a word. I wondered if that was because of the signing, or the general strain of the murder investigation.

"So," I said, "that seemed to go pretty well."

When I got no response, I said, "Who was he?"

That worked. Both of them said, "Huh?"

"The man who asked the question. About writing in the first person."

"Oh," Winnington said. "Just a jerk. There's one in every crowd."

"Oh?"

"Some guy thinks he's so smart, and wants to show off in front of everyone. It's no big deal. Happens all the time."

"Wait a minute. You've seen this man before?"

"No. Not him. But enough guys *like* him. Always trying to be so clever, and they haven't got a clue. Take the guy tonight. Do you write in the first person? Trying to sound intellectual, when actually it's a dumb question."

"But you've never seen the guy before?"

"Why? He's not important. Just some kook."

"Yeah," I said. "But we happen to be looking for a kook."

"Yeah, I know," Winnington said, "but him? I mean, can you imagine *him* strangling someone?"

I couldn't, nor could I imagine what our cab driver must

have thought of the conversation, assuming the gentleman spoke English.

Moments later we pulled up in front of the Winningtons' apartment building. I waited while Winnington paid off the cab, then saw them inside and put them in the elevator.

Closing the door on my thousand-dollar day.

Hot damn.

I could afford to take a cab home myself. Maybe even slip the doorman a buck, ask him to hail one for me. Really feel like a big shot.

I walked out the front door, wondering how much of a schmuck I'd feel like if I actually did that, and prepared to step out in the street and hail my own cab, when a car suddenly swerved in to the curb and screeched to a stop right where I was standing.

I jumped back instinctively. My nerves were on edge, and I was fully prepared for someone to roll down the window and start blasting away at me.

A drive-by shooting.

To my horror, the moment I had that thought, the passenger-side window started down.

What could I do? Fall to the ground? Jump behind the plump doorman I'd just decided not to give a dollar to for getting me a cab?

Or stand there like a fool and get shot?

Before I could decide, a voice said, "Hey, get in."

I blinked.

Leaned down, looked in the window.

It was Sergeant Thurman.

What he said blew my mind.

"Come on. Let's get some coffee."

24.

You have to understand.

I believe I mentioned working with Sergeant Thurman before. Hoping I never would again. And the fact he wasn't very bright.

Well, that's an incredible understatement.

I don't know how to put it strongly enough.

Let me try.

I guess the bottom line is, he beat me up. That really says it all. Everything else is an intellectualization. But when the fists come crashing into your body, delivered by someone that strong, rational thought goes out the window. You know the term, a gut reaction? Try getting punched in the gut. Hard. Again and again.

True, he had motivation. I was holding out in a murder case, and he knew it. But that doesn't justify what he did. Nothing justified what he did.

Still, I had chosen the high road. Instead of showing him up, I had let him in on the solution to the crime, let him help me trap the killer. And that, coupled with the fact that in this case I was cooperating with the cops and had told them everything I knew, somehow made me okay in his book.

Which truly blew my mind. When I got up this morning,

Sergeant Thurman buying me a cup of coffee had seemed as likely as me being elected President of the United States. I still wasn't President, but I was having coffee with Thurman at a deli on Madison Avenue.

"So," Thurman said, "whaddya think?"

I thought this was a pretty strange ending to a thousand-dollar day. But I had a feeling that wasn't exactly what he meant. "About the case?"

"About the guy. What do you think about the guy?"

"I think he's a kook."

"Besides that."

"Probably a would-be writer, pissed off because Winnington's published and he's not."

Thurman nodded. "Good. I like that. Fits just fine."

"It's a long way from wanting to be published to killing a publicist."

"Maybe, maybe not," Thurman said. "We got crank phone calls. That's how it starts, see. The guy makes crank phone calls, he gets sucked in. Next thing you know, bam, he gets backed into a corner and has to kill."

The problem with Sergeant Thurman was his logic didn't extend very far.

"Backed into a corner how? What's his connection with this publicist?"

"The phone number."

"Huh?"

"She had the phone number. If she was the way he found out the phone number, then the whole thing fits."

"She wasn't the way he found out the phone number."

"Why not? If the guy's a writer, maybe he knew her."

I shook my head. "There's only two writers who were up there who could have seen the number." My eyes widened. "Are you telling me he's him?"

"Who?"

"What's-his-name. The guy she said was up there. The one who kept paying her to read his manuscripts."

"No, not him. This guy is Noah Sprague. I don't remember who your guy was, but it wasn't that. This guy lives on West Seventy-eighth Street. Apartment in a brownstone. Appears to live alone."

"Seventy-eighth?"

"Yeah. Why?"

"It's walking distance. Could be why the guy showed up at the store. Just happened to be there."

"I don't buy that," Thurman said. "I like him for this. I think he's the type. What did your client say?"

"Huh?"

"About the guy. What did Winnington say?"

"Winnington is not my client."

"Yeah, yeah, right. It's the wife. Big deal. We know who's payin' the bills. Anyway, what did he say?"

"Says he's never seen him before."

"Oh?"

"Far as he knows. Says he's a kook. Says there's one at every signing. It's no big deal, he doesn't think much of it."

"Even with the phone calls?"

"He can't see this guy strangling anyone."

Thurman made a face. "Fucking amateurs. Same old story. Don't they watch TV?"

"Huh?"

"Every killer gets caught, the neighbors all say, oh, he's such a nice guy, I can't imagine him hurting anyone."

"It's not quite the same thing."

"You think not? If this guy's the killer, it's *exactly* the same thing. Did Winnington say anything else?"

"About what?"

"About the guy? Winnington say anything about the guy?"

"No. Like I say, he never saw him before. He was just a guy trying to show off how smart he was, when actually he was really dumb."

"So Winnington was pissed off?"

"Not pissed off, really. But he thought the guy was stupid."

"About writing?"

"Yes."

Thurman paused. I could practically see the wheels going in his head, trying to work it out. "What the guy said about writing—what was that again?"

"About writing in the first person."

"Yeah, right." Thurman frowned. "Just what does that mean?"

Explaining literature to Sergeant Thurman? If I could do it, I could walk on water. Maybe the presidency wasn't out of my grasp, after all.

"Well," I said, "a first-person narrative just means your hero is telling the story. The writer uses the word *I*. Instead of saying, '*He* went down the street,' the writer says, '*I* went down the street.'"

Thurman looked baffled. "*Who* went down the street?"

"Bad example. Okay, say you were the hero in the story. The writer writes, 'Sergeant Thurman went down the street. He saw the bad guy, drew his gun.' That's writing in the third person."

"Third person? What third person?"

"He. He is the third person."

"Who?"

I grimaced. "Another bad example. Never mind the third person. Anyway, the point is, one way to tell a story about you is to say, 'Sergeant Thurman did this. Then he did that. Then he did this, that, and the other thing.' Okay? That's the example. 'Sergeant Thurman went down the street. He saw the bad guy, pulled a gun.' That's one way to tell the story.

"The other way is, the writer pretends he's Sergeant Thurman, and says, *I.*"

"He says *you?*"

"No, no. He uses the word *I* to tell the story. The writer pretends he's you. He says, 'I was walking down the street. I saw the bad guy and I pulled my gun.'"

"He pretends he's me?"

"For the sake of the story. Let me put it another way. It's not that he pretends he's you. He pretends that *you're* telling the story. See what I mean?"

"I'm telling the story?"

"That's what the writer pretends. He says, 'I'm Sergeant Thurman, I'm a homicide cop, I was working on the case and a strange thing happened. I was walking down the street, I saw the bad guy, and I pulled a gun.'"

Thurman frowned again, took a deep breath, and exhaled very noisily, after which he rubbed his head. "Okay," he said. "I think I've got it. First person means I'm tellin' the story?"

"That's right."

"And your client says that's no good?"

I didn't correct him again about Winnington not being my client. "He said it wouldn't work for suspense."

"Then I bet it wouldn't. That guy's sharp."

I sighed. I wasn't about to argue, but for my money, Kenneth P. Winnington was a pompous, self-satisfied windbag, and it occurred to me if I could ever get published, the first thing I would want to do would be write a suspense novel in the first person just for the satisfaction of proving him wrong.

When I didn't answer, Thurman said, "Did he say anything else?"

"Not really. How come you didn't ask him yourself?"

Thurman shrugged. "You were ridin' home with them. I figured you'd ask him."

"What if I didn't?"

"A detective? Of course you're gonna ask him."

"Even so, Thurman. Why get it secondhand?"

Thurman shrugged. "No reason to let the guy know what I'm thinkin'."

"Yeah? Why not?"

"Are you kiddin' me? It's the wife bein' threatened, right? Husband/wife thing, the husband's always the first suspect."

"Husband/wife thing? You mean the phone calls?"

"Of course."

I stared at him. "He's not making the phone calls. He was there when they came in."

"Sure, but he could have an accomplice."

"An accomplice?"

"Yeah. Maybe even an unwitting one. In which case, he'd be the next to go."

"You suspect Winnington?"

"I *don't* suspect Winnington. I mean, I don't think he did it. On the other hand, I don't think he *didn't* do it. He *is* a suspect, I just don't *suspect* him."

For Sergeant Thurman, that was rather clear thinking. I was actually impressed. "Are there any other suspects?"

"Oh, sure. Aside from Winnington and his wife—"

"His wife?"

"Yeah, why not? Wouldn't be the first person faked a crime against themself."

"What's her motive?"

"What's anybody's motive? I have no idea. You just asked me for suspects. She's one, so's the secretary. For my money, neither one of them is as good as Winnington himself, but there they are. Then you got the agent and the woman at the publishing company."

"His editor."

"Yeah, her. Talked to both of them this afternoon. For my money, I can't see either one of them doin' it. But that don't mean they didn't. Aside from them, I still got those two would-be writers to track down."

"Wannabes."

"Huh?"

"That's what she calls them. Wannabes."

"Not any more, she doesn't. So I gotta track them down—not that either one sounds promising. For my money, this Noah Sprague's our man."

"You've got absolutely nothing on him."

"Yeah, but I will. You're still doin' this Caller ID shit, right? I'll pick him up tomorrow morning when he leaves his house. If he makes a call, he's mine."

"Are you serious?"

"Why not? You're still on the job, aren't you?"

"Yeah, but—"

"Didn't you say the calls come through nine fifteen?"

"Usually. Actually, today they didn't. There was just the one call—the one on the tape. What happened with that, by the way?"

"Happened with it?"

"Yeah. You get anything?"

"What's to get? It's a voice on a tape. You get another voice, you try to match 'em up. You can't do much with one. The trouble is, it's a whisper. My guy in the bookstore—he doesn't sound a thing like him. Got a whiny, candy-ass voice. But let him whisper—I think it's a good shot."

"You're really tailing him tomorrow?"

"Sure thing. You wanna wrap this case up as quick as you can, don't you?"

I smiled at Thurman. A shit-eating grin.

Clearly MacAullif hadn't told him I was working for five hundred bucks a day with no completion bonus.

25.

He even drove me home. Jesus Christ, a ride home from Sergeant Thurman? Pinch me, I must be dreaming.

He dropped me off on Broadway, a block from my house. He would have driven me to my door, but I had to go to the fruit stand. I bought a quart of milk on the corner, then walked over to West End.

I passed my car on the way. It was where Alice and I had left it earlier that afternoon, on the north side of 104th. Which was too bad, because tomorrow was Thursday.

I must explain. We have alternate side parking in New York City. The north side of the street is the Monday, Wednesday, Friday side, and the south side is the Tuesday, Thursday, Saturday side. Actually, with the financial crunch, parking has been suspended on Wednesday and Saturday for years to save the city the cost of cleaning the street, which is what alternate side parking was all about to begin with. The signs still say Monday, Wednesday, Friday and Tuesday, Thursday, Saturday, because the cost of replacing them was prohibitive, and would have wiped out what the city was saving by not cleaning the street. Everyone just knows that Wednesday and Saturday don't count.

Anyway, how alternate side parking works is, for three hours everyone on the bad side of the street double-parks on the good side, so the street sweeper can come through.

I was on the good side, which was bad. I was on the uptown side of the street, which was no parking Monday, Wednesday, Friday. Which meant it was on the good side of the street, and didn't have to be moved. Which was bad, because Alice had to move it to drive Tommie to the East Side Day School. Alternate side parking hours in our neighborhood are 8:00 to 11:00. By 7:30, everyone is double parked, and if you're on the good side of the street, you can't get out. On the other hand, if the car was on the bad side of the street, Alice and Tommie could get in the car at five to eight, and take off. But with the car on the good side, I'd have to be out of the house by 7:00 to move it to make sure it wasn't blocked. Which was a pain in the ass, but something I was used to doing.

But only if I had to.

I would much rather not.

Which is why, when I spotted a parking space on the south side of the street right across from me, I reacted like Pavlov's dog.

Holy shit, there's an extra half hour's sleep right across the street.

I quickly slipped my keys out of my pants pockets and unlocked the car door.

That's when I noticed something was wrong.

Son of a bitch, they'd done it again! Smashed the back window! Damn it to fucking shit hell!

Sorry for the invective, but this was one of the occupational hazards of living in New York City and parking your car on the street. On the one hand, you save the three hundred bucks a month you'd have to pay for a garage. On the other hand, you pick up your share of parking tickets, and your car gets broken into every now and then.

The car thieves used to pick the door lock, but lately they'd taken to smashing glass. The window they broke was always the same, the small triangular one behind the rear door. Evidently, being small it was easier to smash, and doing so allowed them to reach a hand in and unlock the door.

The really aggravating part was they never stole anything, because there was never anything to steal, but each time they did I had to replace the glass at sixty-five bucks a whack at the auto glass place at 23rd Street and the West Side Highway. This made the fourth or fifth time in the last few years, and it was happening with such regularity that I was beginning to suspect the auto glass place, which had my name, address, and license plate number, after all, of sending guys to my neighborhood every now and then to smash the window so they could fix it again.

While I was standing there thinking that, my alarm went off, on account of I put my key in the door. I unlocked the door, punched in the numbers on the code alarm, shutting it off. The alarm would have gone off when the window was smashed too, but shut itself off after one minute. That's because I'm a responsible citizen who has the type of alarm whose purpose is to frighten off the car thief, not to wake the neighborhood, like the ones that go off at two in the morning and keep on for hours, owned by irresponsible citizens that the majority of New Yorkers have dubbed with the affectionate term of assholes.

Anyway, I looked at the backseat of my car, which was covered with little chunks of safety glass, the window having shattered into a million pieces. I'd have to clean it up before Alice took Tommie to school. And she'd have to be the one to fix the window this time, since I'd be on the job.

That train of thought reminded me of my original intention. Broken window or not, the car needed to be on the other side of the street.

I started to get in and felt something.

Holy shit. The car thief had left something on the seat. What the hell could that be?

I hopped out of the car again—actually, I'd never really gotten in—but I stood up and looked down at the seat.

It was a newspaper, folded up. But not the way a newspaper folds. It was wrapped around something.

A bomb?

I mean, let's get paranoid here. But the thought actually crossed my mind, could this be a bomb? Should I call the bomb squad? Should I get the hell out of here? Should I turn and run?

But, no, I'd almost sat on the thing, and it didn't feel like a bomb. There'd been a give to it. An almost soft and squishy feel. And now I noticed a faint odor.

An odor?

Which, as I leaned closer, was actually rather strong.

What the hell?

Well, no guts, no glory.

I took a breath, reached in.

Grabbed the edge of the newspaper.

Spread it open.

Peered inside.

I gawked.

It was a pile of dead fish.

26.

"Sergeant Thurman wants to be my friend."

"Huh?"

"Yeah. I think he likes me. The way I see it, this could be the start of a beautiful friendship."

MacAullif squinted sideways, favored me with his most pained and put-upon look. "What the hell are you talking about?"

I gave him a rundown of my meeting with Sergeant Thurman. "Well," I said. "Whaddya think?"

MacAullif shrugged. "Well," he said, "it's a first date. You wanna take it slow."

"Fuck you. Whaddya think of the case?"

"You mean, what do I think of Sergeant Thurman's *opinion* of the case?"

"I guess that's what I mean."

"Sure you do. Pardon me, but didn't we just have this discussion yesterday? Weren't you in here telling me you had to talk to me about the case because you couldn't talk to Sergeant Thurman?"

"Oh. Well . . ."

"So now you're in here telling me you *can* talk to Sergeant Thurman, you *did* talk to Sergeant Thurman, you were up practically all *night* talking to Sergeant Thurman, and now you wanna talk about that."

"When you put it that way . . ."

"When I put it any way at all, I just can't win with you, can I?"

"Well, now there," I said, "it sounds like you're just jealous I'm talking to another officer."

"Right," MacAullif said. "That'll be the day. You wanna talk to Sergeant Thurman, talk to Sergeant Thurman, just don't do it in my office 'cause I happen to have work to do."

"Fine," I said. "The only problem is, I can't talk to Sergeant Thurman right now, because he happens to be out chasing down a suspect."

"Oh?"

"Yeah. The guy I told you about. From the signing. He's following him around to see where he goes."

"You mean to see if he makes the phone call?"

"Exactly. Only problem is, there wasn't any call this morning."

"How do you know?"

"I'm on the beeper. The minute they get the phone call, I'll get a page."

"How come you're not stakin' out phone booths?"

"I was. When the nine fifteen call didn't come through, I hung it up and came here."

"To tell me about Sergeant Thurman?"

"That's just part of it."

"What's the other part?"

"Someone gave me some fish."

"Huh?"

I told MacAullif about finding the dead fish in my car. "So what do you make of that?"

"What do *you* make of it?"

"Well, it's like in *The Godfather*. A Sicilian message."

"Right," MacAullif said. "But that wasn't just fish. That was wrapped up with the guy's bulletproof vest. What was his name?"

"Luca Brasi."

"Right. That was the message. Luca Brasi sleeps with the fishes. What were these fish wrapped up in?"

"The *New York Post*."

"Rupert Murdoch sleeps with the fishes? Doesn't fly."

"I know. So what do you make of it?"

"There's two possibilities. One, someone's trying to scare you. Two, your car was robbed by an absentminded son of a bitch just caught a mess of fish."

"I find that hard to swallow."

"No shit. So you consider the warning. You say, is this cause and effect? Did someone put fish in my car because I'm involved in a murder case?"

"Is that how it plays for you?"

"It doesn't play at all. It's the most incredible piece of bullshit you've ever brought me. It is as unlikely as you having coffee with Sergeant Thurman. The odds of either event are miserable. The odds of both happening in a single evening are astronomical. Are you sure you're not making this up?"

"MacAullif."

He looked at me, cocked his head. "You're not kidding, are you? You're actually shaken up by this? Otherwise, you probably wouldn't be here. This bullshit about Sergeant Thurman notwithstanding. Is that what's happening here? You getting freaked out about a load of fish?"

"Hey, give me a break," I said. "Yesterday was not aces to begin with. It started out with me looking at a dead body. One I'd seen alive just the day before."

"I wasn't attacking your manhood," MacAullif said. "Just

making an observation. The fact is, it shook you up. And rightfully so. You tell Thurman about the fish?"

"I haven't seen Thurman since last night. Like I said, he's out tailing a suspect."

"Uh-huh. You gonna tell him when you see him?"

"Damn."

"What is it?"

"You always put your finger on it, MacAullif. That's exactly the point. I don't really want to tell Thurman."

"Why?"

"Because he won't understand."

"What's to understand? Someone put a load of fish in your car."

"Yeah, but he won't know what to make of it."

"So what? Neither do you."

"What are you getting at?"

MacAullif opened his top drawer, took out a cigar, began drumming it on the desk. "What am I getting at? Damned if I know. But you tell me this and a red flag goes up. You want to keep this from Thurman because you don't think he'll interpret it correctly. Well, big deal. On that basis, you should keep the whole fuckin' case away from Thurman. But no, you're talkin' to him about that just fine. I would say, you don't want him to see what a pussy you are, scared of a couple of fish."

"Thanks a lot, MacAullif," I said. "You've cleared everything up for me."

"You don't like that assessment?" MacAullif said. "Lemme try another one. You're scared to death the guy might actually *do something* about the fish, and then you'd feel indebted to him."

I shuddered. "Christ, what a scary thought."

"Yeah," MacAullif said. "Anyway, has schmoozing with Sergeant Thurman in any way altered your opinion of his abilities, or the likelihood of his solving this particular case?"

"Give me a break. The way I see it, the only chance he's got at all of solving the case is if the guy he's tailing happens to make another phone call or confesses."

"Hardly a ringing endorsement," MacAullif said. "So the bottom line is, you're not going to tell Sergeant Thurman your fish story, so you bring it to me. What did you do with the fish, by the way?"

"Threw them in the garbage."

MacAullif made a face. "So this is how you preserve the evidence. Thank god you're not a cop."

"I wasn't going to worry my wife and kid by obsessing over a bunch of dead fish."

"Maybe not, but what were they like?"

"Like?"

"Yeah. Can you describe the fish? What kind were they?"

"I don't know. I think they were bluefish."

"You think?"

"Yeah, I think. I mean, a fish is a fish."

"Yeah, well, were they whole fish? Had they been cleaned and gutted? Were they packed in ice?"

"Whole fish. Wrapped in newspaper."

"Were they cold?"

"They were dead."

"Were they cold like they'd been packed in ice, then taken out of ice, or packed in ice that had melted?"

"They were cold like room temperature cold. If they'd been packed in ice, it was too long to tell."

"Uh-huh," MacAullif said. "Well, that's one thing you could do."

"What?"

"Trace the fish."

"Huh?"

"Well, why not? Assuming they were put in your car deliberately, you got someone wanted to fill your car with fish. Think what that means. The person has to know it's your car. And, he has to know where your car is. When did you leave your car in this spot?"

"Yesterday afternoon. After I left your office, I went back to my client's, heard the tape recording, found out I had a signing to go to that night. In between, I went home to change, tell my wife I was involved in a murder, little things like that. Only she couldn't get a parking space after picking up the kid at school, so when I get home the car's on Broadway at a meter. I met her on her way to move it."

"What time was that?"

"About four in the afternoon."

"Any trouble getting a spot?"

"No more than usual. Took us about fifteen minutes, driving around."

"This is four in the afternoon?"

"Yeah. Why?"

"Then there's a couple of things that you can do. One, you check fish markets in your neighborhood, see if anyone bought a bunch of fish around then."

"Oh, come on."

"What's wrong with that?"

"Are you kidding me? It's a *Saturday Night Live* sketch. Go into a fish market, ask 'em if they sold any fish. All they *sell* is fish."

"Yeah," MacAullif said, "but if you think about it, it's not that bad. All they sell is fish, but this is a particular sale. Most people buy a fish, they'd like it cleaned. Or a larger fish, they want a piece. This is a guy buys several whole fish, wants 'em just like they come. Betcha there are not that many orders just like that." MacAullif pointed with the cigar. "Plus, whaddya wanna bet this guy doesn't ask for a particular fish—like he doesn't say, You got any sea bass, or whatever—he just looks around at what's there and says, Give me four of those."

I frowned. "Yeah. Maybe."

MacAullif grimaced. "Aw, you're such a pain in the ass. You hate it because you think you'll feel stupid doin' it. That every store you go in that isn't the one, you'll feel stupider still. That's the part you never get. That ninety percent of legwork is strikin' out. Well, fuck it. I'm not sayin' you *have* to do this. I was only sayin' you *can*."

"Yeah, I know," I said. "Fine. Thanks for the hint. What was your other idea?"

"I forget."

"You're not gonna tell me because I didn't like your idea about the fish?"

"I hate to cause you any grief."

"Fuck you, MacAullif. What's the other one?"

"Taxicab."

"Taxicab?"

"Yeah. You drove around for fifteen minutes parking your car. If this is not coincidence you were given the fish, then the fish giver knew where your car was parked. And how would the fish giver know that unless he saw you park it there? For him to have seen you park it there is either a monstrous coincidence, or he must have been following you. When you go to Broadway, you're on foot, so we can assume he's on foot. When you get in the car, he hails a cab. So you're lookin' for a cab someone hailed on Broadway yesterday afternoon made figure eights around your neighborhood fifteen minutes and stopped on the same block as your car."

"Son of a bitch," I said.

"You like that better than the fish?"

"Actually, I do. I'm sure hundreds of people bought fish yesterday. Probably not that many drove parking patterns in a cab."

"Uh-huh. So how you gonna handle it, go out to Broadway start hailin' cabs until you find the right one?"

"That might take some time."

"You got any better ideas?"

"How about calling cab companies?"

"They probably wouldn't speak to you on the phone. You'd have to go around, flash ID, tell a good story. Still, they won't want to do it 'cause it's a pain in the ass."

"Right," I said. "It's not like I had an official reason for asking, like I was a cop or something."

MacAullif didn't acknowledge the hint, just said, "Yeah, you gotta talk fast, flash the ID, maybe slip the dispatcher a couple of bucks. You're makin' enough that shouldn't hurt, and what the hell, you charge it to expenses anyway."

"You're suggesting I hand out bribes?"

"Gratuities. Huge difference. Good thing to remember in your line of work. Well, you gonna do it?"

"Huh?"

"Gonna try to trace the cab?"

"I will if I get time."

"Huh?"

"I'm still working on the crank phone calls."

"You don't think the two things are related?"

"Possibly."

" 'Cause if they were, workin' on one would be workin' on the other."

"I see what you're saying, but . . ."

MacAullif grinned. "But tracing the taxicab is almost as unappetizing a prospect as tracing the fish. I know you all too well. So go on, get out of here, play it any way you want to. I made my suggestions, now it's up to you. So go on, do whatever you want."

MacAullif raised his cigar. "Just one thing."

"What's that?"

"I don't know if the fish means anything or not. If you're not gonna look into it, you won't know either. But just in case it does . . ."

"What?"

"Watch your back."

27.

Great.

I *had* been watching my back. I'm paranoid to begin with, and getting a load of dead fish is not the sort of thing that makes me any less so.

I left MacAullif's office feeling rather bad. I had hoped MacAullif would pooh-pooh the fish. Tell me I was being silly and wasting his time. Instead, he suggests I investigate and tells me to watch my back.

Big help.

My beeper hadn't gone off, meaning the mystery caller hadn't checked in, so I went back to my office to see what I could do about tracing the cab.

I got out the NYNEX Yellow Pages and looked up Taxicabs. To my surprise, there was less than half a page. In all of New York City? Somehow that didn't seem right.

Closer inspection revealed most of the taxi services listed were the type you phoned for. Which made sense, but what I mean is, they were not taxicab dispatchers so much as car services. In fact, some actually were car services—I found Carmel listed, which is a service Alice and I sometimes use to get to the airport. But what about regular fleets of cabs?

I looked at the listing again.

After the heading Taxicabs, in parentheses, was the letter D. What the hell did that mean?

There was no explanation on the page.

I turned to the front of the yellow pages, where I found no explanation either, though I did find the table of contents. About halfway down the page was the heading "How to Use This Directory." It was on page 2, but was not as immediately accessible as that would lead one to believe, as that was page 2 of the Introductory Pages, following some thirty-odd pages of the Inside Interest Pages, which include airport information, diagrams of theaters and sports stadiums, not to mention several pages of NYNEX coupons.

I located page 2. Captioned "How to Use," it told you in three steps, labeled steps one, two, and three, how to look up something in the yellow pages. In case you're wondering, the short answer was alphabetically.

I found what I wanted on page 3. The third paragraph under the heading "Buying Information" read: "There are some businesses which have the dual interest in serving both the individual consumer and the business buyer. These businesses are identified in the index and in the body of the book with the letter D, signifying that the heading appears in both the Manhattan Consumer and the NYNEX Business to Business Yellow Pages editions."

Aha. Mystery solved.

I looked at the top of the page. The heading read "Manhattan Consumer Yellow Pages."

No wonder I couldn't find the listings. I was in the Consumer section. I needed the Business to Business.

I flipped to the back of the book. The alphabetical listings started again. Here was the Business to Business. Where were taxicabs?

I located them quickly, under the heading "Taxicabs."

But that's all there was. Just the heading. No listings. What the hell was going on?

Then I noticed on the side of the page it said "Index."

Index?

I flipped to the front of the Business to Business section and read "NYNEX Index. A guide to the headings that appear both in this directory and in the NYNEX Business to Business Directory."

Of course. This wasn't the directory. This was just the index, telling what was *in* the directory. The Business to Business Directory was a whole different book.

Which I didn't have.

I leaned back in my desk chair, rubbed my head.

The phone rang.

I picked it up, growled, "Hello."

It was MacAullif. "You can forget about tracing the cab."

"Huh?"

"There's no record anywhere of any cab driving that route," he said, and hung up.

28.

I found Sergeant Thurman hanging out in front of a brownstone on West 78th Street. I parked my car halfway down the block and walked back.

"What's up?" I said.

Thurman jerked his thumb. "He's in there."

"Oh?"

"Went out for coffee, went right back. Been there ever since."

"You been here all morning?"

"If I hadn't, I wouldn't know he was there."

"How long you gonna stay on him?"

"Long as it takes. He's the guy."

"Oh, come on."

"You don't think he's the guy?"

"I suppose he could be. But it's a long shot."

"Oh, yeah? Well, get this. He's single, he lives alone. He has no job. His last job was drivin' taxi, but he lost his license for too many moving violations. Nothing serious, just rinky-dink shit like runnin' red lights and makin' left-hand turns durin' the wrong time, you know, like when it's no left turn from seven to ten. The sort of shit only a real loser would lose his license for.

"That's him, by the way. Loser from the word go. Which is just the guy we're lookin' for."

"Yeah, but—"

"Plus he's a writer. Again, nothin' big. Contributes articles to the free papers. *The Westsider. Manhattan Spirit.* Not like he makes any money doin' it, it's just so he can call himself a writer."

"How'd you get all this, sitting here in the street?"

Thurman grinned. "Hey, I'm a sergeant. People work for me."

"Why don't you assign one of them to this?"

"No way. He's my boy. I want him."

"You find any connection to Winnington?"

"Not yet. But I'm sure it's there. So, whadda you up to?"

I hesitated. For a moment I wondered if I should tell him about the fish. It was only a second, but that was enough. My thoughts immediately began performing back flips. Tell Sergeant Thurman? Why, in the name of reason? I just got through telling MacAullif I couldn't tell Sergeant Thurman. So then I turn around and tell him. Why? To betray MacAullif? To pay him back for making me feel stupid about tracing the taxicabs, for letting me go through the whole charade while he was actually doing it himself? Or was that the reason—because MacAullif did the taxicab I wanted Thurman to do the fish?

The thought occurred to me, maybe MacAullif was *doing* the fish. Although I knew he wasn't. Tracing the taxicabs was routine. It was the type of thing cops do all the time. They undoubtedly had a system in place. For MacAullif it probably took only one phone call.

Fish would be different. There would be no system set up for fish. It would require contacting each and every store. MacAullif wouldn't do it, and neither would Thurman—why the hell was I having such thoughts?

All of that went through my head in a flash, and if I showed any of it, I'm sure Thurman didn't notice, because I just shrugged and said, "Not much."

"Still working for Winnington?"

"Yes, of course."

"What you doin'?"

Good question. "Still trying to trace the calls. They haven't had one today."

"I could have told you that. The guy hasn't been out. But how did you know there hasn't been a call?"

"I'm on the beeper. When they get a call, they beep me."

"That's nice. When your beeper goes off, you'll know I got my man."

"If it's him."

"Oh, it's him. Ten to one I could pick him up right now, bring him in, get him to confess."

"Then why don't you?"

"Tell you why. Fuckin' Miranda and the rest. No matter how you treat a guy these days, half of what he tells you ain't worth shit. A sorry state of affairs, a guy says he did it, don't hold up in court. But that's what we've come to. So, even if I can get a guy to confess, I'd rather catch him with the goods. I'm stickin' with him, when he makes the call, he's mine."

It was just about then that I realized what Sergeant Thurman had done. He'd equated the killer with the caller, so he was now attempting to trap the caller.

As was I.

Sergeant Thurman and I were both attempting to do the same thing. I was, in effect, competing with Sergeant Thurman to see who could stop the crank caller first.

A depressing thought.

However, that being the case, it occurred to me Sergeant Thurman had chosen his course of action. Typical of the man, he had jumped to a hasty conclusion in naming a suspect, and would now bend all of his energies toward proving that one person guilty of the crime.

Most likely at the expense of everything else.

"You trace down those people yet?" I said.

"Who?"

"Those two writers. The ones who called on her."

"I will if I have to."

"If you have to?"

"If I nail my killer, who cares?"

Who indeed. I left him there on stakeout, went off to do the job myself. If Thurman wasn't going to do it, someone had to. Besides, if I was really competing with Thurman, I couldn't bear the thought of seeing him win. Not that that seemed even a remote possibility.

I drove a few blocks just to get away from Thurman, and stopped at a pay phone.

Just my luck, neither of the wannabe writers was home. Both had answering machines, but I left no message, not knowing what I wanted to say.

Damn.

Right back where I started. On the job with nothing to do.

Except retrace old ground.

As I flipped through my notebook looking up the numbers, the irony of what I was doing was not lost on me.

Sergeant Thurman was a homicide cop, attempting to solve a murder by finding out who was responsible for making crank phone calls.

I was a detective, hired to find out who was making the calls.

It appeared the only way to do it was for me to solve the murder.

29.

"That cop is not very bright."

"You noticed that?"

Abe Feinstein took a bite from his enormous corned beef sandwich. We were in the Stage Deli on Seventh Avenue, which makes enormous sandwiches. I had offered to take him to the deli where we met before, but when he heard it was me, he'd opted for here. I guess he knew a sucker when he saw one. Which I guess I was. I was only having coffee myself, and figured to pick up the tab. Or at least pony up the cash for it while Abe put it on his credit card.

Whatever it cost me, it was worth it to hear his assessment of Sergeant Thurman.

"Noticed?" Abe Feinstein said. "The cop comes walking in with the word *dumb* on his forehead. It's written on his shirt. It's tattooed on his eyelids. The man breathes dumb."

"What did he want?"

"He wanted to solve a murder by asking me a lot of stupid questions. Some of the same questions you asked me, but you had a reason. This cop, he hasn't got a clue."

"He ask you where you were at the time of the murder?"

Abe Feinstein raised his finger. "That's one dumb question. The first time he asked it was dumb. The second time he asked it was dumber. The third time he asked it was dumbest. Each time I say the same thing, I am in my apartment, I am alone, I am not out killing a publicist for not doing justice to my author's books. Why? One, because I'm not a killer. Two, because it doesn't make sense. As a person with any normal thought process could see."

"It does seem absurd."

"You noticed? Congratulations, welcome to the world of the rational, the sane."

He grabbed his sandwich. "Now, Sherry, I'm sorry she's gone. A scheming, cunning, shrewish, conniving, hard-edged bitch of a woman." He nodded gravely. "She will be missed."

"Can you think of any reason anyone would want to kill her?"

"Absolutely. She was a major pain in the ass. Many people wanted to kill her. But do it? Pish tush. Not the sort of thing you do. Kill a gutsy old broad for being brash."

"If it had to do with the phone number."

"That's something else. If it had to do with that, it didn't have to do with her. I mean, as a person. I mean, she wasn't killed because of who she was, only because of what she had. Could have been anyone with the phone number."

"Exactly."

He looked at me sideways. "Are you telling me I'm in danger?"

"I wouldn't think so. But I wouldn't rule out the possibility, either. If I were you, I would be on my guard."

"Are you kidding me? I am always on my guard."

"So what did the cop want to know? Aside from your whereabouts at the time of the crime."

"That was about it. The guy didn't want to know squat. Didn't know squat himself." Abe raised the sandwich, cocked his head. "You know what? It was more than that. He acted like *I* didn't know squat. That's it in a nutshell. The guy gave the impression he was askin' me questions 'cause it was his job, but he didn't expect me to know jack shit."

"And you do?"

"Not at all. But he don't know that. So where the hell does he get off makin' that assumption?"

"What *did* he ask you about?"

"Asked me about Kenny. What's it like workin' with the big writer. I didn't tell him, like I told you, what I think of Kenny's talent." Abe Feinstein raised his hand, made a whizzing gesture over his head. "Not to that cop. No point. Then he asked me if him and his wife get along. You could see that idea coming a mile away—is he the guy behind harassing his wife?" Abe held up his hand. "Not that I say this to him—that I know that's what he's getting at. I don't fly defensive, say, Kenny wouldn't do such a thing. I just answer like the dumbest schmuck in the world, Oh, yeah, they get along fine. And he accepts that answer like the dumbest schmuck in the world. Only thing is, I'm play-acting and he's not."

"Uh-huh," I said. "He ask you about his editor?"

"Oh, yeah. In fact, I think he actually saw her first."

"Oh?"

"I think so. I'm not sure. Either he'd just come from there, or he was just going there. So he must not have mentioned anything she said. 'Cause if he did, I'd be sure. And I'm not. Anyway, I think he asked me if there was any connection between Sherry and her and I said not that I knew of. Again, I don't think he really gave a damn."

"Uh-huh," I said. "Actually, I was thinking of the other one."

"Other one?"

"The other editor. The one you told me about. Who did his first book."

"Doug Mark."

"Right. Did he ask you about him?"

"No."

"Are you sure?"

"Absolutely. The name never came up." He looked at me. "You suspect Doug Mark?"

"I don't suspect anyone," I said. "I'm just gathering leads. Unlike Sergeant Thurman, I want as many as I can get."

"You want to tell me why Kenny's first editor might have killed his present publicist?"

"Not particularly."

"I didn't think so."

"The point is, we don't know anybody's motive yet. They're both in the industry, they might know each other. Suppose this Doug Mark was the guy making the calls. And Sherry Pressman was the source of the phone number."

"So he kills her to keep you from finding that out?"

"Actually," I said, "that doesn't sound half bad."

He grimaced. "Hey, don't be as dumb as the cop. You think this guy harbors a grudge four, five years, then gets revenge on Kenny by making phone calls to his wife? I tell you one thing, I am very glad as an agent I don't have to pitch that plot."

"All right, if that's a stupid idea, then you tell me—who do you think killed her?"

"One of her writers."

"Huh?"

"No, not like Kenny. I mean the suckers. The ones she was taking for a ride."

"And who was that?"

"All of them. The whole bunch. If you ask me, any one of them could have done it, and who could blame 'em?"

"You mean for charging a reading fee?"

He waved it away. "That's just part of it. It's her whole attitude, you know. It's not just they were suckers, it's she *treated* them like suckers. Treated them with contempt. Made fun of them behind their backs. Called them wannabes, did you know that?"

"She told me."

"Figures. She told everyone. Except them, of course. Happens to be a derogatory term, one writers would particularly resent."

"I didn't know that."

"Yeah, well, you're not in the business. Trust me on this. The woman was laughin' at 'em, and rippin' 'em off. If you were a writer, wouldn't you wanna kill her?"

I didn't tell Abe I *was* a writer. Considering my credentials, I didn't think he'd be too impressed. Instead I excused myself, went to the pay phone, called the two writers again. What Abe had just told me had boosted their importance up a notch. But they were both still answering machines.

While I was at it, I tried Doug Mark. I didn't have his number, so I called information to get it. Only they had no listing. Either the number was unlisted, or he didn't live in Manhattan.

I got back to the table to find Abe Feinstein had moved on to a piece of peach pie.

"You happen to know Doug Mark's number?"

"Not offhand. I would have it at home."

"Does he live in Manhattan?"

"As I recall. It's been a few years."

"Would that be his home or work number?"

"I'm not sure where he's working now."

"You're not sure he's working?"

"No."

"But you're an agent. Wouldn't you keep track of where editors are working?"

Abe smiled. "My authors are well placed. They are not

169

looking for publishers. They have them. All near the top of the tree."

"And Doug Mark is not?"

"Are you kidding me? Why do you think Kenny left him? He's someone you start with, then move on. Kenny went up. Doug Mark didn't. Whether he's working now I could not say."

"But you have his number?"

"Absolutely. Haven't called the man in years, but his number I will have."

"Can I call you later and get it?"

"Be my guest."

"Thanks. And you be mine," I said, picking up the check.

30.

Elizabeth Abbott appeared shaken by Sherry Pressman's death, which seemed out of character for the crisp, efficient, on-top-of-everything editor. I wondered if this was perfectly natural, or if the woman had something to hide.

It turned out to be a little of both.

"Shocking, absolutely shocking," she said. "That someone could do such a thing."

"You have no idea who that might be?"

"No, of course not. What an idea."

"How well did you know Sherry Pressman?"

"That's just it. I hardly knew her at all."

"She *was* Kenneth P. Winnington's publicist."

"Yes, of course."

"Didn't you deal with her on that basis?"

"To an extent," she said.

And her eyes shifted.

And I caught it. The alert detective. Son of a bitch.

I controlled myself, refrained from dancing up and down. "Did you have any trouble with Sherry Pressman?"

"No, of course not."

"Of course not?"

"Well, not what you'd call trouble. We didn't always see eye to eye."

"Oh?"

She flushed. "I didn't mean it like that."

"Like what?"

"You're making it sound like we didn't get along."

"Did you?"

"Yes, of course."

"Then what was the problem?"

"There wasn't any problem. It was just . . ."

"Yes?"

"Well, I can't say I approve of the way she was handling Mr. Winnington."

"Oh?"

I must say, my one-word responses were working. It seemed the less I said, the more she tried to justify herself.

"Yes, well, I'm sorry to say it, but that's a fact. It seemed to me for the amount she charged she could have done more."

"You know how much she charged?"

Elizabeth Abbott flushed again. "I know generally. That is, I have an idea. But what she actually charged him, no, I don't. I just feel she could have done more."

"Did you make these feelings known to Mr. Winnington?"

"Why are you asking this?"

"I'm interested in your relationship with the decedent. Apparently there was some friction there." I smiled. "I am not insinuating that you killed her. I'm just trying to find out the score."

That statement did not put Elizabeth Abbott at her ease. "That I killed her?"

"I don't for a moment think you did. Unfortunately, she was killed right after I talked to you."

"What do you mean by that?"

"I mean the timing is unfortunate. I talked to you, I talked to her, and she dies."

Elizabeth Abbott shivered.

"Not that I think you're in any danger," I put in hastily. "I'm merely talking about the sequence. I saw you, then I called on her. If the police wanted to make something of it, they could suggest you might have followed me to her."

Her eyes were wide. "Followed you?"

"Yes, of course. You knew I was going to call on Sherry Pressman. You followed me to see if I did. The minute I left, you went in and killed her."

"What are you saying?"

I put up my hands. "I'm not saying a thing. I know you didn't do that. I'm telling you how the police can reason. Weren't they here yesterday talking to you?"

"Yes, of course."

"Well, didn't they ask you questions like that?"

"Like what? Did I follow you to her house and kill her? No, they most certainly did not."

"Uh-huh. Now, the cop who questioned you . . ."

"Oh. Him."

"What about him?"

"What indeed. A walking stereotype. You know how long he'd last in one of my novels?"

"Your novels?"

"I mean one of my authors' novels. You think I'd let him get away with that?"

"I'm sure you wouldn't," I said. "But what did he want to know?"

"The same thing you did. When did I get the phone number? Who did I give it out to? Stuff like that."

"He didn't want to know about your relationship with Sherry Pressman?"

"Not really. I must say, he didn't appear that bright." She looked at me. "Is that a tactic on his part, do you suppose, to appear stupid? To lull you into a sense of false security?"

"Not that I know of. Anyway, did he ask you what you did that afternoon?"

"What I did?"

"After I left. Did he ask you if you went out? Or if you were in all afternoon? Basically, did he ask you for an alibi?"

"An alibi?"

"Yes. Did he ever say what were you doing between the hours of such-and-such and such-and-such?"

"No."

"He didn't?"

"No. Why would he? Anyway, I told him I was here all day."

"You did?"

"Yes, of course."

"Why?"

"Because I was."

I hoped Elizabeth Abbott edited better than she spoke. Grace and clarity did not appear to be among her virtues.

"So you told the cop you hadn't gone out all day, although he didn't ask you?"

She frowned. "I beg your pardon?"

"Just trying to get things straight in my head. I happen to know this cop. I know he's not too swift, so I'd like to pin things down. But the point is, you did assure him you were here all day?"

"Yes, of course."

"Fine," I said. "Now then, it's been a while since the cop talked to you and you've had a chance to think this over. So tell me, can you think of anyone who might have wanted to kill Sherry Pressman?"

"Not at all. It simply makes no sense."

"Is that how you see it?"

"Absolutely. You must understand, I deal with this sort of thing all the time. In books, I mean. And if I ran across this murder in a manuscript, I would have the author take it out. Why? Because it makes no sense."

"You don't think she was killed for the telephone number?"

She shook her head. "It's the flimsiest of motives. Give me a break. It's so bad you can't even state the premise fairly. You say killed for the phone number. But that's not even it. The idea isn't that she was killed to *get* the phone number. The idea— and correct me if I'm wrong—is that the killer already *had* the phone number, and killed her to cover up that fact."

"What's wrong with that?"

"Aside from being convoluted and stretching credulity, it wouldn't work."

"Why not?"

"Because if she was really the source of the phone number, you're already on to that. You were already investigating the people who might have learned the phone number from her. And you've already called on her and asked her who they are. If one of them is a killer, what good does it do that person to kill her? You already have the information."

"So the killer would have to be someone I don't know about."

"How is that possible?" She smiled and shrugged her shoulders. "You see what a fine line of belief you're drawing here? For the scenario to work, the killer has to know you're after his name. Know that Sherry Pressman could provide it. Know that Sherry Pressman won't provide it the first time you talk to her—because otherwise killing her would be totally ineffective—but might provide it at a later date if not silenced. So, for that premise to work, that very faint possibility has to be

175

somehow strong enough to make the killer take action." She shook her head. "It's a bad book."

"It's not a book."

"Yes, I know. But it still has to make sense, doesn't it?"

"Yes, it does," I said. "Listen, could you do me a favor?"

"What's that?"

"You know Mr. Winnington's former editor—what's-his-name—Doug Mark?"

She frowned. "What about him?"

"Would you happen to have his phone number?"

"Oh. I might. Let me check."

She flipped the Rolodex around to the M's, thumbed through it.

"No, it doesn't seem to be here."

"Well, thanks anyway."

"Hang on. I'll see if my assistant has it." She picked up the phone, pushed a button. "Kelly? Do me a favor. See if you can find a phone number for Doug Mark. Thanks." She hung up the phone. "She'll find it. What do you need it for?"

"Just like to ask him some questions."

"Oh?"

"Well, we're looking for anyone who had a reason to resent Mr. Winnington."

"Are you kidding?"

"Well, wouldn't Doug Mark fall into that category?"

"Give me a break. Authors change houses all the time. You think he's the first editor ever got dumped? I'll give you the phone number, sure, but I think you're on the wrong track."

"Uh-huh," I said. "Do you happen to know where Doug Mark is working now?"

"No, I don't."

"So it's possible he isn't."

"I suppose so. Why?"

176

"Might be a little more basis for resentment if the guy can't even get a job."

"I suppose," Elizabeth Abbott said, but her manner showed what she thought of the idea.

A woman came in the door. Young, attractive, in a pale blue pantsuit. She had a piece of paper in her hand.

"Here you are," she said, holding it out to the editor. "Doug Mark's number."

"It's for him."

"Oh. Here."

"Thanks," I said. I took the paper, looked at it. It was a 212 number. "Is this his home number?"

"That's right."

"You don't have his work number?"

"He's not working at the moment."

"Oh?"

"No. He's between jobs."

"How do you know that?"

"He told me."

"Kelly," Elizabeth Abbott said. "When did you speak to Doug Mark?"

"Sometime last week."

"When last week?" I said.

She looked at me, frowned. Looked back at the editor. "Elizabeth?"

"I'm sorry," I said. "I'm a private detective. You're aware that a publicist named Sherry Pressman was killed?"

"Yes, of course."

"Well, I'm investigating it. That's why I need Doug Mark's number. If you spoke to him last week, I'd like to know why and I'd like to know when. I'm not nosy, it's my job. It may have absolutely nothing to do with anything, but I'd appreciate your help." I turned to Elizabeth Abbott. "Is that putting it fairly?"

"I think so. Kelly, if you know anything that might help . . ."

"Yes, of course," Kelly said. "I just don't remember. Let me think. Friday the mechanical on the cover came in. So it wasn't then. Thursday—what happened Thursday? No, it wasn't last week, it was this week. It was Monday."

"You talked to him Monday?"

"That's right. Monday afternoon."

"Did you call him or did he call you?"

"Huh? Oh, no, it wasn't on the phone. It was here."

Elizabeth Abbott and I both said, "Here?" I know it happens in the movies a lot, people speaking in unison, but it's not that common in real life.

"That's right," Kelly said.

"What was Doug Mark doing here?" I said.

"I don't know. He said he just dropped in." Kelly turned to Elizabeth Abbott. "Didn't he tell you?"

"Me? No. I didn't see him. I didn't even know he was here."

"That's funny," Kelly said. "I thought he came to see you."

"Well, he didn't. Why did you think that?"

"Because that's where I saw him."

"Where?"

"Coming out of your office."

31.

Doug Mark was a tall, thin man with a face so lopsided he gave the impression he was just on the brink of falling over. This was even more remarkable in that he was sitting down. He had ushered me into the living room of his modest Chelsea apartment, gestured to the couch, and then taken the easy chair opposite.

"What can I do for you?"

I was tempted to say, "You could tilt your head a little to the left so I could see you straight on," but figured that would not be tactful. "It's about Sherry Pressman."

"So you said on the phone. I told you I knew nothing about it, and you came anyway. I don't mean to be rude, but why are you here?"

"Sherry Pressman was Kenneth P. Winnington's publicist."

"Yes, she was."

"And you were Kenneth P. Winnington's editor."

"I was five years ago. I can't see why that matters now."

"Are you familiar with Mr. Winnington's wife?"

His eyes widened. "Oh," he said, "there's a way to put it. *Familiar.* Do you know how many meanings that has? Are you *familiar* with the connotations of that word?"

"I'm not asking if you knew her in the biblical sense. I'm asking if you knew her at all."

He smiled what was, of course, a lopsided smile. "Very good," he said. "Very well put. I think you'll find Kenny married after we parted company."

"Then you never met his wife?"

"Didn't I just answer that?"

"No, you didn't. For someone who's so precise with words, I would think you'd know that."

He smiled again. "Good point. Are you a lawyer? No, you said you were a detective. Well, whatever you are, that's a very good point."

"I'm flattered," I said. "But you still haven't answered the question."

"Whether I'd met his wife? Or, since we're being precise, whether I'd *ever* met his wife. See, the *ever*, supposedly a clarifying word, actually muddies the issue. It means I have to consider is it possible she was at some dinner party I was at, or perhaps some even more unlikely instance that had nothing to do with anything. Do you see what I mean?"

"I certainly do. Mr. Mark, a burglar caught red-handed with the family jewels could not blather more inanely. Now, would you like to congratulate me on that verbal construction, or would you like to answer the question?"

"I have never to my knowledge met his wife. I wasn't invited to the wedding. I recall seeing her picture in the paper. Pictures can be very misleading, but she appeared young and attractive." He cocked his head, which almost gave me vertigo. "Was there anything else?"

"Yes. Have you called Mr. Winnington lately?"

"I beg your pardon?"

"Kenneth P. Winnington. Have you called him on the phone?"

"What has any of this to do with the death of this publicist?"

"I don't know. That's why I'm asking questions."

"Yes, but you must have a reason for asking. Pardon me, but what the hell is going on?"

"I'd be happy to tell you if you'd just answer the question. Have you called the Winnington residence at any time in the last month?"

"Of course not. Why would I?"

"I don't know. But someone did."

"What do you mean?"

"Mrs. Winnington has been receiving crank phone calls. Death threats."

"Death threats?"

"That's right."

"That's why you wanted to know if I knew his wife? You were asking me if I made death threats over the phone?"

"Did you?"

"I most certainly did not. Why in the world would I do a thing like that?"

"Because her husband dumped you."

He blinked and his mouth hung open.

At an angle.

"So that's your theory—I hated him, so I started harassing her?"

"Did you?"

"No, of course not. What a stupid idea."

"But you did hate him?"

He drew back, tucked his chin in, folded his arms. "That's putting it a little strongly. I resented the fact that he left. You couldn't begin to understand why."

"Would it have anything to do with the fact that Winnington wasn't a very good writer and wouldn't have gotten published at all if you hadn't rewritten his first novel wholesale?"

181

Doug Mark looked at me sideways. I can't begin to describe what that was like. "Who told you that?"

"His agent. I bribed him with a pastrami sandwich."

"Ah, good old Abe. Not one to pull his punches. So he's putting that story about?"

"I don't know if he's putting it about. He told me because I wasn't in the industry. He seemed happy to be able to tell someone. Anyway, is it true?"

"That I rewrote his book? Of course I did. I gave him two shots at it. When he couldn't hack it, I stepped in. Now, if you want the god's honest truth, I knew when I bought it I'd have to step in."

"But you bought it anyway."

"Sure. I knew it could be a best seller with a little work. Turns out I was right."

"It must have been rather upsetting when Winnington changed publishers."

"Don't be silly. I knew he would. We were a small house. Of course he's gonna move up. I resented it, sure, but harbor a grudge? Is that what you're getting at?"

"Are you saying you don't?"

"Of course not. That's ancient history. I never give the man a second thought."

"Then why were you in his editor's office on Monday afternoon?"

Doug Mark froze with his head cocked, his mouth open, and one finger raised. A hell of a tableau. He blinked and then smiled. "Wow. Pretty impressive. You just lobbed that in there all casual so I never saw it coming. If it actually meant anything, you'd have nailed me cold."

"Do I sense another bout of artistic stalling coming on?"

"Not at all. What was I doing in her office? Frankly, I was

looking for work. I happen to be out of work, and I need some."

"And you thought Elizabeth Abbott might have something for you?"

"Not exactly. But if you want to work in publishing, you need to inquire in the industry."

"But Elizabeth Abbott didn't see you. She was surprised to find out you'd been there."

"Yeah. I missed her. I spoke to another woman, who I believe is her assistant."

"Right. Who saw you coming out of her office. And I'm wondering why you would go into her office when no one was there."

"Yes, but I don't know no one's there until I go in, do I? I popped into Elizabeth Abbott's office, she wasn't there. I popped back out, I met her assistant, end of story. Why is this so important?"

"You happen to glance at Elizabeth Abbott's Rolodex?"

"Her Rolodex? Why would I do that?"

"Are you saying you didn't?"

"Yes, I'm saying I didn't. What's the idea?"

"Kenneth P. Winnington changed his phone number. Because of the crank calls. Only a few people had it. Elizabeth Abbott was one."

"So?"

"Sherry Pressman was another."

He blinked, put up his hand. "Wait a minute, wait a minute. Let me be sure I understand this. You're telling me Sherry Pressman was killed because she had Kenneth P. Winnington's phone number?"

"It's a possibility."

"And I'm a suspect—is that how you see it?—I'm a suspect

because I was in Elizabeth Abbott's office, and she also has Kenneth P. Winnington's phone number? Is that the situation?"

"Not exactly."

"But it's the reason you're here?"

"I suppose you could say that."

He shook his head disparagingly. "What a weak plot."

I wish people would stop saying that.

32.

I had a feeling I was being followed. Which is a really creepy feeling, and one that's hard to shake. I should know. I've had it before.

The only thing is, when I thought about it, it occurred to me that one time I thought I was being followed it turned out I wasn't. On the other hand, another time when I had no idea I was being followed, I was. So my feelings on the subject were not necessarily reliable.

Even so, when I came out of Doug Mark's brownstone apartment house on West 22nd Street and headed for Ninth Avenue where I'd left my car, I had the strangest feeling that someone was watching me.

For one thing, it was after dark. It had taken me a while to get hold of Doug Mark. He hadn't been home in the early afternoon. Which is why I'd wound up going home and getting my car. That and the fact I'd wanted to make sure the window had gotten repaired all right.

Don't get me wrong. I'm not saying I was double-checking on Alice. In such matters, Alice is probably ten times more competent than I. It was just that the whole fish incident was so unsettling I kind of needed to see the car back together again in order to feel better about it myself.

In that respect the car was just fine. The window had been repaired and the glass had been cleaned up, and the only hint there'd ever been a problem was a faint trace of eau de poisson, detectable by only the most discerning nose.

So I'd taken the car and driven downtown when I'd finally reached Doug Mark.

On my way to it now, I could have sworn I was being watched.

If you've never had the feeling, I don't know how to describe it. But take the experience of walking home late at night, feeling unarmed and vulnerable. And walking a little fast because it's very quiet and there's no one on the street. And if a mugger *should* be lurking between parked cars, should suddenly appear, well what the hell would you do then?

Now, take that feeling and magnify it by the fact that someone you know has been killed. And maybe, just maybe, the fact you're being followed is somehow related to that.

Creepy enough for you? Probably not. I'm sure I haven't done it justice. I don't have Kenneth P. Winnington's gift. Can't paint the horrific picture. But the fact was, I was on West 22nd Street between Eighth and Ninth Avenues. It was dark. The street lights were not doing their job. And there was no one in sight. Not one person.

And as I walked toward Ninth Avenue, I could feel eyes on me.

Sense someone there.

Moving.

Coming after me.

I stopped. Froze. Listened for footsteps.

Heard none.

Looked all around me.

Saw nothing.

My right hand went inside my jacket. Left breast pocket. Where a gun would normally be. Where my camera was now.

I gripped the camera, held it, as if ready to jerk it out and flash it in the face of my attacker, like Jimmy Stewart in *Rear Window*. Only I couldn't see myself doing that, somehow. No, the camera was a bluff. I was telling the stalker, hey, don't mess with me, I got a gun. Of course, that would only work if the stalker didn't know me well, but what the hey.

I was not standing there like a clod thinking all this. We're talking split seconds. It takes time to tell, no time to do. I stopped, listened, looked around, my hand's in my jacket bluffing a gun. A second later I'm on the move, stepping off toward Ninth Avenue with firm purpose. Marching with determination as opposed to resorting to flight. A fine distinction, but one's own.

I went past a parked van behind which no one was lurking. Came up on a rather dark building entryway into which I could not see. Time to cross the street?

Time to panic?

Time to run?

Certainly not time to stop.

I strode on by, trying hard not to look as if I were in training for an Olympic event.

The next building had a rather well-lit entryway. I stopped in front of it, looked around.

Saw nothing.

Which should have reassured me. But actually had the opposite effect.

I pushed on.

The next building was abandoned, the doors and windows cinderblocked up. Which meant no lights at all.

In the empty lot next door, where a brownstone had been, there was just rubble now. Broken glass and brick.

A crunching sound.

Someone in the rubble.

Horrible associations.

I remembered another rubble-filled lot a few years back where I'd gotten shot. Was that what was triggering this panic now? The feeling of not being in control? The feeling of one's thoughts beginning to swirl and twist and dissolve into the ether?

I shook my head to clear it, pushed on.

Nearly to the corner, nearly to Ninth Avenue now, just three more buildings.

Jesus Christ, get a grip.

I tried to humiliate myself, tell myself I wasn't doing anything special, brave, or heroic. What seemed like running the gauntlet to me consisted of merely coming out of a building and walking half a block to my car. Were I to succeed, this would probably not be written up in the papers as the world's greatest achievement by a private eye.

Were I to fail . . .

Jesus Christ, get a grip.

I shivered, strode for the corner. It was all I could do not to break into a run.

The street light on the corner was out, natch, but still, just reaching the wider avenue was something. And surely there would be someone on it.

There wasn't.

Deserted for blocks.

Come on, people, this is New York City. Where the hell is everybody?

The car was halfway down the block. A short block, the up-town/downtown block. Not like the long half block I'd just come. I stepped right along down the wider sidewalk, which allowed me to walk in the middle, out of reach of both the buildings and the parked cars.

And there was mine, the ancient Toyota, waiting patiently like a faithful steed. I strode out in the street, fitted the key into the lock of the driver's side door. Home free.

And yet.

My eyes darted over the car, looking for a broken window, or any other indication of forced entry, my mind, in flights of fancy, envisioning an attacker, crouched down in the back seat, waiting until I took the wheel to spring up, reach forward, slip the thin wire around my neck.

Like hell.

Before getting in I opened the rear door, made damn sure no one was there. That done, I hopped in, locked the door, punched off the code alarm, and started the car.

Then sighed with relief when it didn't explode.

As I pulled out of the parking space, it occurred to me it was a good thing I hadn't had that thought a few seconds earlier, or I might never have started the damn car.

But I had, and I was in it, and I was safe. And once I'd hung a right on 21st Street and another on Tenth Avenue, I was headed uptown and on my way home, and everything was just fine. And from what I could tell from looking in my rear-view mirror, no one was following me at all.

But I still couldn't shake the feeling.

33.

Alice wasn't impressed.

"You had a feeling?"

"Yes."

"A feeling you were being followed?"

"I've explained it the best I could."

"You've explained it several times. It still doesn't make any sense."

"Because it's a feeling. How do you explain a feeling?"

"You don't, of course. You explain all the things that contribute to the feeling. In this case they don't add up, so you say, of course they don't, it's just a feeling."

"That's not fair."

"You want some more rice?"

I was at the kitchen table eating salmon, rice, and broccoli. Alice and Tommie had already eaten. She'd zapped the fish in the microwave to warm it up for me, and it wasn't half bad.

"Starve a cold, feed paranoia?" I said, as Alice spooned me out more rice.

"Aside from that," Alice said. "Do you think you learned anything?"

"That's the whole problem," I said. Or at least, tried to say. I had salmon in my mouth. "Every time I think I'm getting somewhere it all seems so stupid. And everybody says so. All these damn publishing types. About what a lousy plot. That's the trouble with a real-life crime. It just doesn't necessarily have to make literary sense."

Alice looked at me. "What the hell does that mean?"

I rubbed my head. "I don't know. I really think I'm losing it. It's just on the one hand I got Sergeant Thurman, who's a total moron. Who's gone off the deep end obsessing about this one poor schmuck. Who's just sitting on him, waiting for him to make a phone call. Which leaves me with everything else. Which is pretty ironic, seeing as how the phone call is the thing I was hired to handle. And the murder case is Thurman's business. But somehow it's all got switched around."

"No, it hasn't," Alice said. "The phone call's still your business. As far as you're concerned, the murder is just a distraction."

"Oh, come on."

Alice put up her hand. "No, it's true. You were hired to stop the phone calls. That is your primary focus in the case. I take it there were no calls today."

"No, there wasn't."

"Of course not. Because if there were, Sergeant Thurman would either have been proved right or wrong. If he's right, the case is over. So you assume he's wrong. Also, because with Sergeant Thurman, that's a very natural assumption. As soon as that happens—as soon as there's another phone call—Sergeant Thurman will get off this suspect and back on the investigation. And maybe then you'll feel like the case is right side up again."

I said nothing, ate more salmon.

The idea of Sergeant Thurman being in charge of the case, meaning things were right side up again, was not reassuring.

Tommie popped in from the living room, said, "I beat World Four," and popped out again.

Tommie was playing *Yoshi's Island* on Super NES. It was a game that had something to do with the dinosaur eating enemies and laying eggs that it then threw at other enemies. I didn't fully understand it, which made me feel old. In the past, Tommie and I had always played Nintendo together. Now he was growing up, and I was growing into an old fogy, and how fast the years were flying by.

"You were saying," Alice said.

"Huh?"

"About this editor. Aside from his opinion that nothing made sense, what was your impression of him?"

"I'm not sure."

"That's not particularly helpful."

"I know, but there you are. On the one hand, the guy tells me he doesn't know Winnington's wife, and couldn't care less what happened to him. On the other hand, the guy is out of a job, and probably wouldn't be if Winnington hadn't dumped him five years ago. And this Monday he was in Elizabeth Abbott's office, where he could have gotten Winnington's new number off her Rolodex."

"But if he had, what would he need with the publicist?"

"That was his point exactly. And I don't have an answer. But just because I don't have an answer doesn't mean it isn't true. He was in her goddamn office. And when *I* was in her goddamn office, and asked her to check the Rolodex, Kenneth P. Winnington's number was right there on top. Where it would have been if this guy had turned to it to find it. And he was in her office when she wasn't there. And he *claims* he was there looking for work. But he never did speak to Elizabeth Abbott, and might not have spoken to anybody, if her assistant hadn't happened to see him coming out of her office."

"It is distressing," Alice said.

"Is that all you have to say about it?"

"Well, what do you expect me to say? You want me to make it make sense?"

"It would be nice."

"It certainly would. But we don't have all the facts yet. And the ones we have don't add up."

"Great," I said.

I stood up, took my plate over to the sink.

The phone rang. Alice scooped it up, said, "Hello," then, "Oh, hi, Clara."

Which effectively ended our conversation. When her friend Clara called, Alice would be on the phone for hours.

"Hold on, Clara, let me change phones," Alice said. "Stanley, I'm going to take this in the bedroom. Hang it up for me, will you?"

"Sure."

"Oh, and I got clothes in the dryer. Can you get 'em out?"

"When are they done?"

"Now. First two dryers."

"Where's the cart?"

"It's down there. Thanks."

I waited until Alice picked up in the bedroom, then hung up the phone, and went to get our clothes out of the laundry room in the basement.

Which was too bad. I was going to go in the living room and watch Tommie play *Yoshi's Island*. Compared to which, folding laundry held no real allure.

Ah, well, the private detective's work was never done. I armed myself with quarters and dimes, just in case the clothes were still damp, went out in the hallway, rang the bell, and took the elevator down to the basement.

The laundry room was deserted at that time of night. All

the washers and dryers had stopped. The place was quiet as a tomb.

I went over to the dryers to check my clothes. Sure enough, the dark load was still damp. No real surprise there—the dark load was large, and the jeans took a long time to dry.

But the white load was damp too. That didn't figure. It was much smaller, mostly socks and underwear, and by rights it should have been dry. The fact it wasn't could be blamed on the machine. That was the trouble with the dryers. There were four of them, and they didn't always work efficiently. And the real problem was, you never knew which one.

I knew now. The culprit was dryer number one. I took my clothes out of it, moved them to number three. Then fed in sixty cents—two quarters stacked and a dime—for fifteen minutes, which, with the clothes just damp, should be enough. I put another sixty cents in the other dryer for the dark load, then pushed the plungers into the coin slots and started the machines.

With an incredible racket, the clothes began to whirl.

Great. Fifteen minutes and they'd be done. I could either stand here like a fool and watch them, or go ring for the elevator, take it upstairs, and have to turn around and come back down almost as soon as I got there. I mean, when you add in the time waiting for the elevator and going up and waiting for the elevator and coming down, what would I have, a whopping five minutes? I mean, was it worth even doing?

I stood there like a schmuck, vacillating, wasting more time, the choice of going upstairs becoming a more ridiculous one with each passing second.

And the lights went out.

Suddenly, just like that, the laundry room was dark.

My first thought was a power failure. But, no, the racket

from the dryers assured me that was not the case. It was just the lights.

And just the laundry room lights. Through the door at the far end of the room a faint light was shining in from the basement hall.

So what happened?

Who turned out the lights?

The thought made me shiver. Which was stupid. Here I was, safe and sound in my own building. We had manned elevators. No one could get in.

So what happened to the damn lights?

Even with the light coming in the door, it was pitch dark in my end of the laundry room. With my hand ahead of me, I groped my way around the table for folding clothes, and headed for the door. Where, if my memory served me well, the light switch was.

Yes, there it was, right next to the door. The silhouette of the metal box that controlled the lights in the room. Had someone switched it off?

Before checking that I checked the doorway, peered around out into the basement hall. There was nothing there. A long, empty hallway overhung with pipes. Dusty, dimly lit, just what you'd expect in an old apartment building. But empty, not a soul in sight.

So who turned out the lights?

Back to the light switch. I could see the box, but not the switch itself—it was too dark. I reached out, felt it with my hand.

The switch was up. Surely that meant on. Nonetheless, I clicked it down.

Nothing.

Back up.

Nothing.

Didn't that mean no one had turned off the switch?

Well, at least not there. But what about the fuse box? Someone could have thrown a circuit breaker.

Who?

Jesus Christ. I had to tell myself again, no one could get into the basement. There were no stairs down from the lobby. The only way to get to the basement was in the elevator.

Except for the back door.

The thought chilled me. Despite the fact I knew full well that, one, the back door was locked, and, two, the back door led to a courtyard that was accessible only by an iron gate that was locked and topped with razor wire.

Even so, the decision to ring for the elevator and go upstairs didn't seem quite so stupid as it had.

I came out of the laundry room into the basement hallway, stood in front of the elevator, contemplated doing just that.

And heard a noise.

Yeah, I know, I'd been hearing the noise from the dryers. But out of the laundry room around the corner in the hall, that noise was faint and muted.

This noise was sharp.

And from the other direction.

From the other end of the hall.

Where the door to the courtyard was.

That was around the bend at the other end of the hall. Or one of the bends. To the right was the boiler room. To the left the door to outside. So surely it was the boiler I heard. Some clang from the boiler.

Wasn't that it?

No, it wasn't.

It was the rustling of paper.

Jesus.

As if drawn by a magnet, I turned, took two steps down the hall.

And felt a chill.

But this time it was real. Cold air on my forearm, on my cheeks.

A draft.

From where?

Another step. Yes, damn it. Cold air.

Common sense told me to get out of there. Turn around, ring for the elevator. But I didn't want to turn my back on it. I had to know. Somehow, I had to know.

The sound again.

Or was it?

And once again, I couldn't tell, from the left or from the right?

Another step. My eyes darting around. In the shadows. In the dim light. Making sure. There is no one in that doorway, and the door is locked. That is not a prowler, that is a fire hose. That is not the fuse box, where the hell is it?

Suddenly I'm at the end of the hall. And I can't hear the dryers at all anymore. Or the sound that drew me there. But if I take one more step and look to the left, I can see the door to the courtyard.

I turned, looked at the back door.

It was open!

As I looked, horrified, the rustling sound came right behind me.

I jumped a mile. Wheeled around. Nearly wet my pants.

Nothing. No one there. Just . . .

The door to the boiler room.

He's in there.

Or was he?

Suddenly, I realized I had my back to the door.

The open door.

I turned, flattened my back against the wall, so I could look in both directions.

The sound again. From the boiler room. Never mind the door. He's in there.

I stepped on something. Looked down. It was a piece of pipe. I reached down, snatched it up. Held it like a weapon. It was a gooseneck, probably from a kitchen sink. It must have looked ridiculous, the wrong shape for a weapon. I didn't care. I held it up, ready to strike, crept toward the boiler room door.

No light inside. Wouldn't you know it. Just a metal staircase leading down. Not for me, thanks. It's back to the elevator for me, gang. This has all been a lot of fun, but—

It happened so fast I didn't have time to react.

A shadow shot from the doorway, whizzed by my face before I could even move the pipe. Startled, I dropped it. It clanged on the cement floor.

With a yowl of rage and fright, my attacker darted through the hallway and out the back door.

It was a cat.

It's hard to describe what I felt then. Relief, yes, but my heart was pounding, my adrenaline surging. And I had been absolutely, positively wired. The realization it was a cat punctured this, and it rushed away like air escaping from a balloon.

I exhaled, slumped back, leaned against the wall.

That's when it hit me.

That's when I realized, this was it, this was when it happened. In movie after movie, this was how it played out. The incredibly tense scene, the sudden shock, then the comic relief—oh, it's just a cat—the hero relaxes, then, bam!, the killer strikes.

Only it didn't happen. And, I slowly realized, it wasn't going to happen. Because it wasn't a movie, and no one had written the script. There was no prowler, no killer, no lurker in the dark. And the only one who'd gotten in the open back door was the cat.

And no one had thrown the circuit breaker, cutting the lights. The bulb in the laundry room had simply burned out.

I rang for the elevator, went upstairs, got a new bulb and a flashlight. Then I went back to the laundry room and answered the age-old question, how many private detectives does it take to change a light bulb? I changed it, then folded the laundry, feeling as foolish as you might imagine.

I still couldn't help looking over my shoulder as I did.

I needn't have bothered.

The killer wasn't stalking me in my basement that night.

The killer was somewhere else.

34.

Doug Mark hadn't been strangled.

He'd been shot.

He was sitting on his living room couch, right where I'd left him. As always, his head was askew. Only now the asymmetrical picture was compounded by the circular hole in his forehead and the red racing stripe that ran down his left cheek.

To be honest, racing stripe wasn't the first image that came to mind. I've had things published myself—magazine articles, to be sure—still, the line of blood reminded me of nothing so much as the stroke of a copy editor's red pencil. The circular hole and the straight red line were a delete symbol.

Someone had edited Doug Mark out.

I looked up from the body to find Sergeant Thurman standing there glaring at me.

"Well?" he demanded.

It was a question I was ill prepared to answer.

It was nine thirty in the morning. I'd been beeped off my stakeout of the 34th Street pay phone. I'd been glad when the beeper went off. I thought it meant my client had gotten another phone call. Which would have proved Sergeant Thurman wrong. Instead, two cops had picked me up and brought me here, where I'd encountered Doug Mark's corpse. Exactly what that proved was yet to be determined.

"Well?" I said. "What do you mean, well?"

"Don't play games with me. Do you know this man?"

"Of course I do. His name's Doug Mark. He was Kenneth P. Winnington's first editor."

"Is that right?"

"Don't you know?"

"I'm asking the questions here."

"Then ask some that make sense. If you know enough to drag me in here, you must know who he is."

"Don't fuck with me," Thurman said. "I want some answers and I want 'em now. How do you know this guy?"

"I saw him yesterday."

"Here?"

"Yeah."

"When?"

"Four thirty, five o'clock."

"What did you want with him?"

"Information."

"No shit. Don't be a wise ass. What were you doing here?"

"Looking for someone with a reason to hate Kenneth P. Winnington."

"Come again."

"Winnington dumped him. I figured he qualified."

"That's pretty thin."

"Then why's he dead?"

The look on Thurman's face was priceless. I had a feeling when his thought process caught up with him he might punch me in the nose.

Fortunately, we were interrupted by the arrival of the medical examiner, a black man with white hair and wire-rimmed glasses. He squeezed his portly figure into the room, insinuated himself between the coffee table and the couch, and bent over the body of Doug Mark. After a few moments he straightened up and declared, "This man is dead."

"No shit, doc," Thurman said. "You think you could tell me when?"

"He's dead right now."

The two cops who had brought me up grinned.

Thurman didn't. "You think you could tell me when he *died?*"

The ME appeared unruffled. "Yeah, I could take a crack at that. When would you *like* him to have died?"

Thurman's eyes narrowed. "I wouldn't *like* anything. I'm wondering about five o'clock yesterday afternoon."

The ME nodded. "Could have died then. We'll get him down to the morgue, run some tests."

"Fine, you do that," Thurman said. He wheeled back on me. "I want some answers, and I want 'em fast, and I want 'em straight. How'd you get a line on this guy?"

"From the agent."

"What agent?"

"Winnington's agent. What's-his-name. Abe Feinstein."

"He sent you here?"

"No, he just told me about him. Coming here was my idea."

"But he gave you the address?"

"Actually, it was the editor who gave me the address."

"The editor?"

"Winnington's editor. Elizabeth Abbott."

"How come she gave you the address?"

"Because the agent didn't have it?"

Thurman's eyes narrowed. "You giving me a runaround?"

"I'm giving you the straight facts. They just don't happen to make sense."

"No shit."

"How'd you connect me?"

"I'm askin' the questions here."

"Yeah, but why? How'd you know to pull me in?"

"What's a matter, you hard of hearing?" Thurman said. "I ask and you answer. That's how it works. But never mind. Since you seem to be having trouble, why don't you cool out and think things over."

Thurman turned to the cops who'd brought me in. "Okay, he's ID'd the body, now run him downtown."

The cops took hold of me, piloted me out the door.

My head was spinning. What the hell was going on? I seemed to be having more than my usual trouble figuring everything out. And it wasn't just the shock of finding Doug Mark dead. Sure, that was a kick in the head, what with me having just talked to him and all that. But, aside from that, it occurred to me that absolutely nothing made sense.

Why the hell had I been dragged in here? More to the point, why had I been dragged in here if Sergeant Thurman didn't know about Doug Mark? I could understand it if Sergeant Thurman had connected Doug Mark to Kenneth P. Winnington, and decided to question me on that. But that still wouldn't make a lot of sense unless he knew I'd called on him. I suppose he could have learned from Elizabeth Abbott or her assistant at the publisher's, since they'd given me the address, but how could he have possibly gotten to them so soon?

I had no idea.

The only thing I knew for sure, the only satisfaction I could take from this, if one can use such terms about a gruesome murder, was that the death of Doug Mark accomplished one thing. It blew Sergeant Thurman's theory out of the water. Which was probably what was eating him up, and why he was so pissed off just now. Unless the nebbishy writer Sergeant Thurman was sitting on had actually killed Doug Mark, in which case the murders would be solved, this murder exonerated him. Just as it would have had there been another telephone call.

Yeah, that much I knew. Which basically meant I knew nothing. But I kept thinking about it, and going over it in my mind, because it was easier to do that than to think about the other thing that I was trying not to think about.

The fact that in one way or another, by leading the killer to him, I had probably caused Doug Mark's death.

35.

"Why am I here?"

ADA Frost did not favor me with a baby-faced smile. This morning he looked particularly grim. "Sit down," he said.

We were alone in his office. The two cops had driven me downtown, ushered me into his office, and left.

I'd have left too, if I could. But there was no reason to make a fuss. I took the offered chair.

"I'll ask again," I said. "Why am I here?"

"You mind telling me about Doug Mark?"

"Doug Mark is dead."

"So I understand. What's his connection with you?"

"Do I need an attorney here?"

"You tell me."

"That's a new one. I tell you?"

"Absolutely. If you killed him, you need an attorney. Frankly, I find that rather unlikely, but in that case you do. Otherwise, there's no reason we shouldn't just talk."

I considered calling Richard and the whole nine yards. The prospect was unpleasant. More than likely we'd get the other two lawyers in here too, and start that whole merry-go-round again. And this time I had nothing to hide—it wasn't like I was trying to keep my client's name out of it. There was no reason for me not to talk since Frost didn't really peg me for the murder. For the moment I just felt bad, and wanted to get it over with.

"Okay," I said. "Talk."

"I would prefer to hear from you," Frost said. "How do you know Doug Mark?"

I gave him a rundown of what happened.

"That's very interesting," he said. "You got Doug Mark's phone number from Kenneth P. Winnington's publisher yesterday afternoon. Till then, you had not met the man, talked to the man, had no idea where he lived."

"Uh-huh."

"You went to the publisher, secured his number, and called on him last night."

"That's right."

"And he admitted being in this editor's office. Elizabeth Abbott. Where he could have gotten Winnington's new number."

"Yes, he did. Although he claims he didn't get it. And even if he did, why would that be a reason to kill him?"

"I have no idea," Frost said. "I'm merely assembling facts."

"Oh, yeah? Well, you have some I don't," I said. "Because this man is found dead, and two cops drag me up to his apartment before Sergeant Thurman even knows what's happening." I put up my hand. "Not that it's that unusual for Sergeant Thurman not to know what's happening, but you know what I mean. Sergeant Thurman dragged me in without knowing my connection to Doug Mark. Now why did he do that?"

"Why do you think?"

"I have no idea. Please, fill me in."

Frost leveled a finger. "You understand this goes no further. This is something we plan to withhold."

"What, for Christ's sake?"

Frost leaned back in his desk chair, laced his fingers together, put his hands behind his head. "The crimes are not at all similar. Sherry Pressman was strangled. I understand this man was shot."

"Yeah. So?"

"So, basically, there's no connection. Except for the rather tenuous one that both of them at one time or another had worked with Kenneth P. Winnington."

"Why are you stating the obvious?"

"I'm not stating the obvious. The obvious connection is you. You called on both people. Both people subsequently died."

"How'd you know?"

"Huh?"

"How'd you know I called on Doug Mark?"

Frost smiled. He raised one finger. "Ah. There you've hit on it." He cocked his head. "Are you telling me you have no idea?"

"Yeah. I've no idea."

"Really. Of course, you didn't see. Still, I would have thought."

"Would you mind not talking in cryptic half sentences? Just what the hell is going on?"

"I guess I should explain," Frost said. "Doug Mark had a girlfriend. Didn't live with him, but she had a key. She was supposed to meet him for breakfast this morning. When he didn't show, she went to wake him up. You know what she found."

"So?"

"So she called 911. A cruiser responded. Unfortunately, one of the cops was green."

"Green?"

"Yeah. Rookie cop. Rookie mistake. It was his first murder scene."

"What did he do?"

"What he did was disturb the corpse. Not that unusual, really. Actually happens all the time. I mean, you gotta make sure

207

the guy's dead. Not that there was any doubt in this case. Anyway, the long and short of it is, the kid touched the body and there you are."

"Where? Where the hell am I? You having fun dragging this out?"

"No, I'm not," Frost said. "It might surprise you, but I'm not enjoying this at all. Anyway—and this is the part that doesn't leave this room—it happens the rookie cop took something off the body."

"You're kidding."

"I wish I were. But that's a fact. His partner saw him do it, but by then it was too late." Frost grimaced, raised his hand. "I'll tell you something else off the record. Nine cops out of ten see that happen, wouldn't say a word, they'd simply put it back. But, oh no, this cop's a stickler, does everything by the numbers, and who's to say he's not right. Anyway, instead of replacing it, he bags it, marks it, and sends it in."

"So what was it?"

"It was this," Frost said. He picked up a plastic evidence bag from his desk. It was a small bag, about six by nine, with a white piece of paper in it. He held it up for a moment, then passed it over.

I took a look and gawked.

On the paper, in longhand, were two words.

Stanley Hastings.

36.

I stared at Baby Face Frost. "This can't be right."

"Oh? Why not?"

"It makes no sense."

"Oh, yeah? It makes sense to me. You call on people, and they die with your name in their hand."

"That makes sense to you?"

"It establishes a pattern."

"A pattern of what? I didn't kill these people."

"I never said you did."

"I'm glad to hear it. Particularly after you advising me I didn't need a lawyer."

"I don't think you do."

"You don't peg me for these crimes?"

"Give me a break. Even for the most dedicated private detective, that would seem overzealous."

"I'm glad you can joke about it. It shows you're a real fun guy. You mind telling me what the hell is going on?"

Frost shrugged. "What you see is what you get. The guy was holding that paper in his hand. You have any idea how it got there?"

"None at all. What's more, I don't think he wrote it."

Frost raised his eyebrows. "Oh?"

"Handwriting should be able to tell that, shouldn't they? Whether he wrote it?"

"What makes you think he didn't?"

"Because I didn't see it there. When I called on him. It's a page from a notebook, right? Small spiral notebook. Torn off at the top. Well, I don't remember seeing one around." I put up my hands. "And that's not even the point. The point is, the killer put this in the guy's hand deliberately. That's the only thing that makes sense. In which case, the killer either wrote it himself, or he got Doug Mark to write it. At least that's how I figure it."

"And why would the killer do that?"

"To frame me. Obviously."

"Obviously? But it's such a clumsy frame. It wouldn't fool anyone."

"I'm delighted to hear it. But you gotta remember. You know me. This is not our first case. The frame isn't at all convincing because you know I didn't do it. But the killer doesn't know that. The killer thinks any evidence implicating me will be taken at face value. See what I mean?"

"Granted," Frost said. "I'm perfectly willing to accept that theory, that the killer is trying to frame you. In fact, I practically have to accept it, since it happened twice. Once, you put down to coincidence. Twice is hard to ignore. So, if we accept the premise the killer is trying to frame you, the question is why?"

"Only one reason I can think of."

"What's that?"

"They want me off the case."

Frost frowned. "Interesting. Interesting theory, that. What is it that you're doing that's dangerous to the killer? The obvious answer is the phone calls. You were hired to trace the phone calls. But the cops are working on that too. So what would be the point of eliminating you?"

"Well . . ." I said.

"Well what?"

"Not to toot my own horn, but if you think about it, isn't it slightly conceivable that the killer might be afraid I might be onto something, but wouldn't consider Sergeant Thurman a threat?"

Thurman arrived just then, came crashing into Frost's office without so much as a by-your-leave, and said, "The body's on the way to the morgue. What's his story?"

Frost shrugged. "Says he's been framed."

"Gee, that's a new one," Thurman said. "You discuss the paper?"

"Yes, we did."

"How's he explain that?"

"The killer put it in his hand."

"How convenient."

"I suppose it makes more sense that *I* would put it in his hand, in order to implicate myself?"

"Don't talk wise," Thurman said. "Why didn't you tell me about this guy?"

"What?"

"Yesterday. When you called on him. Why didn't you fill me in?"

"I had no idea he was important. I was merely running down leads."

"Oh, yeah? Well, it's my case, I'm in charge, I wanna know what those leads are."

"I'll tell you anything you wanna know."

"I don't mean *now*," Thurman said. "I mean *then*. You have to tell me *then*."

"That's beyond my capabilities."

Thurman's face was getting redder by the minute. "Don't crack wise. You know what I mean. This is a murder investigation. Anything you've got, I want."

"I don't have anything," I said. "Like I said, I'm just chasing leads."

"What made you chase this one?"

"I told you. He had a reason to hate Winnington. That's what I was looking for."

"So why didn't you bring it to me?"

"Are you kidding? You wouldn't have listened. You're so fixated on the guy from the book signing. Now that that's over with, maybe you'll listen to reason."

"Over with?"

"Yeah. Doesn't this murder exonerate him?"

"Not at all."

I stared at Thurman. "You don't think the murders and the phone calls are related?"

"Of course I do."

"So if the guy didn't kill Doug Mark, that lets him off the hook, doesn't it?"

Thurman said nothing. Merely glared.

"Well, doesn't it?"

"No, it doesn't. The man is guilty."

I blinked. "I beg your pardon?"

"That's the guy. He did it. No doubt in my mind."

"Wait a minute," I said. "I don't understand. The guy either went to Doug Mark's or he didn't. If he didn't, he's off the hook, right?"

Sergeant Thurman said nothing.

ADA Frost cleared his throat. "While the autopsy report is not yet in, it would appear Doug Mark was killed some time yesterday in the early evening."

"Yeah. So?"

"The crank calls your client has been receiving all took place during the day. During normal business hours. Nine to five. There was no reason to assume the caller would make one at any other time."

My eyes widened. I turned to Sergeant Thurman. "You *lost* him?"

"I didn't lose him. He wasn't under twenty-four-hour surveillance."

That's when I snapped, blew up, went off the deep end.

"I don't believe this. I absolutely don't believe this. I'm sorry, but it's too damn much." I wheeled on Thurman. "Not only did you fuck up and let the guy go, but now you're using that as an excuse to argue that the guy is guilty? I mean, of all the stupid, idiotic, numbnuts things I've ever heard, this takes the fucking cake!"

It occurred to me long about then that my honeymoon with Sergeant Thurman was probably over.

37.

MacAullif was amused. That figured. MacAullif was in one of those contrary moods where anything that pissed me off probably made his day.

"It isn't funny," I told him.

"Depends on where you sit," MacAullif said. "Now me, I'm not involved in this case at all, and I like it a lot."

"I'm glad you're having so much fun. It happens two people are dead."

"Yeah, yeah, and it's tragic and all that," MacAullif said. "But, you know, I'm a homicide cop. Any case I get, someone's likely to be dead. Some of them are sad, some of them are funny, and that's how it is."

"This isn't funny."

"Right. You led the killer to both victims, so you're Typhoid Mary, and it's all your fault. I know the way you think. You happen to be full of shit, but nothing I can say is gonna change that, so we skip over it and move on. Not counting that, what have you got, you've got Sergeant Thurman looking like a Keystone Kop again. And you expect me not to laugh."

"He's got the wrong man."

"So? For Sergeant Thurman this is not a unique situation. I wouldn't let it worry you. If he's really the wrong man, eventually it will become obvious. I mean to the point where even Sergeant Thurman will see it. Meanwhile, it's pretty damn funny."

"Meanwhile, I need a course of action."

MacAullif grimaced. "Jesus Christ, what a pain in the ass. What'sa matter, you been watchin' too much TV, you need a course of action?"

"I'm getting paid to do a job. I'd like to do it."

"Aha, that's different," MacAullif said. "You want to justify your employment. And here I thought this was all motivated by guilt."

"Never mind guilt. But if I'm leading the killer to these people, I'd rather not lead him to anyone else."

"Except me."

"That's not funny."

"Yeah, well, just between you and me, I'm not really worried. But let me see if I've got this straight. The reason you're in here talkin' to me now is because you're afraid to talk to anybody else?"

"That's not exactly true."

"It's close enough," MacAullif said. "Okay, you wanna talk, talk, then let me get on with my life."

"Let me ask you some questions."

"Shoot."

"Why is the killer framing me?"

"That's your question?"

"It's one of 'em."

"It's a pretty good one. If I were in your place, I'd probably want to know that too."

"MacAullif."

"What, you're pissed off I don't have an answer? All right, I got an answer. In fact, I got several. Which is the whole problem. I don't have *the* answer. The right answer. The one you're lookin' for. But you want some answers, here goes. Why is the killer framing you? First off, to draw suspicion away from himself. That is generally the purpose of a frame. The killer frames someone to get himself off."

MacAullif took out a cigar. He didn't unwrap it, just drummed it on the desk. "Now we got a little problem here in that the frame is not very good. In fact, it's bad, it's terrible, it's horrible, it stinks to high heaven, and why would anyone even bother to try?"

"Exactly my point," I said.

"So we look for another reason."

"Have you got one?"

"Sure."

"What's that?"

"Because you're there." MacAullif shrugged. "Same reason they climb the mountain, right? But that's basically it. You happen to be there. The killer knows that, so the killer underlines it. It may not frame you for the crime, but it certainly involves you in the case."

"Why does the killer want to do that?"

"How the hell should I know? We don't know if it's convenient, or if it's personal. Which is the flip side of because you're there. You're not framed because you're *there*, you're framed because you're *you*."

"I beg your pardon?"

"The killer hates you. It's strictly personal, and the killer's doin' this because he hates your guts." MacAullif looked at me. "Is there anyone whose toes you stepped on during this investigation?"

"Not that I know of."

"Well, let me put it another way. Is there anyone involved in the case you don't particularly like?" As I raised my eyebrows, he added, "Not counting Sergeant Thurman."

"Oh." I frowned. "Well . . ."

"Well, what?"

"Well, there's no one I actively dislike. On the other hand, I find Kenneth P. Winnington to be arrogant and condescending."

"I'll buy that."

"But, even if he were aware of it, I can't see him killing two people just to teach me a lesson."

"Of course not. But if he *were* killing two people and didn't like you, he might take advantage of the opportunity to tweak your nose."

"Are you serious?"

"I'm offering you theories. What's wrong with that one?"

"Then Winnington would have to be behind the whole thing."

"Of course. It's his wife who's being harassed, isn't it? The husband's always the most likely suspect."

"He's not making the calls."

"No, he would have an accomplice."

"You really think so?"

"No," MacAullif said irritably. "How many times do I have to say it? I'm talking theory. It's just one theory, and it isn't even the best one."

"What's the best one?"

"That you're stepping on the killer's toes. That you're getting close, the killer sees you as a threat, and tries to head you off."

"But I'm *not* getting close."

"Yeah, but the killer doesn't know you're incompetent. He thinks a detective's on his tail."

"Thanks a lot."

"That give you enough to go on?"

"That gives me nothing I didn't already know."

"What about your load of fish?"

"What about 'em?"

"You find out where they came from?"

"I haven't had time."

"You had time to get this editor killed."

"That isn't funny."

"No, it's not. So, you don't know about the fish. But it must have occurred to you it goes along with the notes."

"The notes?"

"The notes with your name on 'em the victims are clutching. It's far-fetched, theatrical, larger than life. The type of thing you'd expect to find in a book."

"Yes, of course. So what?"

"In one of Winnington's books?"

"I don't think so."

"Oh? Have you read one?"

"No."

"Then how do you know?"

"Surely if there was a similarity, someone would have mentioned it."

"Oh? Who'd you tell about the fish?"

"No one."

"So how'd they know to mention it?"

"I didn't mean the fish."

"You mean the notes?"

"Yeah."

"The notes are no big deal. It's a fucking cliché. The victim dies with a clue in his hand. You could have the same thing in half a dozen books and no one would think a thing of it. It's only when you throw in the fish."

"All right, I get the point. I'll find out if there's anything similar in any of his books."

"Good," MacAullif said. "Quite frankly, I doubt it. But I wouldn't pass it up."

"You have any more bad advice?"

MacAullif frowned, rattled the cigar back and forth between his fingers and his thumb. "You say this guy was shot?"

"That's right."

"And the other one was strangled?"

"Uh-huh. What do you make of that?"

"First off, you don't have your typical serial killer. 'Cause he doesn't change his MO. So, your first consideration is, did the same person commit both crimes?"

"Don't you think so?"

"What I think's not important. We're examining possibilities here."

"Don't be a pain in the ass. I know we're talking possibilities. What's your opinion?"

MacAullif leveled the cigar at me. "You wanna hear what I have to say? Then don't give me this cut-to-the-chase bullshit. I gotta lay out all the possibilities, see which ones I like. The problem is you like to jump to the conclusion without going through all the steps. Which is probably why you're so often wrong."

MacAullif leaned back in his chair, scratched his nose with the cigar. "Where was I. Oh, yeah, did the same person commit both crimes. Well, that's one possibility. In its favor is the notes with your name on 'em. And the connection to Winnington. Is there any reasonable hypothesis that explains those facts *without* the same person committing both crimes? I would say there were two. First scenario, copycat crime. Second killer, familiar with details from first crime, recreates note in hand. However, killer is not true copycat in not mimicking means of death.

"Second scenario, conspiracy. Accomplice of first killer commits second crime. Uses own method of death while carrying out general theme."

"Uh-huh," I said. "And do you think either of those are the case?"

"Not really. My gut feeling is the same person killed them both."

"Then why use different means?"

"Actually, that's not so hard," MacAullif said. "Because the first one was strangled and the second one was shot. Instead of the other way around."

"What do you mean?"

"The first killing may not have been planned. The guy's talkin' to this woman, suddenly realizes he has to kill her. He has no weapon in hand, so he strangles her. After that, he's upped the ante, it's a no-limit game, he knows it, and he arms himself. So the second one he shoots."

MacAullif shrugged. "The other theory is merely sexist. The woman he can strangle, the guy he has to shoot."

"But why? Why does he do this at all?"

"He does it to cover up his complicity in the crank phone calls. Though what's behind that, and why it's so important, I have no idea."

"Why it's so important?"

"Covering it up, I mean." MacAullif spread his arms. "Before the first murder, what have you got? A few crank phone calls. Big fucking deal. If you catch the guy, what's he gonna get? A slap on the wrist, and don't-do-it-again. To avoid this he commits murder? Way out of proportion, don't you think?"

"Yes, I do. But the fact is, it happened."

"Right. Which strongly indicates the first murder wasn't planned. It was an impulsive action, taken on the spur of the moment. Of course, once the guy goes that far, there's no turning back." MacAullif raised his finger. "The only thing against that scenario is . . ."

"Yes?"

"The fish. If the killer dumped the fish in your car, then we are dealing with something really sick. In which case, Thurman is wasting his time tailing this would-be writer. Instead, he should be tailing you."

"Me?"

"Sure. Both victims died after you called on 'em. How did the killer know that? Most likely he was following you. If this were my case, I'd put a tail on you and see who shows up."

"You think I should suggest that to Thurman?"

"I think you should stay as far away from Thurman as you could possibly get. All I'm sayin' is, watch your back."

"No shit. Any other insights?"

MacAullif frowned. "I keep coming back to books. The victims are a publicist and an editor. The client is a writer. Or the client's husband, or whatever. But the fact is, he is. And what's more, he writes mysteries."

"Actually, he writes suspense."

"What's the difference?"

"It's a different kind of book."

"I didn't think it was a different kind of vegetable. *How* is it different?"

"Actually, I don't really read suspense."

"So you don't know?" MacAullif said. "You're telling me you don't know?"

"You make it sound like a federal crime."

"Fucking up a murder investigation *should* be a federal crime. Thurman's doing it, that's no reason you gotta do it. You got a suspense writer involved in a murder plot. Everyone connected to the suspense writer's career starts dropping dead. Do you suppose there might be a connection?"

"I get the point."

"Do you? Good. Here's another one. This guy Sergeant Thurman's sitting on—what do you know about him?"

"Not much. Why?"

"Just because Sergeant Thurman thinks he's guilty doesn't mean he isn't."

I exhaled. "Right. I'll consider the possibility."

"And those other writers—the wannabes, from the publicist—you ever track 'em down?"

"Not yet. But . . ."

"Right," MacAullif said. "You don't want 'em to die. Too bad you broke up with Thurman. You could call on one of 'em, he could stake him out and see who tries to kill him."

"Or you could."

"In your dreams. It's not my case, and I'm not goin' near it. In fact, I shouldn't even be talking about it." MacAullif pointed the cigar at the door. "In case you didn't recognize it, that's your exit cue."

"Any last advice?"

"Yeah. Why don't you talk to Rosenberg?"

"My attorney? Why?"

"The son of a bitch." MacAullif snorted. "Maybe you could lead the killer to him."

38.

Richard was pissed. "Why didn't you call me?"

"There was no need."

"No need? Are you kidding me? You spilled your guts."

"Richard, no one thinks I did it."

"And what difference does that make?"

I sighed, ran my hand over my head. "Give me a break, Richard. This isn't some game I'm playing with these guys. This is a murder case."

"Exactly my point. You're involved in a capital crime. You have to watch your step."

"Richard, I'm not guilty."

"What difference does that make? You think an innocent man never went to jail?"

"What's the matter? Are you willfully misunderstanding me? Frost knows I didn't do it."

"The murder, yes," Richard said. "But there's obstruction of justice, withholding evidence, tampering with a witness."

"I'm not doing *any* of those things," I cried in exasperation.

"Yes, but they don't know that. And you do not have the swiftest cop in the world in charge of the investigation. You're cooperating with him now, but if you should get on his bad side . . ."

"Oh."

"Why do you say, oh?"

"Well, I told him to go fuck himself."

Richard rolled his eyes. "Probably not the brightest move you could have made. See what happens when you don't call your lawyer?"

"If you'd been there, *you'd* have told him to go fuck himself."

"Perhaps. But I would hope in less actionable terms. You mind telling me what inspired this bonehead play?"

"I couldn't help it. He thinks this guy from the book signing's guilty. So he puts him under surveillance. Then he knocks off because it's five o'clock. The murder happened after five, so now he says the guy could have done it, 'cause he wasn't watching him."

"Makes sense to me," Richard said.

"Sense? You call that making sense?"

"It's perfectly logical. If no one was watching him, the guy *could* have done it."

"Yeah, but he *didn't*," I said. "If someone was watching him, we could have *eliminated* him from having done it. Then we could get on with the case. Instead, Thurman's fixated on this guy, and he's not doing anything else."

"What would you like him to do?"

"Right now, get hit by a truck."

"Uh-huh," Richard said. "Perhaps I should have phrased that differently. In terms of the investigation, what do you think should be done?"

"I don't know."

"And yet you fault Thurman for not doing it."

I exhaled. "Jesus Christ. This is not my day. Everyone's a pain in the ass."

"Everyone?"

"You, MacAullif. Not to mention Frost and Thurman."

"How about your client?"

"Haven't seen her. Her, or her husband. I called, but they weren't home. Most likely downtown answering questions about Doug Mark."

"Oh, I doubt that," Richard said.

"Why?"

"Because *they* are smart enough to call their lawyers. They did for the first murder, so they automatically will for the second. It's a simple learning experience. Practically a conditioned reflex. Even the lower animals are capable of it."

Richard's irony seemed more than the situation warranted. Which clarified his present mood. He wasn't at all concerned I might have implicated myself with Frost. He was pissed off at missing out on the action. If the other attorneys were there, he didn't want to be left out of the loop.

"A point well taken, Richard," I said. "The fact is, Winnington and his wife have nothing to do with it. It will turn out they haven't had any contact with the man in years, their attorneys will advise them to cooperate fully with the police in all aspects of the case, and the only bone of contention, the only reason the lawyers will be there in the first place, will be to see what they can do in terms of controlling publicity."

"Granted," Richard said. "Toward that end, I'm wondering if *you* said anything that might result in bad publicity for your client."

"Are you kidding me?"

"Not at all. As your attorney, that is one of the things I would have been looking out for. Because there is nothing worse than putting yourself in the position of being sued by your own client. Since I wasn't there, I can't tell if that happened."

"It didn't happen."

"Oh, no? When I asked about your client, your best guess

225

was she and her husband were dragged downtown. Immediately after you gave a statement to the police. One might wonder if there was any connection."

"One might if one were an incredible hair-splitting pain in the ass," I said. "The murdered man was Kenneth P. Winnington's first editor, who had reason to hate his guts. You think the police aren't going to have him in?"

"And how did the police happen to *know* that?" Richard said. "Correct me if I'm wrong, but it seems to me they heard it from you."

I rubbed my head, reminded myself again that there were two people I should never argue with, my wife and my lawyer. "That's fine, Richard," I said. "Guilty as charged. But Winnington's not going to sue me, and one way or another his connection with Doug Mark would have come out. Anyway, I'm sure his attorney, what's-his-face—"

"Barney K. Rancroft."

"Right. I'm sure Mr. Rancroft has advised Mr. Winnington to cooperate fully in exchange for keeping his name out of it."

"That may not be possible," Richard said. "This is, after all, the second crime."

"Yeah, but no one knows that. And the means were different. So it won't be written up as a serial killer."

"Even so," Richard said. "The publicist was one thing. They withhold the bit about the phone calls, because they would anyway, and they play Winnington down. The papers mention him, but in passing, and only because enterprising reporters dig it out. The story is Publicist Murdered, and Winnington is mentioned as being her most famous author. But that is it, no other connection is made."

Richard shook his head. "The editor is a brand-new ball game. The story is Editor Murdered, and if it comes out Kenneth P. Winnington is *his* most famous author, that is a connection even the stupidest reporter is going to make."

"I know."

"As if that weren't bad enough, you've got the piece of paper with your name on it." Richard rolled his eyes. "Thank goodness the police don't suspect you of anything. Most people, confronted with evidence like that, would think, oh gee, I gotta protect myself. You, knowing better, decide to talk to the ADA and curse out the investigating officer."

"That's the other thing," I said.

"What is?"

"The notes. The papers with my name on 'em."

"What about 'em?"

"Nobody buys 'em. Frost thinks they're too obvious for a frame. So does MacAullif. Thurman probably takes 'em at face value, but that's just Thurman. The way I see it, they're so crude and obvious there's practically no point."

"So?"

"So, what's your opinion? Aside from the fact I should have called my lawyer."

Richard pursed his lips, nodded. "The notes are a deliberate slap in the face. They are not meant for the cops, so much as they are meant for you."

"Do you think so?"

Richard shrugged. "Either that, or they are a clumsy attempt to frame you for the crime. And a rather half-hearted attempt, at that. In which case, I would say the killer used them not because they related to you, but because they were at hand. At least the first one. The killer sees the note lying there, thinks what a dandy clue for the cops, and sticks it in the victim's hand. The second body, there's no note, but the killer decides there should be. So he holds the guy at gunpoint, forces him to write one. He has him tear it out of the notebook, then shoots him in the head."

"You really think that happened?"

"If the note is in the victim's handwriting I think it's a strong possibility. In which case the killer has a bizarre sense of humor, or really hates you, or is somewhat unhinged, or any combination of those three. Then there's another thing."

"What's that?"

"The whole business with the notes is very unreal. It's one of those things that seem stranger than fiction."

"You don't know the half of it."

"What do you mean?"

I told Richard about the fish. "So what do you make of that?"

"It's either absolutely nothing, or something very sick. If it's deliberate—if the fish were put in your car for a purpose— then you're absolutely right, it's just like the note. It's something straight out of a book. So the first question would be, is there anything like it in any of Winnington's books?"

"That's exactly what MacAullif said."

"Really?" Richard cocked his head. "Gee, doesn't that make you sort of wonder?"

39.

"Tell me about your books."

Kenneth P. Winnington frowned. "What?"

"The books you write. Suspense novels. Tell me about 'em."

Winnington frowned, leaned back in his desk chair, and gestured with his drink to his wife, who was curled up in an easy chair sipping a drink of her own. It occurred to me no one had offered me a drink. Not that I wanted one. Still, no one had.

"We just got back from talking to the police," Winnington said, "and we're a little stressed out. Among other things, we ID'd Doug Mark's body."

"You saw him at the morgue?"

"Yes. Why?"

"I saw him at the crime scene. It wasn't pleasant."

"No, it wasn't. It's been a hell of a day. Then you come in here and ask me about my books as if nothing had happened."

"I'm sorry. I didn't mean to skip the amenities. I had a reason, but it can wait. How'd it go with the cops?"

"Not well. First thing that ADA did was ask us for an alibi."

"Did you have one?"

"No, we didn't," Winnington said irritably. "And the way he asked the question there was no way that we would."

"What do you mean?"

"He says, Tell me what you did yesterday. He doesn't tell us when the crime happened, ask us what we were doing *then*. No, he says describe the whole fucking day."

"What's wrong with that?"

"Are you kidding me?" He gestured to Maxine again. "Either we claim we were together all day long, or risk winding up without an alibi. The way I understand it, we don't have an alibi."

"You know that for sure?"

"No, it's just the impression I get from the questions that were asked. I still have no idea when the guy died."

"Yesterday, sometime after five o'clock."

"How do you know?"

"Because that's when I saw him."

"What were you doing calling on Doug Mark?"

"Looking for someone with a reason to hate your guts."

"You mean you thought *he* might be behind the crank phone calls?"

"It had occurred to me."

"That's absurd."

"I admit his murder probably exonerates him. Anyway, yesterday he was merely a lead. Today, he's important enough to wind up dead. Would you have any idea why?"

"No, I wouldn't."

"How about you, Mrs. Winnington?"

"Me?" Maxine said. "I don't even know Doug Mark."

"Uh-huh," I said. "Well, would it surprise you to know he was in Elizabeth Abbott's office Monday afternoon? He was there alone, and at a time when her Rolodex was turned to your new unlisted phone number."

She frowned. "What are you implying?"

"I'm not implying anything. I'm telling you why I considered Doug Mark a suspect. Anyway, that's why I called on him.

And why he wound up holding a piece of paper with my name on it."

I put up my hand, turned to Winnington. "Now then, this is what I was getting at before. The crimes strike everyone as something straight out of a book. You write books. It's logical to ask if there is any connection."

"That's absurd."

"Oh, really? Why?"

"I have nothing like that in any of my books. Corpses clutching clues. That's not suspense. That's mystery fiction. That's whodunit."

"That's exactly why I'm asking," I said. "I'm not up on suspense. My experience is mostly mystery fiction. I know there's a difference, but I'm not that clear on what it is. I'm asking you because you know. Now, let me give you another example."

"Example?"

"Yeah. The phone calls. The ones you've been getting. Threatening anonymous phone calls. Is that suspense or mystery?"

"It could be either. It depends on how they're used. If they're used to frighten, to terrify, that's suspense. If they're merely a plot device, they're mystery."

"Uh-huh," I said. "Well, let me ask you this. Is there any similarity to your books?"

"You mean the crank phone calls?"

"Yeah."

Winnington shook his head. "Not at all. I've never used anything of the kind."

"All right," I said. "Another example. Someone breaks into the protagonist's car, leaves a pile of dead fish on the front seat."

"I beg your pardon?"

"Anything like that in your books?"

231

"Absolutely not."

"Would that be suspense or mystery?"

"That would be simply weird," Winnington said. "You'll pardon me, but is there a point to all this?"

"I'm just trying to work things out. We got a problem in this case. The cop in charge is not too bright. He's sitting on the guy who walked out on your signing. If he did it, fine, the case is solved, and no one will be happier than I will. But if he didn't, we have to fend for ourselves." I pointed. "Now, you're a suspense writer. People connected with your career die. Your literary career. Which happens to be suspense. So I need to know about that. I'm asking you because you happen to be the best source of information. You not only write it, you talk about it. Like at the signing. When you talked about writing in the first person. You get questions like that all the time, so you not only know how to do what you do, you know how to explain it. I need to have it explained. On the off chance it will help. Can you do that for me?"

"Yes, he can," Maxine said. She got up, crossed behind his chair, put her hands on his shoulders, leaned in. "Sweetheart, I'm the one being threatened here. Then these killings. I'm scared. If this can possibly help, do it, please."

"Of course," Winnington said. He looked up at me. "What do you want to know?"

"Okay, I got what you said about writing in the first person. That it doesn't work in suspense because you can't deliver the ticking bomb. Besides that, what's the difference between mystery and suspense?"

"Okay," Winnington said. "The basic difference is, a mystery is a whodunit. Generally speaking. There's some private eye novels where this is not the case—the killer is known in advance, the problem is tracking him down. But generally speaking, when you talk about a mystery, you mean a whodunit.

232

Which is your basic play-fair mystery, with a bunch of suspects with various motives, all who might be guilty. And the killer is one of them, and his identity is revealed at the end of the book. At which time the protagonist enumerates the clues that led to the solution."

Winnington shrugged and smiled. "I know that's rather simplistic, but that's basically it.

"Suspense is entirely different. Generally speaking, they're not whodunits. Oh, you can have a suspense novel that *is* a whodunit, but it's not at all necessary. In suspense, often the identity of the killer is known from the very start of the book." He broke off, looked at me. "Didn't we go over some of this before?"

"Just generally, and not much more than that. I'd be grateful if you could elaborate."

"Uh-huh. Well, like I said, the identity of the killer isn't particularly important. Even if it's *not* revealed at the beginning of the book. Because the revelation, when it takes place, is not a real revelation. For instance, you have a book where women are being raped and murdered by a serial killer. The serial killer is not important in himself, he's merely an instrument of terror. We don't know who he is until the end of the book when he's revealed, but it's not a true revelation. Why? Because he's not revealed to be anyone in particular."

Winnington frowned. "That's not exactly what I mean. Let me give you an example. At the end of the book the cops find out the killer is Joe Blow from Brooklyn. Well, that's not a startling revelation, because the reader has never heard of Joe Blow from Brooklyn. Joe Blow from Brooklyn is not a character in the book. It's just a name. See what I mean? Revealing the killer is not a true revelation. Because we're not showing him to be anyone in particular, we're just giving him a name."

"Isn't that cheating the reader?"

"Not in suspense. It would be in mystery. The killer has to be someone we met before. One of the characters in the book. So the reader can go, Aha, I suspected him when he showed up at the party in Chapter Six."

"Uh-huh," I said. I was not happy. "So, if I understand what you're saying, if for some cockeyed reason these killings represented someone acting out a suspense plot, there's no reason to believe the killer would be anyone we know?"

"Exactly," Winnington said. He raised one finger, and there was a gleam in his eye. Rather than being troubled by what he was saying, he had slipped into full lecture mode. "Because in suspense, the killer is not a person so much as a force of evil. In this way, suspense is very similar to horror. Have you seen the movie *Alien?*"

"Sure."

"There you are. Perfect example. The alien is a killing machine. A source of sure death. There's people running all over the ship, if they find the alien they die.

"A suspense novel is the same thing. Here's a woman coming home from work, she goes into her apartment, starts switching on the lights. If the serial killer's there, she's dead. Is he there, or is this just a false alarm, a tease? See what I mean?"

"Uh-huh. And the serial killer's not necessarily anyone she knows?"

"Right. Or even anyone the *reader* knows. See the difference? Because we're not in the first person, we're in the third person omniscient. And we've been describing events all over the place. And the serial killer isn't anybody else except the serial killer."

"Uh-huh," I said. "And why is he doing what he's doing?"

"That's not important either. Oh, maybe it will come out in the end—he was abused as a child, he hated his third-grade teacher, he took too many drugs in the '60s or freaked out in

Viet Nam. That's not important. What's important is the guy's doing it, and he might do it to *her*."

"Her?"

"The heroine, the protagonist, the woman in the book. She might be in danger."

As he said that, I couldn't help looking at his wife.

Neither could he.

He frowned, looked back at me. "Now then," he said. "The calls have stopped. We haven't had one in two days. Not that you'd notice, what with everything going on. But the fact is, there hasn't been a single call. Now what do you make of that?"

I stopped to consider. What the calls meant to me was the next time we got one it would prove Sergeant Thurman wrong, so the fact that they'd stopped had been frustrating. But beyond that, I hadn't given the matter that much thought.

I did so now. "Well," I said, "one possibility is he's graduated from talk to action. For a while he got off on making threats. Then he killed. Now threats no longer satisfy him."

Maxine shuddered. "Jesus Christ."

"I know," I said. "I'm sorry. But that could be the case. It also could be he's just too busy."

"To make a phone call?" Winnington said.

"Yeah, I know," I said, "but it's not just making a phone call. If he was calling from his own phone, sure. But he's making the calls from pay phones around the city. So maybe he hasn't had the time to go out and do it.

"Or maybe . . ." My eyes widened and I raised one finger. "Someone's with him. Say the guy's married, his wife's around, and he can't get away to make the call."

"He wasn't having any problem before," Winnington said.

"Yeah, but we don't know the circumstances. I'm making this up off the top of my head. Say that for some reason or other the situation has changed, and someone is around who inhibits the guy from making the call."

"But not from committing murder?" Winnington said, sarcastically.

"I admit I don't have it all worked out yet," I said. "You asked for possibilities. Those are possibilities. If you want my opinion, I'd say that murder has made it a brand-new ball game. There may not be any more phone calls because we've upped the stakes, and we're in a no-limit game."

"If the phone calls just stop . . ." Maxine said.

"Yes?"

"We'll never know who's making them."

"If the caller is the killer, we will."

"Great," Maxine said. "If someone kills me, you'll know. That's really comforting."

I frowned. "Have the police offered you protection?"

"No."

"You might request it."

"You think that would do any good?" Winnington said.

"There've been two murders. They might be willing to put a guard on your apartment."

"You think that's necessary?" Maxine said. "You don't think we're safe in here?"

"Great," Winnington said. "Get her agitated over nothing." He turned to his wife. "Yes, of course we're safe in here. We have doormen and elevator operators. No one can get into the building." He turned back at me. "Why did you put *that* idea in her head?"

"I'm sorry," I said. "Yes, of course you're safe in here. Don't give it another thought." I put up my hands. "I really should be going."

Winnington leaned forward, pushed a button on his desk. "David will show you out."

"Uh-huh," I said.

I turned, headed for the door.

The phone rang.

I stopped, turned, looked.

It rang again.

For a moment, we froze. All three of us, looking at the phone. Then Maxine got up, crossed over to it, pressed the button for the speaker phone.

"Hello?" she said.

A hoarse whisper filled the room.

"The publicist was a warning. You're next."

40.

I left the Winningtons to call the police, and got the hell out of there. Not that I wasn't interested and all that, and not that I wouldn't have liked to be on hand to see Sergeant Thurman proved wrong. But, as it happened, I had other things to do.

A phone call to MacAullif had traced the number on the Caller ID box to a pay phone on Broadway and 106th. Which was all I needed to know. I'd been afraid to do anything for fear of leading the killer to someone else. But if the guy was on Broadway and 106th Street, he wasn't tailing me.

The first order of business was the wannabe writers. Linda Toole was still an answering machine, but Wilber Penrose was home, and wasn't at all reluctant to talk. When I told him it was about the Sherry Pressman murder, he told me to come right up.

Right up turned out to be a second-story walkup over a butcher shop at Broadway and 108th Street. That gave me a bit of a turn, being only two blocks from the site of the phone call. And just when I was feeling so good about putting some distance between me and the killer. I had to tell myself that it was just coincidence, and the guy would not be hanging out on Broadway and 106th just on the off chance I should happen to come by. Even so, I must admit I drove up Amsterdam to

110th, and then down Broadway to 108th, just so I wouldn't have to pass the corner.

I left my car at a meter, found the address, and got buzzed in.

Wilber Penrose was waiting on the landing. He was a little man with horn-rimmed glasses and a bald head ringed with a fringe of curly white hair. Though, I guess ringed isn't quite right, since there was no hair on his forehead—it occurred to me a good editor would have taken that right out. Anyway, the guy seemed glad to see me.

"Come in, come in," he said. "This is a terrible thing. Just a terrible thing."

I agreed that it was, and allowed myself to be led into what proved to be a modest one-bedroom apartment, the living room piled floor to ceiling with manuscripts and books. Again, piled is the wrong word—most of the books were in bookcases. It was the manuscripts—or at least what I judged to be manuscripts, the five-hundred-page paper boxes—that were stacked in piles. The clue that these were manuscripts came in the form of titles scrawled on the ends of the boxes, such as, *Three Who Fell*, *Date with Death*, *Kick Him When He's Down*, and, so help me, *The Naked Secretary*.

Wilber Penrose seated me on the couch, then swiveled around his desk chair, and sat facing me.

"So," he said. "What do you want to know?"

"I understand you were one of the last people to see Sherry Pressman alive."

His eyes widened. "Yes. Isn't that incredible? It's a case of real life copying art."

"Oh? How is that?"

"My book. *Death in the Afternoon*. We were just talking about it."

"*Death in the Afternoon?*"

"Yes. It's the last thing I talked to her about. And then she gets killed. Just like that."

"Just like in your book?"

"Exactly."

"Wait a minute. You mean the plot from your book?"

"The plot?"

"You're telling me the same thing happens in your book? A woman is strangled?"

"Strangled?"

"Yes."

He shook his head. "No, no, no. The killer in my book is a slasher."

"Slasher?"

"Yes. He uses a straight razor. Cuts his victims up."

"Uh-huh," I said. "So how's the Sherry Pressman murder like your book?"

"Oh," he said. "Well, she was killed, of course."

I took a breath, raised my eyebrows. "That's the only similarity?"

"Well, isn't it a fantastic coincidence?"

"Unbelievable," I said. "And when was the last time you saw Sherry Pressman?"

"Monday afternoon."

"At what time?"

"Between two and three."

"You went to her apartment?"

"Yes, I did."

"What for?"

"To discuss my manuscript. *Death in the Afternoon.*"

"About a slasher?"

"Right. But there's a lot more to it than that."

"I'm sure there is. And that's what you and Sherry Pressman talked about?"

"That's right."

"She had read your manuscript?"

"Yes, of course."

"Because you paid her to do so?"

"Yes. But not just to read it. To evaluate it. To offer criticism, ideas for a second draft."

"And that's what she did?"

"Absolutely."

"Had you done this with her before?"

"Yes, I had."

"How many times?"

"You mean how many books had we discussed?"

"That's right."

"Three."

"Including that one?"

"No. Three other books. *Death in the Afternoon* was the fourth."

"And how much did you pay her?"

"Five hundred dollars."

"Each time?"

"Yes, of course."

"For evaluating your books, and making suggestions on how to improve them?"

"That's right."

"Did you implement her suggestions?"

"I beg your pardon?"

"Did you rewrite your manuscripts along the lines she suggested?"

"Yes, of course."

"What then?"

"I beg your pardon?"

"What happened to them then?"

"Nothing happened to them. They're right here."

"Yes, but if you paid her to improve the books, and then you improved them as she suggested . . . Well, wasn't there some kind of follow-up? Wouldn't she read your rewrite?"

"Oh, yes, of course."

"So what was the next step? What happened then?"

His eyes narrowed. "Why are you asking this?"

"I'm trying to get an idea about your relationship with the deceased. I trust this is just a business relationship?"

"I beg your pardon?"

"I mean, you weren't seeing her socially? You weren't dating her or anything, were you?"

"Good heavens, no."

"So your relationship was a business relationship?"

"That's right."

"You paid her to evaluate manuscripts that you had written. She offered you advice on how to improve them."

"Yes."

"So what happened after you improved them?"

Penrose frowned. "Why do you keep asking this?"

"Because I'm not getting an answer. You say this is the fourth book you discussed with her. What about the other three? After you fixed them up, what happened to them?"

"She read them again and told me what she thought."

"What did she think?"

"She felt they had improved, but not enough to warrant publication."

"Did you agree with that assessment?"

"I beg your pardon?"

"Did you think she was right? That the manuscripts weren't publishable."

"Not necessarily."

"You mean you think they *were* publishable?"

Wilber Penrose looked pained. "I find it difficult to discuss my work in this fashion. Yes, I think what I wrote was good enough to be published. But that's just my opinion. Unfortunately, my opinion doesn't count."

"And hers does?"

"To a certain extent, yes."

"So if she doesn't like something, that's the end of it?"

Penrose took a deep breath, blew it out. "No, it's not the end of it. Just because she doesn't like something doesn't mean I give up. I've tried elsewhere."

"Oh? For instance?"

"I've tried to get an agent. So far I've been unsuccessful."

"But you've tried?"

"Why are you asking?"

"I'd like to get the whole picture here. What agents have you shown your stuff to?"

"Abe Feinstein."

I blinked. "I beg your pardon?"

"I've shown my work to Abe Feinstein. He didn't take it, but he seemed impressed."

"Wait a minute," I said. "You've shown a manuscript of yours to Abe Feinstein?"

"I most certainly have. And I'm not at all discouraged he didn't take it. Being rejected by Abe Feinstein puts me in rather famous company."

"I'm glad to hear it," I said. "Tell me, when did this happen?"

"I beg your pardon?"

"When did you give your manuscript to Abe Feinstein?"

"About a month ago."

"Really. Is this the same book you were discussing with Sherry Pressman?"

"What, *Death in the Afternoon*? No, that's just a first draft. I'm revising it now. I can't wait till he sees that one."

"So what was the book you gave to Abe Feinstein? The one he rejected?"

"One I wrote last year. *Kick Him When He's Down.* Sherry didn't think it was publishable, and I wanted a second opinion."

"Uh-huh," I said. "Tell me something. How'd you get the book to Abe Feinstein? I wouldn't imagine he reads everything that comes along."

"He doesn't," Penrose said. "I used Sherry's name."

"Oh?"

"Well, sure. After all, she was the one who brought it up."

"What?"

"Abe Feinstein. She said if the manuscript improved enough, she'd show it to him."

"So she was the one who gave him the manuscript?"

Penrose shifted in his seat. "Well, no, actually, I did. She wasn't going to. Felt it wasn't up to snuff. I didn't agree. So I called him myself, used her name. Good thing I did. Now the guy's read one of my books, we got a working relationship, he'll be all primed for when I give him *Death in the Afternoon.*"

"Uh-huh," I said. "And was Sherry upset that you used her name?"

"Not really. She did take pains to point out she'd been proved right. Which I think is a close point. True, the guy didn't take it. But he was impressed."

"And this is a big-time agent you're talking about?"

"Are you kidding me?" Penrose said. "He's Kenneth P. Winnington's agent."

"And who is Kenneth P. Winnington?"

Penrose looked at me as if I'd just arrived from another planet. "Who is Kenneth P. Winnington? Just the *New York Times* number-one best-selling author, that's all. I can't believe you don't know that."

"Oh, yes, of course," I said. "Tell me, what do you think of his work?"

"Winnington?"

"Yes. How do you like his books?"

Penrose made a face. "Frankly, I can't read them. The man's an overrated hack."

"Oh?"

Penrose put up both hands. "Please, please, don't quote me on that. That just slipped out. You're not going to write that up, are you?"

"Write it up?"

"Yes. Please. That was off the record. Please don't use that."

So. Penrose had taken me for a newspaper reporter, which was why he'd been so eager to tell his story. He'd envisioned a lot of free publicity, boosting his career.

I'd been slow to catch on because my mind had been somewhere else. When Penrose mentioned Abe Feinstein, the pieces began to fit.

Here was your horribly frustrated wannabe writer. Getting his manuscripts read at five hundred bucks a whack. Then he gets an entry to a prominent literary agent. The agent rejects him. But the agent represents a famous author. A best-selling author. One the writer regards as a hack.

Well, that would be a pretty galling situation, wouldn't it?

Suddenly, Wilber Penrose living two blocks away from that pay phone took on a whole new meaning.

Anyway, Penrose's stock as a suspect had risen considerably. So if he wanted to think of me as a reporter, I saw no reason to disillusion him. In fact, just to cement the idea, I whipped out my notebook, flipped it open, and jotted a few notes at random, saying, "The name of your book is *Death in the Afternoon*? And that is the one you were discussing with Sherry Pressman?"

Penrose practically beamed. "That's right. That's the one I'm working on right now."

"And that's the one you were discussing with her the last time you met?"

"That's right."

"Did you talk about anything else?"

Penrose blinked. "I beg your pardon?"

"Aside from the book, did you talk about anything else? Other writers, people she handled, perhaps?"

"People she handled?"

"Yes. Did she have anyone famous in her stable?"

Pennington looked at me narrowly. As a reporter covering the story, I should know that. "Kenneth P. Winnington," he said.

"Oh, she handled him too?"

"She was his publicist, yes."

"Oh, and did Mr. Winnington's name come up in the conversation?"

"It may have. Why?"

"Don't be silly," I said. "Anyone famous adds importance to the story. So, in what context did she mention him? Perhaps as an example of his work?"

"I didn't say she mentioned him."

"You said she might have. Can you remember if she did?"

"Not offhand."

I frowned. "Would I be correct in assuming she has referred to him from time to time, and you just can't remember whether she did on this particular occasion."

"I suppose so. I don't see why it's so important."

"Did she ever mention having his unlisted phone number?"

Penrose blinked. "I beg your pardon?"

"Just wondering if you ever got a peek at her address book." Bingo.

Talk about a guilty reaction. Wilber Penrose was no poker player. The answer was all over his face.

"Oh, now, look," he said. "Why do you want to ask me that?"

Because Sergeant Thurman was too stupid to, was the thought that came to mind. I did not voice it, just fixed him with a steely gaze and said, "What were you doing in that book?"

Penrose began to fidget. "Oh, well, now, look," he said. "You gotta understand."

"Understand what?"

"Well, Abe Feinstein has an unlisted number."

"Abe Feinstein?"

"Yeah. And if Sherry wasn't going to show him my book, I figured I would."

I suppose that could have been it. It also could have been a pretty good attempt to cover up. I decided to keep him off balance with another quick shift. "Know any editors?"

"Editors?"

"Yeah. You know any editors? For instance, this guy Winnington—you happen to know his editor?"

Before he could answer, my beeper went off. Talk about poor timing. Not only did it interrupt the flow, but from the way Penrose was looking at me, my newspaper reporter status, already shaky, was undergoing a serious reevaluation.

I shut the beeper off, asked to use the phone. I wondered what Penrose would think if he knew I was calling the unlisted number of Kenneth P. Winnington.

I also wondered if he *knew* the unlisted number of Kenneth P. Winnington.

Winnington answered on the first ring.

"It's Stanley Hastings," I said. "What's up?"

"They got him!"

41.

Sergeant Thurman was being modest. Which was hard to take. An arrogant Sergeant Thurman was bad enough. A modest one was almost unbearable.

"Hey, no big deal," Thurman said. "Not exactly the toughest case in the world. It's like I told you, the guy makes the phone call, he's mine."

Which is exactly what had happened. Sergeant Thurman, in the course of his surveillance, had observed wannabe writer Noah Sprague making a call from a pay phone on the corner of Broadway and 106th Street. When the Winningtons called the police with the time and phone number of the latest crank call, damned if they didn't get a match.

"So what's his story?" I said.

"No story," Thurman said. "The minute he saw what was going on he called a lawyer and clammed." He jerked his thumb at the one-way glass, through which I could see Noah Sprague seated at a table in the interrogation room. "That's why he's alone in there. The way the stupid rules work, the guy wants a lawyer, you ask him another question you lose the case."

"So he hasn't talked at all?"

"No."

"So how do you know he's the guy?"

"Are you kidding me? He made the call."

"Maybe so. But you don't have him on the killings."

"What, are you nuts? Didn't you hear what he said? *The publicist was a warning, you're next.* How much clearer could it be?"

ADA Frost came bustling up, looking pleased as punch. "Lawyer's on the way over. I can't wait. Ten to one he'll want to play *Let's Make a Deal.*"

"You're gonna deal?" Thurman said.

"Probably not," Frost said. "But I can't wait to hear the offer. Aside from the harassment, I got two separate murder counts. If I get any sort of conviction on one, even manslaughter, I turn around, try him on the other, and it's bye, bye, birdie. I'm telling you, this is one plea bargain attempt I gotta hear."

"Even if the guy hasn't talked?" I said.

"It doesn't matter," Frost said. "This is the type of case you almost rather they didn't. I mean, you got an open and shut case. The only chance the guy has of getting off is if his attorney can find some way of proving someone violated his rights. Not talking to him at all is a plus."

"Yeah, but it leaves a few gaps. Like you say, you got two separate homicides. One's a strangling, one's a shooting. Won't it be hard to make the guy for both?"

"Not really," Frost said. "I make him for the publicist first. I get any conviction at all, I go after him for the other." He shrugged. "By the time we get there we should have evidence up the wazoo. We're getting a search warrant for the guy's apartment. This is the type of dunce, what do you bet he held on to the gun?" Frost pointed through the one-way glass. "I mean, just look at the guy. Is this your mastermind criminal here? No, this is just your poor schmuck playing games and getting in over his head. The way it works is, the guy is gonna spill his guts to his lawyer, and his lawyer's gonna wanna deal."

I frowned. "I don't know."

"Yeah, well, I do. It's a nice one to solve. Everybody's happy. Except maybe Winnington. Because there's no way we keep his name out of it once this guy talks. Though he shouldn't mind the publicity so much now the thing's resolved."

"Don't you see some problems in this?"

"Like what?"

"Well, look at the guy. Can you really see him strangling someone?"

"Give me a break," Thurman said. "You seen as many homicides as I have, you got no problem at all seein' this guy strangling someone."

"Yeah, but—"

"But what?"

"Well, you know the wannabe writers—the ones paying to have their manuscripts read? Well, I just talked to one of them. Wilber Penrose. And I gotta tell you, he looks real good for the killings. He's a frustrated writer. He was paying the woman a lot of money to read his books. He knows Kenneth P. Winnington. Thinks he's an overrated hack. He's given his book to Abe Feinstein, Winnington's agent, who happened to reject him. He got his number from Sherry Pressman. Who wouldn't give it to him, by the way. So you know how he got it? He got it by looking in her address book. Or so he says, to cover up a guilty reaction he has when I ask if he's ever looked in that book. And that is the book that has Kenneth P. Winnington's unlisted number in it. And the guy lives two blocks from the phone booth on 106th Street where we traced the last crank call."

"What, are you nuts?" Thurman said. "I don't care if he lives *in* the goddamned phone booth. *This* guy made the call. *I saw him make it.* End of case."

I exhaled. "Jesus Christ."

"Hey," Thurman said. "Don't take it so hard. Sometimes

you're right, sometimes you're wrong. You can't always be right. I'm right this time, but I can't really take any credit. It was an easy case, and it dropped in my lap." He smiled, kicked shit. "No big deal."

It was enough to make you sick.

42.

MacAullif wasn't any help.

"If they closed the case, they closed the case. What's the big deal?"

"The big deal is, what if they're wrong?"

"No," MacAullif said. "The big deal is, what if *you're* wrong."

"Huh?"

"That's the big deal here, and that's why you're in my office being a pain in the ass for no reason whatsoever. They've closed the case, which means you're wrong, you can't bear to be wrong, so you won't let it go."

"That's not it."

"Oh, no? Did Thurman catch the guy makin' the phone call or not?"

"He did, but—"

"There you are. Now, I understand that knocks you out of a five hundred dollar a day assignment, which is too damn bad. But on the bright side, you got more days out of it than you expected. Plus, as a silver lining, you didn't have a bonus arrangement for completing the job. So you don't have to feel bad about getting dorked out of it because Thurman solved the case and not you."

"Jesus Christ, MacAullif. I never even thought of that."

"Then you're dumber than you look. What you're getting paid should be your first concern."

"MacAullif, my concern is if this guy didn't do it, the killer's still out there."

"Yeah, but this guy did it. They have him dead to rights."

"On the phone call, yeah, but on the rest of it?"

"Works just fine for me. What doesn't work for you?"

"Well . . ."

"Yeah?"

"What about the fish?"

MacAullif groaned. "Oh, Jesus Christ. The fucking fish."

"This guy doesn't know me. Why would he put fish in my car?"

"How do you know he doesn't know you?"

"Huh?"

"You're investigating the case. You're hot on his tail. He finds out and starts backtracking you."

"Why?"

"How the hell should I know? The facts aren't all in yet. Didn't you say they got a search warrant for the guy's apartment?"

"Yeah."

"So there you are. Maybe they find a book this guy's written, and maybe it's about people dying clutching notes. And maybe someone gets a pile of fish in their car. Maybe this guy's been told his piece of shit book would never happen in real life, and now he's out to prove everyone wrong." MacAullif exhaled, shrugged his shoulders, spread his arms. "But that's off the top of my head, and that's before a single fact is in. That's why agitating yourself is a waste of time."

"Oh, yeah? Well, the guy I talked to happens to look real good for this."

"So you say. In the unlikely event that you're right, I imagine he'll look real good for it tomorrow too."

"That's not the point."

"What's the point?"

"What if I do nothing and someone dies?"

"Oh, yes," MacAullif said. "I forgot. Your universal guilt. Anything that goes wrong is your fault." He cocked his head. "Tell me something. How do you ever get such an inflated opinion of yourself? That you and only you are responsible for what happens in this world."

"Don't be a schmuck. If I have information that could save someone's life—"

"I would be the first one to urge you to speak up," MacAullif said. "But you don't. The simple fact is you don't. You got some crazy, half-baked theories, and you're so gung ho eager you're ready to act on 'em, even though there's nothing to be done." He nodded. "Yeah, that's it in a nutshell. There's nothing to be done. But you, you're gonna beat yourself up for not doing it."

"I could check out this guy. And the other writer. The woman. I never even got to her."

MacAullif lunged to his feet, wiggled his fingers alongside his head. "Jesus Christ, what have you got in there, snakes? The simpler something is, the more convoluted you wanna make it. Yes, it's possible the man's the killer, yes, it's possible the woman's the killer, yes, it's possible some other guy you've never even *heard of* is the killer. And," MacAullif said with elaborate irony, "it is entirely within the realm of possibility that this poor schmuck the police have in jail happens to be the killer." MacAullif leveled his finger. "Now then, if I am to grant you the possibility, the slimmest of possibilities, that the killer, whoever he might be, just might be planning to strike again— and what's more, might be planning on doing so this very night—well, then, would you like me to calculate the odds for you, that if you were to take it upon yourself to single-handedly attempt to prevent this happening—would you like me to calculate your probability of success? I'm talking about the overall probability, the one in a billion shot that, a, the killer tries something, and, b, you thwart it. Though, again, that is off the top of my head, and perhaps one in a billion is a little high."

MacAullif stopped, looked at me. His face was very red. He exhaled, controlled himself.

"Look. Do me a favor. Do yourself a favor."

He exhaled again.

"Go home."

43.

I got my car out of the municipal lot where I'd been lucky to find a meter, and drove uptown, feeling bad. I was not at all happy with the solution to the case, and not just because it was Sergeant Thurman's. For some reason, it just didn't sit right. Something was bothering me, and while I couldn't put my finger on it, I was sure it was there. Which meant it wasn't something I didn't know, it was something I did.

I know that makes no sense. What I'm trying to say is, it wasn't just that I didn't have enough facts. It was the feeling the police had a fact that didn't fit.

I went over everything in my head, and could get no closer. The real stumper was Sergeant Thurman actually catching the guy on the phone. There was no question the wannabe writer Noah Sprague was the crank caller. While that didn't necessarily make him the killer—which was my contention—it certainly didn't look good.

If the guy was the crank caller, he had to have the unlisted phone number. Sources for that were limited. One was Sherry Pressman, who had been killed. Another was Elizabeth Abbott. She hadn't been killed. But Doug Mark, who had been in her office, and who could have learned the number, had been killed.

So both murder victims had access to the new number. The crank caller had the new number. Didn't that make the crank caller the killer?

Not necessarily. It certainly looked bad. What would certainly look worse would be if the police search of his apartment should turn up any other connection. For instance, if it should turn out Noah Sprague had also submitted a manuscript to agent Abe Feinstein, thereby connecting himself to all three of the publishing industry people who had Kenneth P. Winnington's unlisted phone number, it would be enough to boggle the mind. Bad enough he should be connected to two.

Which bothered me.

It was overkill. No pun intended. But the simple fact was, the guy didn't need the number twice. If he got it from the publicist, he didn't need it from Doug Mark. And vice versa.

It occurred to me, maybe that was what was bothering me. Maybe that was the fact that didn't fit. The fact that as the caller, he would only need the number once.

But that couldn't be it. Because that was true in any case, no matter *who* the murderer was. Now that the police had arrested Noah Sprague, it now applied to him, but no more so than to anyone else, if you know what I mean. That was a fact that didn't fit, regardless of who the killer was. But what was bothering me—or at least what I *thought* was bothering me—was something to do with Sprague himself. There was something that didn't jibe specifically with *him* being the murderer.

But I had no idea what it was.

I drove up the West Side Highway, hit a minor traffic jam north of 42nd Street. Considered whether I should stick it out with the highway, or go up Tenth or Eleventh Avenue. Couldn't decide. Realized I didn't really care, since I was heading ignominiously home with nothing to do.

I sat in traffic, went over the case again.

By rights, Noah Sprague was the man. Aside from the call itself, there was what the guy said. *The publicist was a warning. You're next.* What could be more explicit?

So why couldn't I buy it?

Was it merely the fact that it was Sergeant Thurman pointing it out? Was I such a schmuck that I couldn't accept anything the man did, even if it was obviously right? Was I the worst kind of ignorant, prejudiced, pig-headed fool?

Probably.

More than likely.

Traffic thinned out, and I forged ahead, went up the ramp at 57th Street and onto the elevated highway. Took the highway uptown, got off at 95th and onto Riverside Drive.

I was now near both my home and his.

Wilber Penrose.

The wannabe writer.

My favorite suspect.

Was that it? Was it the proximity? The fact he lived so close to me? That he would have had an excellent opportunity to put the fish in my car? The faint smell was still there on the seat, a constant reminder. Was that what was bugging me, nagging at me, making me unwilling to accept the facts?

No. To look at it logically, Wilber Penrose had connections to both Winnington's publicist, Sherry Pressman, and his agent, Abe Feinstein. Any connection to Doug Mark was as yet unknown.

On the other hand, Noah Sprague had connections to Sherry Pressman and Doug Mark, but not Abe Feinstein.

Or did he? Wasn't this a confusion of cause and effect? The police *assumed* a connection with Sherry Pressman and Doug Mark, because Noah Sprague had Kenneth P. Winnington's unlisted phone number. But his only *real* connection with the two of them was if he killed them. But the police were assuming he

killed them, because of his connection. Totally convoluted rea-
soning, based on absolutely nothing.

Except the phone call. *The publicist was a warning. You're next.*
Practically a confession. Hard to fault the cops on that.

My eyes widened, and I almost slammed into the back of a
bus.

Good god, that was it. That was what was bothering me.

The publicist was a warning. You're next.

But there were two killings. And there had been two at the
time of the phone call. Yet Noah Sprague had referred to only
one. The one that had been reported in the newspapers.

But not the one that had just happened.

The publicist was a warning. You're next.

Wrong.

Doug Mark had been next.

You wanna be a murder victim, you gotta get in line.

The real killer knows two people are dead.

He doesn't name one, and say *You're next.*

I was tempted to turn around and drive back downtown. But
who was going to listen? Certainly not Frost or Thurman. As
for MacAullif, if I brought him another theory based on no
more information than I had the last time I was in his office,
well, it was not a pretty prospect.

No, no one was going to listen to me, not unless I had
something more concrete. I had a theory, that was all, and a
half-baked one at that. If I was going to get anywhere, I had to
work it out.

I turned off Riverside Drive, found a parking space on
104th. Walked up the street to my building, and took the elevator upstairs.

There was mail in front of my door. That's how it works in
my building. The elevator men hand out the mail. They roll a
large wooden box with cubbyholes into the elevator, sort the

mail into it, then go floor to floor, putting the mail in front of each door. By lunchtime it's usually there.

Since it was now two in the afternoon, it was no surprise the mail had been delivered, only that Alice hadn't picked it up. Then I remembered this was the day she was going shopping in New Jersey with her friend Katherine. And Tommie was still in school. Which was good. I'd have the apartment to myself. Maybe I could think this thing out.

I picked up the mail, unlocked the door, and went in.

The foyer was dark. I switched on the lights, and stood there, flipping through the letters.

I must confess, I'm always eager to get the mail. Even though I have no reason to be. Even though I'm not expecting anything. Still, I always treat the mail as if one letter just might have that elusive million dollars in it.

Needless to say, it didn't. As I riffled through the mail I found the Con Ed bill, the telephone bill, the cable bill, a letter for Tommie, an L. L. Bean catalogue.

And a folded piece of paper.

I unfolded it.

It said: 315 Broome Street. 2nd floor.

44.

I rang for the elevator, waited till Jerry, our young elevator operator, brought it to our floor.

"Jerry," I said. "Did you hand out the mail today?"

"Of course I did. Is something missing?"

"No. Did you sort it too?"

"Sure. Who else?"

I unfolded the piece of paper, showed it to him. "Did you put this in my box?"

"What is it?" He took it, looked at it. "No, I didn't."

"Are you sure?"

"Sure, I'm sure. It doesn't have your name on it. How would I know to put it in your box?"

"You've got me there. So you've never seen this before?"

"Not at all."

"Then how did it get in my box?"

"I have no idea. Are you sure it was in your box?"

"It was with my mail."

"In front of your door?"

"Yeah."

Jerry smiled, shrugged. "Well, I'm not the detective here, but just because it was in front of your door doesn't mean it was in your box. Maybe someone put it in front of your door."

"It wasn't on top."

"Huh?"

"It wasn't on top of the mail. It was stuck in the middle."

Jerry shrugged. "What can I tell you. So someone came up to your door, stuck it in the middle."

"How would he get in the building? The downstairs doors are locked, and you didn't let anyone up, did you?"

"No."

"So how could he get in?"

"Maybe it was someone who lives in the building. Wanted to leave you a note, walked up and down the stairs."

"Yeah, maybe," I said. But I didn't think so. "Tell me. Was there anybody in the elevator who didn't belong? Anyone you saw today you didn't know?"

"I don't think so. I—" Jerry's eyes widened. "Fifteenth floor."

"Huh?"

"There was a guy came to see someone on the fifteenth floor. Girl in 15C. Well, I knew she wasn't there—she works during the day—but he insisted on going up, ringing the bell."

"He did?"

"Yes, he did."

"And . . . ?"

"She wasn't there. Just like I told him. So he left."

"But he did go up and down in the elevator?"

"Yeah."

"And this was while you were sorting the mail? While the box was in the elevator?"

"As a matter of fact, I think it was."

"Any chance he could have stuck something in my box?"

Jerry looked pained. "I wouldn't think so. I try to be alert. But it's not the type of thing I'm looking for. Someone adding something to the mail. So I guess it's possible."

"What did he look like? Can you describe him?"

"He was a little guy. A white guy."

"How old?"

"Older than me."

"Older than *me?*"

Jerry frowned, dubiously. Seemed not at all happy with the question. "Yeah, I suppose so. It was hard to tell. The guy was bundled up in a coat and had a hat pulled down. The woman he was calling on, maybe it crossed my mind he was too old for her. But she's pretty young."

"Yeah, yeah," I said. "What about the face? Glasses? Beard? Color of hair?"

"I don't think he had glasses. But I could be wrong. I'm in the middle of sorting the mail. I'm concerned with where the guy goes, not what he looks like."

"Right," I said. "And a beard?"

"No beard."

"You sure?"

"I think I'd remember a beard. But the color of the hair, and how old the guy is—I'm giving you the best I can. Is it important?"

"I don't know," I said.

But it was.

Wilber Penrose was a little man who could have fit the description if Jerry'd been willing to concede he was older than me. Which was a close point. I never really comprehend how old I'm getting, and I'm always surprised by people's ages in relation to my own. What I mean is, some guy I think is old will turn out to be younger than me.

Yeah, I know, I'm rambling. The point is, without being able to pin Jerry down, Wilber Penrose could be it.

I took the elevator down to the lobby, went out into the

street. Went to the pay phone on the corner, fished out my notebook, made the call.

Got Wilber Penrose's answering machine.

Damn.

I'd have felt a lot better if he'd answered the phone. Known he was in his apartment on 108th Street.

Not on the second floor of 315 Broome.

I thought of calling MacAullif, but with what? An address scrawled on a scrap of paper? That'd make his day. There's no way he'd do anything about it, and all I'd get was abuse.

Still.

I guess I just read too damn many murder mysteries where the hero gets a clue and decides not to tell the police.

I dropped a quarter in the pay phone, made the call.

Needless to say, MacAullif wasn't thrilled. "Didn't we just have this conversation?"

"Yeah, I know. Something came up."

"What?"

I told him about the note. To say he was skeptical would be an understatement. I was lucky he didn't just hang up the phone.

"315 Broome, 2nd floor?" MacAullif said.

"That's right."

"Scrawled in pencil?"

"In pen."

"Oh, that makes it better. Much better. Here's what you should do. Rush this down to me right away, so I can get it to the handwriting boys. So they can compare it to this suspect they've picked up. Because maybe, just maybe, while he's been sitting in the interrogation room, he managed to get away long enough to stick a message in your mailbox."

"It wasn't him."

"No shit, it wasn't him. And if it doesn't have your name on it, most likely it wasn't for you. You know what it sounds like to me?"

"What?"

"You have alternate side parking in your neighborhood?"

"Of course."

"You double park your car, you leave a sign in the window sayin' where you are. Well, that's what this sounds like. 315 Broome, 2nd floor. It's the note you leave when you double park your car, so the guy you block can find you and get out."

"Broome Street's in SoHo."

"I know where Broome Street is."

"So what's the sign doing in my neighborhood?"

"What's the difference if it was left by mistake?" MacAullif said. "Look, you made my day callin' for advice. So, you want some advice? Forget about this. Take a nice hot shower, relax, have a drink."

"I don't drink."

"More's the pity. Some way or another, you gotta calm down."

MacAullif hung up the phone.

Shit.

Well, what did I expect?

I dropped in a quarter, called Wilber Penrose again. Which was stupid. What, just in case he'd come home in the last five minutes? Well, he hadn't. The answering machine was still on.

I hung up, considered doing exactly what MacAullif had said.

I couldn't do it.

I got in the car, drove downtown.

There was no traffic on the West Side Highway. I took it down to Canal Street, across to West Broadway, and up to Broome.

315 was an old warehouse on a block of buildings that had

been renovated into lofts. Only 315 had not. The ground floor had a metal grille over the front window, and appeared empty. The front door was glass, through which I could see a long narrow flight of stairs.

That's what the note said. Second floor.

I went up to the front door, tried the knob.

It opened.

Hot damn.

I didn't know if I was pleased or not. I had a feeling I'd rather have been disappointed. But there it was, a long narrow flight of stairs.

The light at the bottom was a bare bulb, hanging from the ceiling.

The light at the top was out.

Which wasn't good. The light at the bottom illuminated only half the stairs. At the top I could vaguely see the outline of a door to the left, and, to the right, another flight of stairs.

But aside from that.

Dark shadows.

Dim alcoves.

And a long, narrow, wooden stair.

I didn't want to go up it. My stomach fluttered at the thought. A tiny wave of apprehension. A gentle reminder you're doing something you don't want to do.

What did I want to do?

I stood still, listened for a sound. Craned my neck. Foolishly. As if an extra inch would let me hear upstairs.

Heard nothing. Dead silence. Not even a floorboard creaking. Not even a street noise from outside.

Dead silence.

What was this damn building, soundproof?

What did I want to do?

I think at that moment, I wanted to go back out, get in my

car, and drive home. What kept me from doing it was the thought, Why did I come here to begin with?

It was the same thought that drove me up the stairs. If I wasn't going to go upstairs, why did I come?

I took a deep breath, blew it out again slowly, the way I'd been taught to relax before shooting a free throw, so many years ago, when my only problem had been finding a pick to get off a jump shot, not should I ascend an uninviting flight of stairs.

I listened again. Heard nothing.

Tried the first step.

It creaked. Not loudly. But in the dead silence, anything seemed loud.

I gritted my teeth, continued up. Step by creaking step.

Loft buildings had high ceilings. It was a long flight of stairs.

Halfway up it got dark as I passed the point where the light from the downstairs bulb no longer reached. Was there light from above? There must be some, because I could see vague outlines. It must be trickling down the stairway from some higher floor.

But not much light. Nothing on the second-floor landing was clear.

I took another step and saw it. A gleam of reflected light. Just for an instant. There in the dark. There above me. In the stairwell. A sudden gleam, like a cat's eye. Could it be a cat? Not that high. Not unless it was on a ledge.

How about a man?

Same thing. Too tall for a man. Unless he was crouched up the stairs, waiting to spring, and—

There it was again. What was that?

And then.

Oh, hell.

A rueful smile as the gleam proved to be the light reflected from the burned out, dangling, bare bulb.

I exhaled, and the tension poured out of me.

Jesus Christ.

I got a grip, continued up the stairs.

I reached the landing. There. Not so bad. Exactly what it looked like from the bottom. A door off to the left, more stairs off to the right. Dark shadows hiding nothing. An empty alcove.

No one there.

I raised my hand, knocked on the door.

It opened.

I don't mean someone opened it. I mean it swung open. Not wide open. Just slightly. But when I knocked, it moved. There was a sound of metal on metal, the sound of the unlatched latch sliding out, pushing the door open about an inch.

I made a decision. The decision was not particularly brave. It was not that I was so eager to get where I was going. It was more that I was not particularly thrilled with where I was.

Anyway, I pushed the door open.

Immediate gratification.

Light.

Not bright, blinding light, by any stretch of the imagination. In fact, rather dim, murky light, from some unseen source. But compared to the landing, it was heaven.

I looked around.

I appeared to be in a vast cavern of indeterminate size, for what little light there was did not extend to the walls or ceiling. I could really only see about ten or fifteen feet in front of me, and—

There on the floor, just inside the door, was a white envelope. And it looked as if . . .

I bent down, snatched it up.

Good lord.

Written on the envelope in ballpoint pen in capital letters was my name:

STANLEY HASTINGS.

It occurred to me, the same lettering as the note in Doug Mark's hand?

It also occurred to me I should leave this evidence intact for the police.

That occurred to me while I was ripping it open.

Inside was a folded piece of paper.

I unfolded it.

There was a message in capital letters and ballpoint pen:

GUESS WHO?

I blinked.

Frowned.

Then something exploded in my head, and everything went dark.

45.

My first sensation was that I was alive.

It was a feeling that gradually became a conscious thought. I didn't know why that was so important to me. That is, why that thought should be consuming me. But it was and it did, and as it gradually took over my consciousness, memory came flooding back.

My god.

Where was I?

What happened?

Who was here?

My eyes, now open, darted around the semi-darkness. Could see virtually nothing.

The next sensation was that I could not move.

What the hell?

I strained my arms to no avail.

And my legs.

I could not move at all.

I was sitting upright in a chair, and I couldn't move my arms or legs.

Or upper body. I strained with my chest, but could not push away from the chair.

My neck was free, though. I could twist and turn my head, look around. Not that I could see anything in the dark.

Except me.

I could see the outline of my body, see where I was.

I was sitting in a hard, straight-backed armchair. My hands were attached to the arms of the chair. In fact, my whole lower arms were. Attached by something silvery, something that glimmered in the dim light.

In a flash, I realized what it was. Gaffer's tape. At least, that's what they called it in the movies. The other name was duct tape. Anyway, it was strong, wide, silver tape. And it was wound around my arms from the elbows to the wrists, taping my forearms to the arms of the chair.

Though I could not see, I realized my legs were taped to the legs of the chair in similar fashion. Just as my chest was taped to the back. Just as larger loops of tape encircled my upper arms, pinning them to the back of the chair as well.

Good god.

Who had done this?

And why?

The who I thought I knew. Wilber Penrose. That's why he wasn't home. He was down here, lying in wait. For what reason I could not imagine, but say that he was. Was it possible? Could that meek, ineffectual little man have done all this? Have planned all this? Have had all this in mind? Even while he sat there, lead-ing me on, play-acting, talking about his books? Could Wilber Penrose be such a cold, ruthless, calculating fiend?

I just used the word *fiend*. Get a grip. Don't panic. Hang on to reality. You've got to find a way out of this.

As if there was anything I could do.

The main thing was not to panic, not to lose control, not to give in to the sheer terror, utter fright.

What is he going to do to me?

And why, why, why? There is no reason. There is nothing I have done. In my whole investigation, there is nothing I have done that is the equivalent of stepping on anyone's toes. No reason to make it personal, put fish in my car, leave notes with my name on them. *Guess who?* I can't even guess why.

I sat there in the semi-dark, strapped to the chair, my mind racing, going over it all, trying to make some sense.

What was it Winnington had said about suspense—the identity of the killer wasn't important. Like hell. But that wasn't what he meant. Not that it wasn't important, that it didn't nec-essarily have to follow the logic of a standard mystery. That it wasn't play-fair. That it didn't have to be a logical suspect, someone you had met before. That it was merely an inexorable source of evil, powering the events.

Did that help me? Not one bit. And I didn't buy it for a moment. The killer was someone who knew me, and someone I knew. *Guess who?*

Guess who indeed.

My mind raced over the suspects, Wilber Penrose chief among them. But there was the other wannabe writer—what was her name? Oh, yeah, Linda Toole. I never met her, but could it still be her? Could she have somehow found out I was on her trail?

No, more than likely it was someone I had met.

Agent Abe Feinstein? Quite possible. Another little old man. No alibi for either murder. The motive I couldn't even begin to guess at. Still, he was certainly possible.

Elizabeth Abbott? Could it be? Did the killer have to be a man? Well, it was a man who put the note in my mailbox. At least according to Jerry the elevator man. Still, a man with a coat and a hat pulled down over his eyes. A little man with no beard or moustache. Could it have been a woman?

My mind took the next unwilling leap.

Could it have been my client?

Could it have been Maxine Winnington?

No, logic told me. Not possible. Entirely too convoluted. She sets up the crank phone calls herself, so she'll have an excuse to hire a private detective, so she can kill him?

Why did I say kill him? No one's trying to kill me. This is all a game.

Isn't it?

Get control.

Keep thinking. Get your mind going. You were thinking about the suspects.

Right. What about the secretary, what's-his-name? I'm losing it, I can't remember anything. Pryne. David Pryne. After all, he was the one who had the unlisted number before anyone else. Sure, he was there when some of the calls came in. But if he had an accomplice making the calls—well, could he have passed for the old man in the elevator, all hunched up in a coat? Well, why not. Jerry wasn't sure how old.

Could it be him?

Was he the one who tied me up and left me here?

At that moment there was only one thing I knew for sure— whoever had done this, it wasn't wannabe writer Noah Sprague, who was currently in the custody of the NYPD.

Sergeant Thurman was wrong and I was right.

Small consolation.

Needless to say, I had been struggling all the while to get free. But I was taped so tightly to the chair that I could not move at all. Nor could I move the chair. Attempting to lurch my body in one direction or another produced absolutely no result. Whoever it was who had done this had me entirely at his mercy. Completely at his whim. For whatever reason I could not fathom.

For whatever reason I was not sure I wished to know.

A sudden creak of the door sent a shock through my body like an electric current. My head snapped up straight. I nearly wet my pants.

Good god, this was it. Whatever was going to happen would happen now.

Then the sound of footsteps creaking on the wooden floor. Slow. Deliberate. Taking their time. Too slow. Way too slow for any practical purpose.

Except to scare me half to death.

Then, from out of the darkness, from out of the shadows.

A shape.

A man.

Or was it?

Could it be a woman in men's clothes?

Hard to tell. It could be anyone.

Wilber Penrose?

A step closer.

A flicker of light on the features.

Not Wilber Penrose.

Thin. Clean shaven. And . . .

No one I'd seen before.

Not Abe Feinstein or Elizabeth Abbott. Not Maxine or Kenneth P. Winnington. Not the secretary David Pryne.

That left . . .

Linda Toole!

The other wannabe? The woman? I never met her, so could it be her?

No.

It was a man. A man's face. Unknown, and yet vaguely familiar too.

The man stopped and stood there, looking at me.

"Well," he said, "did you guess?"

The voice seemed vaguely familiar too. Still I could not place it.

"Who are you?" I said.

The lips curled up into a smile. A leering, gloating smile. But the eyes remained hard.

"So," he said. "You still don't know. Have I changed that much? Yes, I suppose I have. But physically? Well, maybe the facial hair. Picture me with a moustache."

I'm poor at faces, under the best of circumstances. In a movie theater, for instance, where the worst not recognizing the actor on the screen will get me is the scorn of my wife. But here, now, when my life depended on it—to picture him with a moustache, what the hell did that mean? This little man, standing there, gloating at me. What would a moustache do to his appearance that—

I thought I had reached the limit. I thought I was as scared as I could be.

I was wrong.

Because in that instant, with the revelation, it suddenly felt as if all the blood had drained out of my body.

Because suddenly I recognized him.

Suddenly I knew.

Standing before me was one man I had never even thought of, had never expected to ever see again.

Carlton Kraswell.

46.

Yeah, I know. The name means nothing to you. There it was, a revelation that didn't reveal. Just as Kenneth P. Winnington had predicted. Why didn't I listen? I asked his opinion, why didn't I take it? Why didn't I let his logic put me on the right track? But I didn't, and now I'm dorked, and now in all likelihood I'm going to be tortured and die.

I know, I know, I'm rambling, I can't do that, I gotta stay calm, I gotta think clearly, deal with him, find a way out of it. As if such a thing were possible, as if something could be done.

But, Jesus Christ, Carlton Kraswell.

Of all the people in the world, Carlton Kraswell.

My worst nightmare.

You see, many, many years ago I'd sent Carlton Kraswell to jail. For murder. Cold-blooded, premeditated murder. He'd taken a full fall, twenty-five to life. Which was why I was so surprised to see him. There was no way he could be here now.

Yet here he was, large as life, grinning like a banshee.

"So," he said. "Recognize me, do you? Remember me now? Good. It's important that you do. It means a lot to me. Really."

Carlton Kraswell walked forward into the light. Slowly, step by step, until he stood right before me.

"Yes, you remember me, don't you? You remember me now." He reached out, took my chin in his hand, tilted my face toward his. "But not like I remember you."

I recoiled at the touch, jerked my head away.

He raised his finger. "Tut, tut, now. Let's have none of that. I'd like to explain the situation to you."

He reached in his pocket, pulled out something flat, took it in both hands, pulled it open, held it up. It was a straight razor. What little light there was glinted off the blade.

He held the razor up against my face. "I expect you to cooperate. If you don't, measures will have to be taken. I leave it to you to figure what they might be."

He snapped the razor shut, stuck it back in his pocket. Looked at me and smiled. His manner was light and whimsical. He had a jaunty air.

It was positively chilling.

"So, as I was saying, I doubt if you remember me as well as I remember you. After all, to you I was just another case. Chalk it up and on to the next. But to me . . . well, I remember it well."

He chuckled a moment, then his eyes got hard. "Do you remember the night of my arrest? It wasn't just that you gave me to the cops. No, you also taunted me. Gave me a bill for your services. Remember that? Told me I'd paid for my own arrest. Thought it was pretty funny. Do you think it's so funny now?"

"Is that why you're doing this?"

"Shut up." Kraswell raised a finger. "When I want you to talk, I'll say so. If I don't say so, don't talk. If you can't follow this simple instruction, I will have to take certain measures. For instance, I could slice your windpipe, and you would be unable to talk. Unfortunately, in a few minutes, you would also be dead. Now, I don't want that to happen, so please don't talk."

He frowned. "Where was I. Oh, yes, the humiliating arrest.

Humiliating, yes, but how minor. How very minor." He shook his head, exhaled, looked away. "Do you know what it's like in prison?" He put up his hand. "No, don't answer that. That's a rhetorical question. These are all rhetorical questions, so don't speak. I'll tell you when they're not. But do you know what it's like in prison? Do you know what it's like for a man like me? A white man, small and frail? Do you have any idea? Being raped repeatedly by large, black men. Repeatedly. Savagely. Again, and again. To be passed around. Traded for cigarettes. For *cigarettes,* for god's sake. To be forced to perform humiliating, degrading acts. While others watched. Mocked and jeered. Waited their turn." Kraswell's eyes burned. "Do you know what that felt like? Do you have any idea?"

No, I didn't. But I understood. Kraswell's obsessive hatred. His lust for revenge. When he spoke, suddenly everything clicked into place.

Good god, what was he going to do to me?

As if he could read my mind, Kraswell grinned and nodded. "Yes. Yes, you've got it now. You understand the game. Because that's what it is. It's a game called *I win.* Or more to the point, a game called *You lose.* Basically, it's very simple. I want you to suffer as much as I have. Even though I'm not sure it's possible, I'm going to give it that old college try.

"So far, I've merely played with your mind. It was fun, but not that satisfying." He smiled. "Did you like the fish? Did you go nuts trying to figure that out? I was following you that day, saw you get in the car with your wife and drive off. I didn't try to follow you then, but there was no need. Now I knew your car, and I knew where you lived. How hard could it be? I came back that night, walked the blocks near your building. And there it was, right on your street. I broke the window, left the pile of fish. Did you wonder why?"

He pointed at me. "You can answer that."

It was so abrupt it caught me off guard. I blinked. Didn't know what to say.

"Too scared to talk, huh?" Kraswell nodded. "Frankly, I'm not surprised. Anyway, I thought you might enjoy the bit with the fish. Because by then we were already playing the game. Oh, I followed you. I stalked you for days. You got a case. A big case. At least, from your point of view. It seemed only fitting to fuck it up.

"First off was the publicist. She was a big help. She gave me a lot of information. Before I strangled her. I thought that was a nice touch. You have an appointment with the woman and she dies. The note was fortuitous. There on the coffee table was a note with your name on it. So why not put it in her hand. Did you like that touch? That was rhetorical, you needn't answer."

Kraswell chuckled. Shook his head. "Yeah, I know. I'm standing here confessing. Telling you the whole plot. Like a villain in a bad movie. You know the kind I mean? He's got the hero helpless, why doesn't he just kill him? Instead he stands there gloating about what he's done."

He broke off, leaned in to me. "Well, in this case, it's the whole point. I *want* you to know what I've done. I did it for you to know. I don't want you to die. I want you to suffer."

God, what conflicting emotions ran through me at that moment. He doesn't want me to die. Maybe there's a way out of this. Maybe I'll live.

But at what cost? He wants me to suffer, what is he going to do? He's got a straight razor. Is he going to castrate me? And if he did—oh, my god, if he did—would I live through it? Would I want to live through it? Oh, my god.

"Hey, hey." Kraswell had me by the chin. "Pay attention. Look at me. I'm not half done. So, what happens with the second one? Well, that's just the same as the first. You call on him, he dies. Only now I'm prepared. I have my gun. This time there's no note, but big deal, I have the guy at gunpoint, I make him write a note. He's holding it when I shoot—I don't even have to put it in his hand."

He smiled again. "And what gives me the greatest pleasure, what pleases me to no end, is knowing you will go nuts attributing these murders to the case that you're working on, and attempting to figure them out, to make them make sense, to absolutely no avail. My god, it's positively delicious.

"Because, you see," Kraswell said, "I am fucking with your head. That is what I am doing all along, and what I am doing now. I am fucking with you the way you fucked with me. I am putting you through living hell. And what I want you to realize, the concept I want you to come up with, is how far I'm willing to go, how ruthless I'm willing to be. I killed two people for no other reason but to fuck up your head.

"But that was nothing.

"That was foreplay.

"That was an appetizer.

"Guess what I'm going to do now."

Kraswell stood there gloating for a few moments, then turned and walked away. He returned immediately carrying a black bag. It was the size and shape of a gym bag, might have contained his sneakers and basketball.

Somehow I didn't think so.

He set the bag on the floor in front of me, straightened up and smiled. "Do you know what I have here? That was rhetorical again. Don't worry, I'm going to tell you. See, one of the advantages of being in jail—yes, there are advantages too—is that you learn things. All kinds of things. Would you like to know what I learned? Yes, that was rhetorical again. You are going to learn, whether you want to or not. Here, I'll show you."

He bent down, unzipped the bag, took something out.

I watched, not wanting to see, but unable to look away.

I gawked.

Good god.

What Carlton Kraswell was holding was something I'd seen in movies, read about in books, but could not imagine encountering in real life.

It was an alarm clock and a bundle of sticks of dynamite.

Kraswell wasn't looking at it, he was looking at me, and liking what he saw. "Yes, yes," he said gleefully. "You recognize it, of course. It's exactly what it looks like. A homemade bomb. And I have to admit, I had to get over an initial prejudice too. It looks like something out of a cartoon, doesn't it. One of those old cliffhanger serials. But the thing is, that doesn't mean it doesn't work. Believe me, it works just fine. Want me to tell you how?"

Kraswell chuckled again. "Well, guess what. It doesn't matter what you want. I'm going to tell you anyhow. Because that's part of the fun. Let me give you a little lesson here on how this thing works."

Kraswell held up the bomb, pointed out the features. "First off, it's a time bomb. Obviously. Because of the clock."

Kraswell pointed to it. It was a metal, round-faced clock with a bell on top. "Just your basic alarm clock. The wind-up kind. I believe it's fully wound, but let's make sure. Yes, it's fully wound. Both the time and the alarm. You will notice it is set to the correct time, which is now what? Three-eighteen. And the alarm—what's the alarm set for? It's rather small, maybe you can't see. But it happens to be set for eight o'clock."

He frowned. "That's no good. That's too long. How about something a little sooner? Let's say five o'clock."

Kraswell reached to the back of the clock, turned something. "There we go. Five o'clock. All set and ready to go. Just one more thing."

Kraswell reached on top of the clock, pulled the bottom up. "There. Now the alarm is set to go off at five o'clock. And guess what happens when it does. I don't have to tell you, do I? You're not a stupid man. You know perfectly well the dynamite goes boom. Otherwise, why would it be there? But I'm not a cruel man. I'm not going to make you *assume* the dynamite goes off. I'm going to personally assure you that it does. So, the alarm is set for five o'clock. It is now three-eighteen—make that three-nineteen—so, you have a little over an hour and a half to suffer."

He looked at me. Smiled enigmatically.

"Perhaps."

After a moment's pause he said, "But first, a few more preparations."

Kraswell bent down, took a cloth and a roll of duct tape out of the bag. He held them up, said, "Good news. I'm going to solve your rhetorical question problem for you. From now on, you won't have to make that decision, whether to answer or not. Just to show you I'm basically a nice guy."

Kraswell took the cloth, wadded it up, shoved it in my mouth. It was a huge wad of cloth. Not only could I not speak, I could barely breathe. I choked. Gagged.

"Oh, gee, is that too much?" Kraswell said. "I'm sorry, but that's the way it's going to be."

Kraswell took the duct tape, attached it to my cheek, wound it over my mouth, and pulled it tight. He ran it over my other cheek and behind my head. Either the chair had a very high back, or Kraswell had attached a board to it, because he pulled my head back flush with something hard, and wound the tape around it. He continued on around until it covered my mouth again. He wound the tape around a couple more times, then stopped, slashed it off with the razor.

Next he put the tape in the middle of my forehead and wound it around a few times, until my head was attached firmly to the board or the back of the chair or whatever. When he'd finished, I was totally helpless.

I could not move.

I could not speak.

I could not make a sound.

"How's that?" Kraswell said. "I know it's not comfortable, but I'm wondering if it's effective. Can you communicate at all? Tell you what, make a sound for me, any small sound, and I'll figure this is ineffective and take the gag out. What do you say? Go ahead. Can you make a sound?"

I tried. I knew I shouldn't, but still I did. I tried like hell to make a sound. And while my mouth was totally gagged, my nose wasn't covered. I couldn't talk, but by straining hard I could make a high-pitched, whiny hum.

"Oh, dear," Kraswell said. "Well, now, that's no good, is it? I might as well just take the gag off if you can make noise like that."

Kraswell reached for the gag. Then withdrew his hands. "But why bother? Let's leave it on just for show. Oh, I know I said I'd take it off. But I lied. To encourage you to make a sound. Now that I know you can, I'll have to do something else."

Kraswell bent down, reached into the bag. Took out a hypodermic syringe.

"Do you see this? Do you know what it is? Yes, I'm sure you do. But how about this?"

He pulled out something else. It was a small vial.

Kraswell held it up, smiled. "You learn a lot of things in prison. A lot of things. Do you have any idea what this is? No,

I'm sure you don't. Well, it's a serum made from venom. That's right. Poison from a snake. It's used in medical research.

"Nowadays I'm sure it's used intelligently, but way back when there's a little story goes with this stuff. When doctors first discovered it they thought they'd found the perfect drug. Why? Because it paralyzes the muscles. Well, not paralyzes. Paralyzes is a bad word. Makes you think of stiff. What it does really is relaxes the muscles. Renders them absolutely incapable of movement.

"The doctors figured this would be invaluable in surgery. Even with the patient unconscious, the muscle will retract, or spasm, or what have you, and cause the surgeon to make the wrong cut. With this, the muscles don't move. The patient lies there, not a twitch.

"So, the doctors went ahead, tried it in surgery."

Kraswell frowned, shook his head. "There was one small drawback. While the muscles were totally relaxed, the mind was not. The patients never lost consciousness. They lay there, incapable of any movement, of any sign, of indicating in any way that they were awake. They lay there, fully conscious, through the entire operation, and went through the most excruciating pain."

Kraswell paused, smiled at me.

It was chilling.

"So," he said. "What do you say we give it a try?"

Kraswell stuck the hypodermic in the vial, pulled the plunger, drew the serum out.

"Well, now," he said. "We have a bit of a problem. I can't get at your arms. But in the hospital they always manage to get an I.V. in the back of the hand."

He leaned over and inspected the back of my left hand.

"Yes, there's a vein. Let's give that a try."

A moment later I felt the prick of a needle.

"Bingo. Blood in the syringe. We must be there. And away we go."

I could feel it going in.

He withdrew the needle, straightened up.

"And there you have it. We'll have a few more minutes while the serum takes effect. After that, you won't be responding any more, but don't worry, I'll know you're there."

Kraswell shrugged. "Of course in a hospital you'd be on a respirator. We don't have one here. But I'm told your heart and lungs will still function. Though your breathing will be somewhat shallow. And you'll have absolutely no control over it. But I'm told you'll survive. I certainly hope so. It's important to me that you do."

Kraswell put the hypodermic back in the bag, straightened up and smiled. "Let me see. Where was I?"

He looked around.

Saw the clock.

"Oh, yes. The clock. I was telling you about the clock. The clock is set for five o'clock. When the alarm rings, the dynamite goes boom."

He held up a finger. "But that's just one possibility. Please bear with me."

Carlton Kraswell turned, walked away into the darkness. I could hear his footsteps, but could no longer see him.

Suddenly a light went on. An overhead light. A hanging bare bulb.

Carlton Kraswell was standing under it, having just pulled the string.

The light lit up an area of the loft. Not the front door—it didn't quite reach that far—but a portion of the side wall.

Along the wall was a row of lockers. Metal lockers, the type you find in a gymnasium or in a school hallway, a row of fifteen or twenty or them. In the dim light, they glimmered a metallic gray.

Kraswell walked back to me.

He pointed. "See that? See the lockers? It's important to me that you do. So blink your eyes once if you see the lockers, two if you don't."

I did nothing. Looked straight ahead, unblinking.

"Oh, dear," Kraswell said. "Do I sense a lack of cooperation? Or has the serum begun to work?"

He reached in his pocket, took out the razor, flicked it open. "Let's try again while you still have eyes to blink. Can you see those lockers?"

Words can't describe the terror of hearing someone threaten to cut your eyes.

Humiliated and ashamed, I blinked.

"Good," Kraswell said. "Good boy. So, you can see the lockers. Then everything is as it should be. Everything is fine."

He stooped down, picked up the homemade bomb, stood up.

"Now then, you remember the bit about this going off at five o'clock? Yes, I'm sure you remember that. Well, there is the other alternative, and let me just explain that to you now."

Kraswell took the bomb, walked over to the row of lockers. He opened one somewhere in the middle of the row, and slowly eased the bomb onto the shelf on top.

"There," he said. "That was easy. Now comes the tricky part. Watch carefully, because if I fuck this up, I will be blown to bits."

He pulled out a wire attached to the bomb, held it up. "You see this? This is the hard part. This is where I mustn't fumble."

He cut off a small piece of duct tape, put it over the end of the wire.

"Now then, here's my problem. I have to close the locker at the same time I tape the wire. You see what I mean? I'm taping the wire to the inside of the door. But when I tape it, I want the door closed. That's not possible, of course, but I want to do the best I can. Keep the wire short and tight. See what I mean?"

Kraswell closed the locker door till it was open a narrow crack. He reached his hand in with the wire, taped it to the back of the door.

"There. That's pretty good. You see the point? Now I close the locker, and everything is set."

He did. Then walked back over to me.

"There. Now, you remember which locker it is? From here it's probably hard to tell, but, hey, that's half the fun."

Kraswell stuck the duct tape back in the bag, straightened up. "You understand the bit about the wire? It's short and tight, and attached to the door. When the door swings open, it will pull the wire. Pulling the wire sets off the bomb. Even before five o'clock. Five is just your outside limit, your fail safe. If nothing has happened by then, five o'clock, kerboom."

Kraswell smiled. "But then again, who knows."

He looked at me for a few moments, then said, "But first, a few last preparations. You see I have a light over there on the lockers. Which means I no longer need the one over here."

He reached up, pulled the string that turned off the overhead light.

"You are now in the dark. You cannot be seen from the door. Or from the lockers, for that matter. You are more or less hidden from view. But, just to make sure . . ."

Kraswell darted away. Then I heard a rustling sound. The sound of cloth. Then something obscured my view.

"So," Kraswell said. "Curtains. Heavy, black curtains. I'll leave a little gap for you to see out, but no one's gonna see you."

The curtains rustled as Kraswell came through. I could hear him step behind the chair.

"Just a moment. Let me check the sight lines here. I must be sure that you can see. Pretty good. I think I need to open this a bit more. There we go. Full view of the lockers. And if there were more light, you could even see the door. Excellent. Simply excellent."

Kraswell came around to the front of the chair, bent down, looked me right in the face. Then he raised his hand, snapped his fingers once in front of each eye. He smiled.

"Perfect. You can't even blink. But you can still see. You can still hear. You can still think. You probably hadn't even realized. Hadn't even noticed it happened."

I hadn't. I had been helpless to know I was helpless. It was an overwhelming thought.

What would he do now?

Kraswell slipped out through the curtains again. Then turned back to face me. "Just a word before I go. You cannot imagine the satisfaction this is for me. It is my life's work, something I've planned for years. For the next hour and a half, I would like you to think on what you've done, how you've brought this on yourself. But, hey, that's just what I'd like. Your thoughts are your own. I'll leave you to them.

"Here's a phrase I absolutely hate, which is why I say it to you now."

Kraswell smiled.

"Have a nice day."

Kraswell turned, walked over into the light. He stopped, took something out of his jacket pocket. It was an envelope. He looked at it, then bent down and set it on the floor. He straightened up, took one last look around.

His eyes met mine.

He smiled.

Then he was gone.

47.

I heard the door close behind him.

I sat there in mounting dread.

Was that it? Was he really gone? Or was this, like everything else, another one of his psychological tricks?

Would he be back, within minutes, wielding the razor?

Because that, I confess, was uppermost in my mind. So much so, I was relieved he had left, even though he had set the bomb. A fiery death in an hour and a half seemed nothing compared to the immediate threat of a razor blade in the balls.

Then there was another thing.

The lockers seemed fairly far away. Could the bomb blast kill me from there? I mean, how powerful was dynamite, anyway? How many sticks were in the bundle? Eight? Ten? How much damage would it do?

When it went off, would I die?

Or was that it? Was that the point? Just as he said, he didn't *want* me to die. Would I just be horribly maimed?

But if that was the point, why hadn't he done it himself? He had the razor. If he wanted to inflict pain, why not that? It wasn't as if he was too squeamish. He throttled the publicist. Shot Doug Mark. Could torture be beneath him? Not to hear him talk. It was what he lived for.

So why hadn't he done it?

And why the serum? What was the point of that? The horror story of patients under the knife seemed to tie in with the razor. But if he was really gone, if there was to be no razor, then why had he done it? Unless to increase the terror, the added element that my heart might suddenly just stop. Though there seemed no danger of that. My breathing, though shallow, was steady. I wasn't being deprived of air.

So why had he done it? Why had he left me here, utterly helpless, unable to make a sound?

What was the point?

With my peripheral vision, I noticed something I hadn't noticed before.

My left wrist.

The tape around my left wrist had been carefully wound so as to miss my watch. The watch faced up. It had a luminous dial. Even in the dark, I could make out the time.

Three thirty-four.

Son of a bitch.

He'd done it on purpose.

He'd planned it this way.

He wanted me to sit here, watching the minutes tick away, waiting for my execution, suffering the torments of the damned.

Indeed, the watch was the cruelest gesture. Because, much as I dreaded to see it, it was impossible to ignore.

Psychological torture.

I forced my mind away from it, made myself think about something else. The letter. The letter on the floor. What the hell was that? A confession, perhaps? An account of what he'd done? Entirely likely, but confession was the wrong word. It wouldn't be confessing, it would be more like bragging. Claiming responsibility, the way terrorists do for some atrocious act.

The letter would contain a list of my sins. The wrongs I had committed against Carlton Kraswell. The reason he had found me guilty and condemned me to death.

But would I die?

Again, the shadow of a doubt. With the bomb way over there, would I in fact die?

And what about the letter? It was much closer to the bomb than I was. If the blast was strong enough to kill me, wouldn't it destroy the letter too?

So what was the point?

Unless *that* was the point. Had Kraswell left the letter there for the same reason he had done everything else, to fuck up my mind? If so, good god, how it was working.

The minutes ticked by. Four o'clock. That was a biggie. The minute it passed, I knew why Carlton Kraswell had chosen an hour and a half. So I could see four o'clock come and go. I was now in my final hour. The last half hour had been hell. This hour would be worse. Now the minutes would fly. Accelerating, picking up pace. Each successive minute slightly shorter than the last. Good god, four oh one already, which means we're coming up on four oh two.

Stop it. Don't do it. Look away from the watch. Concentrate on something else. Focus your attention. Think on anything. Just don't think on the watch, or you'll go mad.

I tried to think about the case. The stupid, pointless case. Wannabe writer Noah Sprague. Poor, ineffectual, sniveling worm resorts to crank phone calls of an insidious nature. And that's the extent of it. That's all it was. The guy had nothing to do with the killings at all. Yet, irony of ironies, it occurred to me, if I were to blow up, and Kraswell's letter were to be destroyed, Thurman and Frost might still nail Noah Sprague for the murders. After all, he made the incriminating phone call about the publicist being a warning. And he had the new unlisted number. If he couldn't explain where he got that, his ass was grass. Christ, it was entirely possible he'd take the fall.

Of course, his attorney would be sure to raise bloody hell about how Winnington's investigator happened to get blown up while his client was in jail.

Blown up.

Jesus.

Four fourteen.

Nearly down to three quarters of an hour.

Stop it. Get your mind on something else.

Carlton Kraswell. Twerpy little Carlton Kraswell. I remembered the first time he'd come into my office. Nervous, fidgety, tugging at his scrawny mustache.

Feeding me a pack of lies.

That was the unfair thing. I hadn't searched Carlton Kraswell out and sent him to jail. He'd chosen me. Duped me, framed me, set me up. It was only luck I hadn't taken the fall myself. Could he really blame me for striking back? I suppose I had rubbed it in, handing him my bill when the cops made the arrest—good god, I'd never make that mistake again.

But to spend all these years plotting revenge. I mean, it wasn't as if I'd sent him to jail on a whim. The guy killed someone, for Christ's sake. Had I really been unreasonable?

I know, what the hell did it matter? What difference did it make? If he sees it that way, he sees it that way. So what could I do, say you got no right to resent me, you gotta take back your bomb?

Bomb.

Jesus.

And just like that, it's four forty-five.

Four forty-five.

Fifteen minutes.

Unbelievable.

Fifteen minutes to live.

The letter on the floor. What was it about the letter on the floor? It's too close, and it's gonna get destroyed in the bomb blast, so what's the point?

But suppose it doesn't get destroyed in the bomb blast? Then *I* don't get destroyed in the bomb blast, and there's no point at all.

So what if that's *not* it? So what if it's another cryptic message, like the one he left for me? *Guess who?* That was in an envelope lying on the floor. What if it's another one of those?

Well. Small problem there. It can't be for me, because how am I going to get over there and get it? Obviously, I am not. So it can't be another message left to taunt me. If it's a message, it's for someone else.

But who?

No one's gonna read it until after the bomb blast.

Would the letter survive the bomb blast?

Would I?

Full cycle.

Four forty-eight.

Good god.

Four forty-eight.

Well done, Mr. Kraswell. Very effective.

And then . . .

Hope!

A sudden, desperate, exhilarating leap of hope.

The sound of the door latch clicking open.

Rescue!

Or could it be . . . cruel doubt . . . Carlton Kraswell back to gloat one last time?

No. Not likely. By now he's miles away.

No. It's your savior, salvation, it's the cavalry to the rescue, it's a deus ex machina, it's everything you ever hoped for, wished for, dreamed of, desperately within the last hour, it's the answer to your prayers.

I sat there in the chair, holding on for dear life, straining to hear in the darkness what my eyes could not yet see.

The door creaked open.

Yes!

Come in!

Yes!

Then footsteps entering the room. But not the heavy tread of cops. A single person, light of step.

It doesn't matter. Someone. Anyone. Come get me.

The footsteps came closer. A figure appeared in the darkness.

I strained my eyes.

The figure stepped into the light.

My heart stopped dead.

Oh god.

Alice.

48.

And suddenly I knew everything.

Suddenly it was all clear.

In a lightning bolt of horror and revulsion, I saw everything he had planned, everything he had set in motion. Just how it was he had intended me to suffer.

Oh, my god. Victory, Carlton Kraswell. Game, set, and match. I concede, I confess, I apologize, I grovel. I'll do anything, just come back now and make it stop.

Not a chance. Not a prayer. It was happening, and there was nothing I could do but sit and watch.

Not that I didn't try. With all my might I willed myself to shout against the gag, to strain against the tape, to heave against the chair.

To absolutely no avail.

For all my effort, not a muscle moved.

All I could do was watch and hope.

Alice walked in two steps, stopped and looked around.

Her eyes passed right over me. It was excruciating. If she saw me, she'd untie me, get me out of here, there was still time. But there was no way that she could see me.

Her gaze swept the room.

Reached the lockers.

No!

Not the lockers. Don't look at the lockers. Look away.

She did.

She looked down, saw the letter on the floor.

She stooped, picked it up.

Looked at it and frowned.

She tore the envelope open, pulled out the letter.

Unfolded it.

Read it.

Then looked at the lockers.

No!

Good god.

No!

Alice looked at the letter again, then folded it up, stuck it back in the envelope.

She turned and walked over to the lockers. She went to the one closest to her, the one on the far end. She stopped in front of it, reached out to the handle. It was one of those metal handles that slides up and down and has a hole for a padlock. There was a loud, metallic clang as Alice slid the handle up and opened the door. She looked in the locker for a moment, then closed the door again.

And moved to the next.

No, Alice, no. Whatever the note said, ignore it. Ignore the lockers. Get out. Just turn and walk out of here now.

Clang.

Alice raised the handle, opened the second door, looked in the locker.

Clang.

She closed it again.

Clang.

She opened the next.

Good god, which locker was it? From here I can't tell. She's

296

on three, and it's somewhere near the middle. How many are there in all? Why didn't you count them, you moron? Why did you just estimate? If you'd counted them, maybe you'd know.

I counted them now.

There were twenty lockers, as near as I could tell. I was somewhat distracted making my count, distracted by the fact that Alice was moving on. Had opened locker number four.

The locker with the bomb was somewhere near the middle, but with twenty lockers, there *was* no middle. It could be eleven or it could be ten. Either one was equally close. And who's to say it had to be either, and couldn't be nine or twelve.

My god, she's on locker number five.

And it's four fifty-one.

Alice, read my thoughts. ESP. Vulcan mind meld. Sixth sense. Woman's intuition. For whatever reason, stop, get out now.

Clang.

Locker five closed.

Clang.

Open locker six.

Good god, Alice, you're getting faster. One glance and you know the locker's empty. Or, at least, what you're looking for, whatever it is, is not there.

Clang.

Was that six? I'm losing count. Did she just close six? Is it seven she's about to——

Clang.

Be there. Let something be there. Something in the locker. Anything to attract her attention. Slow her down.

Clang.

Damn it. Nothing. What was that? Seven? Surely that's enough. Let her stop there.

Clang.

Be there. Let her find it, take it, and leave. That was your game, right, Kraswell? All a tease. What she's looking for is in this locker, and she's going to take it and walk out the door, now I've suffered enough.

Good god, I've suffered enough. Is this enough for you, Kraswell? Please, let her go. God, let her go.

Clang.

Was that eight or nine? No more. No more. And—

A prayer answered.

Yes.

Alice stopped.

Turned toward the door.

Someone was coming.

Kraswell. Coming back to let me off the hook. He'd had his fun, it was enough, the game was over, we could stop playing now. Carlton Kraswell, my favorite person in the world, come, get her out of here, take her away.

Clang.

Not the locker, but the front door.

Yes.

He's back.

It's over.

It's all right.

Everything is going to be all right.

It's probably not Kraswell, it's better it's not Kraswell, but it's somebody, anybody, and whoever it is is going to take you out of here. Do you understand, they're going to make you stop opening the lockers, and get you the hell out the door. Thank god, thank god, the answer to a prayer.

There came the squeak of the door swinging open. Then the sound of footsteps.

The new arrival stepped into the light.

And broke what was left of my heart.

Tommie.

49.

I sat helpless while the last piece of my world crumbled away.

"Tommie," Alice said. "What are you doing here?"

"Huh?" he said. "I got your note."

"What note?"

"You left me a note. To meet you here."

"I did not."

"Did so. You wanna see?"

"What?"

"I got it here somewhere."

Tommie began fishing in his jeans, pulled out a folded piece of paper. "Here you go." He unfolded it. "Tommie. Meet me three fifteen Broome Street, second floor. Mom."

"I didn't write that."

"Oh, sure," Tommie said. "And I'm not here."

"Let me see that," Alice said.

And she crossed to him.

Away from the locker.

Yes.

Alice took the paper, read it. "Where did you get this?"

"It was in the mail."

"The mail?"

"Yeah. I got home, I looked at the mail. There was a letter with my name on it."

"Tommie, that doesn't make any sense. Why would I send you a letter in the mail?"

"I don't know, but this was it. It said to meet you here, and so I did. And you're here. If you didn't write this, why are you here?"

"I got home, there was a message on the answering machine telling me to meet your father here."

"Dad? He left you a message?"

"No. Some man. He said Stanley was hung up downtown and wanted me to meet him here."

"Oh, yeah?" Tommie said. "So where is he?"

"I don't know."

"So what's with the lockers?"

"There was a letter addressed to me lying on the floor."

"What did it say?"

Alice pulled the letter out of the envelope, handed it to Tommie. He unfolded it, read, "Stanley got hung up. Take the bag in the locker and meet him on the corner of Broadway and Canal." He frowned. "What bag, Mom?"

"I don't know."

"This is weird."

"Yeah."

"What should we do?"

"We gotta go meet Dad. If he's really there."

"Why wouldn't he be?"

"Because I didn't write that letter."

"This letter?"

"No. The one to you. You say it was in the mail?"

"Yeah."

"I saw the mail. There was a letter to you. But it had an address and a stamp."

"Yeah. That was kind of strange. But the envelope wasn't sealed."

"Oh?"

"Yeah." Tommie dug in his hip pocket, pulled out the envelope. "See? It wasn't sealed, just folded over. And, look, there's no postmark. So I figured you just stuck it in the envelope."

Oh, god.

I had held that envelope in my hand.

It had been within my power to notice that it wasn't sealed, that it didn't have a postmark. I could have opened it, read it, known something was wrong.

I could have prevented this.

It's my fault.

"Well, I didn't," Alice said. "I didn't write that letter. And I don't know who wrote this one to me. I have no idea what's going on here."

"So what do we do?"

"We get out of here."

"What about the bag?"

"There probably is no bag." Alice frowned. "I suppose I should make sure."

Alice turned, walked back to the lockers.

Tommie followed.

And there they were, right in the middle of the lockers. Right next to the one with the bomb. If they opened the door it would go off. If they just stood there it would go off. Good god, four fifty-six. And who knows how close my watch is to that damn clock? I didn't notice the time. Either watch or clock could be as much as five minutes off, which means it could happen any second, any second now.

You've got to get out.

Alice, get Tommie out.

"So, which one is it?" Tommie said.

301

"I don't know. I've done all these. I think I was on this one."

Alice grabbed the locker handle.

Clang.

Jerked it open.

Nothing happened.

Oh, my god. Which one was it? I can't tell without counting. One, two, three, four, five, six, seven, eight, nine. That was
nine. Good god, stop there.

"Maybe this one," Alice said.

Clang.

Number ten open.

And it's empty.

Good god, number ten is empty.

Which means it's gotta be eleven.

Good god, please, Alice, don't open eleven.

Clang.

Ten shut.

Alice reached her hand toward eleven.

"This is silly, Mom."

She stopped, turned toward him. "I know it's silly. What do
you want me to do?"

"I think we should find Dad."

"I do too. But if he didn't write these notes . . ." Alice
shrugged. "I mean, if there's no bag, he's not going to be on
the corner, either."

"I suppose."

"So we should see if there's a bag."

"I wanna get out of here. It's creepy."

"Just a minute."

I could see it in slow motion.

Alice turned back to the lockers.

Reached out her hand.

Gripped the handle.

Raised it up.

Jerked it open.

And . . .

Clang.

Nothing.

Absolutely nothing.

Had the tape come off? Had it defused? Was it a dud?

"Empty," Alice said, and slammed the door.

Clang.

Suddenly, in horror, I realized.

That was ten again. Turning her back, she'd lost her place and opened locker ten.

Eleven was next.

Eleven was now.

Stop her, Tommie. Stop her again.

But Tommie said nothing.

Alice reached out her hand.

"Stop!"

A voice from the darkness.

"Don't touch that. Get away from the door."

Carlton Kraswell.

A change of heart.

A last-second pang of remorse.

Carlton Kraswell lurched into the light, followed immediately by MacAullif, who had him by the arm.

"Excuse me, Mrs. Hastings," MacAullif said, "but we have a situation here. I want you to take your son and get out of here now."

"But—"

"There's no time to discuss it. Your son's in danger. Get him out."

Alice said, "Come on, Tommie," and the two of them headed for the door.

MacAullif wheeled on Kraswell. "All right, where is he?"

"We've got to get out of here."

"You wanna get out of here, you tell me where he is."

"There's no time."

"Then talk fast. Where is he?"

"There," Kraswell said.

He pointed with his chin. That's when I realized his hands were handcuffed behind him. MacAullif took him by the arm, pushed him toward me. Seconds later he was pulling back the curtain.

"Jesus Christ," MacAullif said.

He grabbed the chair, tried to move it.

"Bolted to the floor," he said.

He whipped out Carlton Kraswell's razor, flipped it open, began slicing at the duct tape.

Kraswell turned and ran.

MacAullif stuck his foot out, tripped him up, and Kraswell went flat.

MacAullif had one arm free. My left one. I wanted to help, but there was nothing I could do. My arm hung limp at my side.

"Jesus Christ," MacAullif said. "What the hell's wrong with you?"

My second arm came free. But my head was still taped to the back of the chair. Two quick cuts took care of that. Then MacAullif was stooping to do my legs.

As my body sagged forward, I could see my watch.

Four fifty-nine.

We weren't going to make it. Me, MacAullif, or Kraswell, who struggled to his feet. MacAullif must have seen him out of the corner of his eye, because without even turning he kicked him down, and sliced the tape away from my legs.

MacAullif straightened up, pulled me from the chair. My

legs were free, but they were taped together, wound up like a mummy. They would have been useless anyway. MacAullif took one look, cursed, grabbed me around the knees, flung me over his shoulder in a fireman's carry. He turned, grabbed Carlton Kraswell by the scruff of the neck, jerked him to his feet, and pulled him toward the door.

Hanging down MacAullif's back, I saw my watch click over to five o'clock.

MacAullif carried me out the door, dragging Carlton Kraswell behind him.

We had just reached the landing when there was a roar like thunder, and a blast of hot air sent us flying down the stairs.

50.

"I'm sorry," MacAullif said.

He would say that. I grimaced, eased myself into a chair.

"What a pain in the ass," I said. "Save a guy's life and say you're sorry."

MacAullif leaned back in his desk chair, cocked his head. "You know what I mean. This shouldn't have happened at all."

"No argument there."

"It's the parole system," MacAullif said. "It's all fucked up. A guy gets twenty-five to life, he ought to *do* twenty-five to life. You shouldn't expect to see the guy for twenty-five years. But, no, the system's so screwed up if the asshole hasn't managed to kill someone in jail, some bleedin' heart parole board figures, whoop-de-do, rehabilitation, and before you know it the scumbag's back on the street."

"It was a bit of a shock."

"No shit. What can I say? It wasn't my jurisdiction, it wasn't my case. Even so, there's gotta be some system of checks and balances. You send a guy away on a murder rap, the least they can do is let you know when he's getting out."

"Yeah," I said. I settled back in my chair, rubbed my head. "You wanna go on beating yourself up, or you think you might pause long enough for me to thank you?"

"Don't mention it. Wife and kid okay?"

"All things considered. Tommie may need some counseling. Alice too. They were right outside when it went off. With no way of knowing we'd got out."

"I know."

I reached up, tugged at the Band-aid on my chin. Remarkably, a few scrapes and bruises were all we'd got out of it. The bomb blast had thrown us down the stairs. Which was a bit of luck. There wasn't much left of the second floor.

"So, you wanna tell me why you did it?" I said. "Not that I'm complaining, but it seems to me you pooh-poohed the idea on the phone."

"That's true."

"So what brought you down there?"

"Actually, you have Sergeant Thurman to thank."

"You're kidding."

"Not at all. You're lucky he's such a bad cop. The type of cop, once he gets a suspect, he'll twist every bit of evidence to make it fit him."

"What's that got to do with it?"

"This guy he drags in—the crank caller—what's his name—Noah Sprague—he's trying to make a case against the guy. Everything he finds, it points to his guilt."

"So?"

"So, workin' up a case on the guy, he finds a friend of his works at Video Access where Winnington rents his tapes."

"Oh, yeah?"

"Yeah. A little pressure and the guy breaks down and admits giving him Winnington's new unlisted number."

"So?"

"So, I run into Thurman and he's braggin' about how he just found a key piece of evidence, locked up his case." MacAullif shrugged, spread his hands. "Which is all ass-backward. Thurman likes it because it confirms the guy made the call. What he's missing is, if the guy got the number from the video place, there's no connection between him and the publicist at all."

"That's all you had?"

"That's all I need. If the phone number didn't come from the publicist, there's a good bet the crank calls and the killings aren't related. Which means Thurman's got the wrong man. Which means you've got the right one, and that note you told me about just might be pay dirt. In which case, you're walking into a trap."

"Yeah." I took a breath, exhaled noisily. "I'm thinking maybe I'll get out of the business."

"Just because you're no good at it?"

"No, MacAullif. The guy went after my wife and kid."

"Yeah, I know. And how can you endanger them? But think about it. The guy came after you for something happened years ago. You quit now, you still can't erase what's been done. Oh, you're forewarned, you're more careful, you'll check up now, every scumbag ever went to jail, make sure the son of a bitch is still there. Is he comin' up for parole, is he likely to get out?

"But in the end, you can't bury your head in the sand. I mean, would you quit workin' for Rosenberg? Because that's your real job, that's what you do full-time. And negligence work, who's to get upset about that?

"This other stuff—the freelance stuff you fall into—each case is individual, no one's hittin' you over the head, you have the right to say no."

"I know, but . . ."

"But right now you're too close to it to think rational. So take some time off, get away from it all, take a vacation. Things will look different when you've had a chance to calm down. When your wife and kid calm down and stop talking about it.

Once they put it behind them, you will. Then you move on. It hasn't even been twenty-four hours yet. You gotta give it time."

"I suppose."

"If it will make you feel any better, I guarantee you Mr. Kraswell will be gone for a long time. Aside from his little stunt with the bomb, he was carrying the pistol that killed Doug Mark. So he's a cinch for that one."

"That's a break."

"Whether they get him on the publicist too is iffy, unless he gives it up. There's no real evidence there. But he's going down for the other. So I guess it doesn't really matter."

I nodded. Sherry Pressman's funeral was that afternoon.

"Except to her."

51.

I went to the funeral. I'm not sure why. Maybe because I needed a sense of closure. Maybe to see the Winningtons again. Or maybe because I couldn't shake the feeling this woman was dead because of me. Because Carlton Kraswell followed me to her apartment. And killed her just for spite. Anyway, I felt I had to go.

Sherry Pressman's memorial service was at a funeral home on Third Avenue in the East 80s. I drove over, got a parking meter on Lexington a block away. It was only an hour meter, but I figured that was probably as much as I could stand. I fed quarters into the meter, walked over to Third.

The first thing I noticed was how few people were there. The Winningtons were not among them. The only one I recognized was wannabe writer Wilber Penrose. I had no real desire to talk to him. I avoided eye contact, went over to commune with the dead.

It was closed casket, praise the lord. Inside was the woman I'd last seen lying on a slab in the morgue. The woman who'd pressured me to buy Winnington's book. It occurred to me I'd never bought it. I resolved to do so, just for her. I smiled slightly at the irony—the publicist's death resulting in a final sale.

I looked up to see Abe Feinstein come in the door. The agent looked properly respectful in his best black suit, except for the knockout of a young brunette hanging on his arm. She was also dressed in black, but there's black and then there's black. Her clinging little number would have raised eyebrows at the Academy Awards.

The woman spotted Wilber Penrose, and, with a wave far too cheery for the situation, disengaged herself from the arm of the agent, and went flying across the room to meet him, where the two of them proceeded to converse animatedly in low tones.

I went up to Abe Feinstein. "Come to pay your respects?"

"Absolutely. Fine woman. Besides, who knows what client of hers I might steal."

"That hadn't occurred to me."

"You're in the business, it would."

"Uh-huh," I said. "Who's your friend?"

"Her? Oh, that's one of Sherry's authors. Linda Toole."

I blinked. "Linda Toole? Are you kidding? The little old lady with the book about cats?"

"Not so little. Not so old. But a book about cats, she has. I'm handling it for her."

"You are? I thought Sherry said it was awful."

"It is rather bad. The woman can barely write. Still, it is a mystery about a woman with cats. Plus, the cat woman's a cook, throws in an actual recipe for tuna salad." He shrugged. "I got her a two book, hard-soft deal in the mid six figures, she's happy as a clam."

I blinked again. "You what?"

"Hey, what can I tell you? I'm the best. I suppose I should hate myself, instead I cashed the check." He cocked his head. "Are you all right?"

"I've been better. Physically I'm fine."

"I heard what happened. Of course, who didn't." He shook his head. "Bad business. But they got the guy who did it?"

"That's right."

"Can they prove it?"

"Actually, they're not sure about her. But they have him dead to rights on Doug Mark."

"That's good."

"Yeah." I exhaled. "If I were to write a book . . ."

"You? About what?"

"I'm not sure."

"Sounds good."

"Yeah. Well, I'm a private detective. It just occurred to me."

"You write it, give me a call. But don't think because you're a private eye it's gotta be that."

"What do you mean?"

"Well, take this case. You got threatening phone calls, two murders, and a bomb blast." He shrugged. "But it doesn't work. The guy what did it's not involved, he's dragged in from left field from somewhere else. The only way it works is if you set him up in the beginning, but you can't do that, because if you do there's no plot. Life sucks in terms of art."

Abe Feinstein scratched his head. "The other way you do it is true crime. But there you got a problem, because Winnington won't cooperate. That would be bad enough anyway, but on top of it I happen to be his agent, so obviously I wouldn't touch it. But don't let me discourage you. You get an idea, you write it up, and we'll talk."

"Uh-huh," I said.

"You seen the Winningtons yet?"

"I was hoping to run into them here."

"Yeah, well, you won't. They're not coming."

"How do you know?"

"Just their style. He's too big to come. Not his way. He

312

won't come to Doug Mark's service either. Even though he'd have much more reason, all he owes him."

"You sound like you don't like him much."

"Are you kidding me? He's my favorite author. The one that pays the bills. I love the guy."

I excused myself, went outside to get some air.

What Abe Feinstein had told me was upsetting. Not that I couldn't write up the story—I wouldn't have done it anyway, not with Alice and Tommie involved. No, I was just grasping at straws, wanting to do something to get out of detective work. Still, a modicum of encouragement would have been nice.

The real thing that bothered me was the fact that the Winningtons wouldn't be there. I'd be sending them a bill and getting a check in the mail, but I wouldn't be dropping by their apartment anymore. And—I wanted to see them again. As I said, just for a sense of closure. Though I wasn't sure why. Maybe it was because the whole story was disjointed. It jumped from them to the whole Carlton Kraswell thing. And I wanted to bring it back full cycle and wrap it up somehow.

But if it wasn't to be, it wasn't to be.

Why should I feel bad? Why should I feel any worse than Doug Mark, whose funeral they wouldn't be attending?

Whose death I'd caused.

I guess maybe that was it. I guess I wanted to see the Winningtons to reassure myself that what I'd done was not my fault. That someone else had set this thing in motion. That everything I'd done I had been made to do. That I really wasn't to blame.

While I was standing there thinking that, wannabe writer Noah Sprague came walking down the street and into the funeral parlor.

It shocked the hell out of me to see him out on the street. I

313

guess it shouldn't have—the guy wasn't guilty of the murders. The crank phone calls, sure, but that of course would be a bailable offense. No reason why he'd be in jail. Still, it gave me a turn.

I didn't know why he'd come. Whether he'd known Sherry Pressman too. Perhaps once submitted a manuscript to her. Probably not. Surely if that were the case Sergeant Thurman would have ferreted it out. But maybe not. Maybe he knew the woman.

Or maybe he, like I, hoped to find the Winningtons there. Hoped to harass them one more time. Maybe he was still on their case.

Well, if he was, it was nothing to do with me. I'd done with the Winningtons. Bang, over, finished.

As I stood there, thinking that, I smiled.

Thank you, Mr. Sprague.

Thank you for coming, that will do quite nicely.

I can put this behind me now and move on.

And I'd get over it.

And Alice would get over it.

And Tommie would get over it.

And things would go back to the way they were before.

I was confident of that now.

It would just take time.